For My Parents Margaret and Jim Verdick

Thank you for showing me your strength, courage, compassion, and love. You are my heroes.

Love, Stacy

Editor: Elizabeth Goldstein

Cover Design: Designs by Jeff

Author Photo: Joanna Obraske

ISBN: 978-0-9837137-6-0

Library of Congress Control Number: 2014900008

BEFORE THE FALL

www.BeforetheFallBooks.com

10 9 8 7 6 5 4 3 2 1

An Intimate Murder

Stacy Verdick Case

BEFORE THE FALL

www.BefortheFallBooks.com

Chapter One

"This better be good, Louise."

My feet had barely hit the ground as I stepped out of my Dodge Charger. Louise held up her hands in surrender.

"Keep your voice down, Catherine. I'm sorry to yank you back to work."

"You should be. I was about to get sweaty and dirty with my husband."

"Exercising?"

"Just because you're a spinster doesn't mean you have to be bitter."

She held her index finger to her lips. "Notch it down, Catherine."

"Fine." I dropped my voice to a harsh whisper. "I'm serious, Louise, don't you ever leave the office? The Saint Paul Police Department does employ other homicide detectives you know. Give them a chance to solve a case now and then."

Louise used the thumb of her left hand to flick her middle finger nail, which made a tick, tick, tick sound. She narrowed her eyes at me.

"You're a workaholic."

"Detective Montgomery?" A tall, slender woman who looked to be in her mid-fifties crossed the lawn toward us. "Is it okay if I take Chad inside?"

She gestured to a man who sat on the lawn with his back to us, wrapped in a silver shock blanket.

Louise straightened. "Ms. Hind, I'd like to introduce

you to my partner, Catherine O'Brien."

Her eyes trailed up and down me in the cool appraisal of an inventory control clerk sizing up a new shipment. "Nice to meet you." I wished I'd bothered to find a clean pair of jeans before I hopped into the car to come over here. Her lips turned up at the corners, but her expression stopped short of an actual smile, more of a polite gesture.

"Would it be okay to bring Chad into my house, Detectives?" She nodded toward a group of uniformed officers. "I was told they would be bringing his parents out soon."

Ah, now I understood the shock blanket.

"I don't think that Chad could handle seeing his parents in a body bag. Plus, the Saint Paul Police Department probably doesn't want the maelstrom of publicity a hysterical son, crying over the body of his parents, on the six o'clock news will cause."

Pam inclined her head toward the road.

Behind a yellow line of police tape, every local news agency, including the local AM college station, had a crew lined up. All of them ready to catch any gruesome details that we might be willing to share, or might accidentally let slip. After all, the public must have their evening dose of human abhorrent behavior before they go to bed at night, or how could the public rest easily this evening?

"I see your point," I said. "By all means take Chad into the house."

She whirled around, bent over Chad, and whispered in his ear. He stood and followed her inside like a remote controlled toy.

"Pam Hind is the next door neighbor to Mr. and Mrs. Jonathan Luther," Louise said.

"And Chad is Chad Luther son of the deceased."

Louise nodded and trudged across the lawn.

"Chad found the bodies?"

"Correct." She held the front door open.

I stopped on the threshold. "Chad killed his parents. Case closed."

"What brings you to your hasty conclusion?"

"Instinct." I tapped my finger against my temple. "Pure instinct."

Louise gave a dismissive shake of her head.

"Catherine, I hate to argue with your well-honed instincts, but I don't think so. Chad is terribly upset."

"I bet if we grilled him like a cheese sandwich, he'd confess." I folded my arms over my chest. "Come on, we could be home in a few hours. What do you think?"

She leaned on the screen door and held it propped open with her shoulder. "I think at the moment Chad would confess to the Lindbergh kidnapping if someone pressed him hard enough."

"He's really upset, huh?"

"Yes. Hysterical is the word that comes to mind."

I stepped into the foyer. "Then I guess we'll have to do this the old fashioned way."

"Why did you become an investigator, Catherine? You never want to investigate."

I sighed. "I have an overwhelming need for justice."

She rolled her eyes heavenward.

"I do. Most people don't know that about me. If killers would pick a better time to off someone, instead of waiting until I'm about to have a sweaty, freak fest with my husband for the first time in weeks, then you'd see a whole different Detective O'Brien."

Louise pursed her lips and nodded. "So it's more of a timing issue?"

"Exactly."

"I can respect that."

Louise led me through the upper, middle class home of

a family that was far from risk takers. Beige dominated every wall and carpet. The only color in the room came from the neat, symmetrically hung family photos on the long wall above the sofa.

One corner of the living room held a curio cabinet with Hummel figurines, similar to the ones my Grandma Rue collected. While the Hummel figurines looked perfectly normal in Grandma Rue's doily enshrouded living room, they glared like a neon sign in the minimalist beige home.

Spatters of blood snaked up the curio cabinet and onto the walls, like red vines. From the pattern, the blood wasn't arterial spray but cast off.

The lab techs buzzed efficiently around the area with the effortless coordination of a hive of bees. Near their feet lay the body of a woman, face up and eyes wide in horror.

"Mrs. Luther?" I knelt next to the body.

"Yes." One of the techs answered. "We've finished processing her body. You can move her if you need to, Detective. We're just about to take her out of here anyway."

I nodded my thanks and stole a pair of gloves from one of the kits on the floor. I snapped on the non-latex gloves and lifted the edge of Mrs. Luther's shirt.

Louise crouched across from me. "I couldn't count them all."

"My God," I whispered. "Someone really didn't like this woman. What could she possibly have done to deserve this?"

Dotted across her chest were multiple punctures, some appeared shallow, some viciously deep.

Louise lifted Mrs. Luther's arm and turned it palm up. "No defensive wounds. Maybe she died before she endured too much pain."

I checked the arm on my side; no visible wounds, not even a scratch.

"That's odd," I said. "From the look on her face, it

doesn't look as though she died instantly."

I twisted my neck so I shared the angle of Mrs. Luther's head and examined her face.

"This isn't just the look of fear," I said. "It's the look of disbelief. We have photos of her right?"

"Yep, every inch," the tech said.

I closed Mrs. Luther's eyes. Whatever she had seen that had caused her such fear and pain was gone. She didn't need to look at this world any longer.

Louise stood. "Come on. I'll show you Mr. Luther."

Jonathan Luther was a collector of all things train. His death had come two flights up from his wife, in the attic of his home, which he'd converted into a train themed room. His body lay sprawled across the tracks of a miniature Northern Pacific Railroad.

The train, which he'd been playing with at the time of his death, had crashed into his ribcage, but to my amazement, hadn't derailed. The cheap train set my brother and I had played with as kids would derail if you looked at it wrong.

This model was higher quality than the plastic trains kids played with, the wheels held to the track like a real train. The engine car chugged and whistled against the resistance of Luther's body. The wheels slid in place, and the whole line of cars shuddered with the force.

The wounds that gaped in the center of Luther's chest looked as though they'd come from two shotgun blasts.

"Jesus," I said.

Louise reached down and pulled the plug on the Northern Pacific. The black engine and green boxcars whined to a stop.

"The techs finished in here first," Louise said. "I wanted you to see him before they moved anything."

Jonathan Luther had been standing in the center of the tracks. Encircled and trapped by his collection.

I ducked under the track, not a minor accomplishment these days, and surveyed Jonathan Luther up close. I turned my back to him and mimicked his stance, hovering over, but not touching, the body.

"The killer was all the way inside the room."

I stood upright and held my arm straight out in front of me. "The bullets would have come from that direction."

Louise moved around the table and aligned herself with my arm. She was three-quarters of the way down the wall, and directly in front of a café table set, whose chairs had an old steam engine carved into the backrests.

"So what?" Louise asked. "He allowed a killer to walk in with a shotgun, sit down, and chat? What sense does that make?"

"None at all." I turned and scrutinized Luther's face. "He looks surprised. There's no fear on his face at all, just shock."

"He knew his killer," she said.

"What I don't understand is why the killer changed weapons. Why stab the wife and then shoot the husband?"

I ran through plausible answers in my mind but couldn't make any stick. In my years as a detective, I'd seen dozens of multiple homicide scenes, and I didn't remember one where the killer had changed weapons.

"Maybe the killer wanted to kill the wife quietly so he wouldn't alert the husband," Louise said. "So he stabs the wife then shoots the husband."

"Mr. Luther was killed first."

Louise grinned. "Okay, I give. How do you know he was killed first?"

"You saw the cast off on the wall down stairs. If Mr. Luther weren't the first to die, then the killer would have been drenched in blood. We should have found blood all the way up the stairs but they were clean. Plus, Mr. Luther, unless he was an extremely dense individual, would never have stood still while a killer, covered in his wife's blood, carrying a shotgun, waltzed into his train room, and blasted him."

"Touché." Louise nodded. "Nice catch."

"Thanks. Maybe my senses have been heightened by my sexual frustration."

"Yeah, I'm sure that must be the reason."

Louise smirked at me, which was the best I could expect for my sense of humor. Rarely, if ever, would she laugh, and when she did throngs of men fell at her feet, like bugs drawn to a bug light. Poor Louise had trained herself long ago that to be taken seriously she needed to restrain her sultry laugh. Growing up must have been difficult for her, being beautiful and smart, and I don't mean that in a snarky way. In this world, the prejudice that you can either be smart or pretty remained, and God forbid you be both.

Louise defined every man's fantasy woman and every woman's worst nightmare. Tall, slim, and elegant; her mahogany skin and braided hair were flawless.

In contrast, I was short, pale, and too round in certain places to be considered slim. I'm more bumpy than curvy, and more dorky than graceful. I am the anti-Louise.

And maybe I was seeing something at the crime scene that for some reason, Louise didn't.

"So why change weapons?" I asked. "Why wouldn't Mrs. Luther run to a neighbor? She must have heard the shotgun blasts."

Louise stomped on the floor. Instead of a hollow clonk, clonk sound there was a solid whomp, whomp.

"Sounds well insulated to me, and she was two floors down."

"I can hear Gavin routing around in our attic when I'm on the first floor."

"No offense, Catherine but your house is old. This is new construction. High dollar new construction at that."

"You might have a point." I ducked under a set of three

railman's signal lamps hanging from the ceiling that were rewired for electricity. "But my house isn't old. It's a classic Victorian with better architecture, and more style, than this high dollar, cookie-cutter new construction."

"Even so," Louise said. "This place was built to be quiet. My guess is after a long hard day at work, Dad liked to play trains while Mom slept."

"Are we done here?" I asked, not fully convinced by her argument. Especially since I could hear the technicians down the hallway, chattering about last night's Minnesota Wild hockey game. If I could hear them, then a shotgun blast could be heard in the living room.

"I think we're done," Louise said.

"Then I'm going home to my old house and my old husband."

"Fraid not," Louise said. "First twenty-four hours and all."

"But I clocked out over an hour ago."

"You're here now."

Arguing the point with her would be like pushing against a wall of stone, equally immovable and just as gritty when she wanted to be. Plus, she was right. Despite my desire to go home and ravish my husband, I had a responsibility and a job to do.

"Where to then?"

"Let's talk to the neighbors and see if they heard anything. I find it hard to believe that the sound of two shotgun blasts could go completely unnoticed."

Two EMTs bumped a gurney into the room.

"Is it okay to remove the body, Detective?"

Louise swiveled around to face me. "Catherine?"

"Sure." I waved them in. "I think we've seen everything we need to see."

The world as a whole is a strange place, and the people who inhabit this world are even stranger. The Luther's neighbors proved to be the strangest I'd encountered in ten years of law enforcement. Considering the whackos and ice-blooded murders I'd run into, these neighbors could be proud of their over achieving ways.

The street looked benign, an affluent tree lined parkway with a BMW or Mercedes in every other driveway. The neighbor across the street had a pickup truck in their drive, but it turned out to be the yard man's, who happened to be cleaning up the left behinds from the oak and maple fall deposits. Pretty to look at until they rotted into brown slime piles on your grass.

We questioned every neighbor on the block but no one heard the gunshots. They lived behind triple pane glass where the temperature was never too hot or too cold. Only one had dared to steal a glance out their insulated glass when an older car, rusted in too many places and not carrying the pedigree of a classic automobile, sped down the street.

"I knew right away they were up to no good." Bernice Leigh, who claimed a relation to Janet Leigh, rocked on the edge of her tufted, chintz ottoman.

"Well maybe not right away." She rolled her hand dramatically in the air. "At first I thought the car could belong to one of the boy's friends who visit the Luther's from time to time."

"Did you know the Luther's very well?" Louise nibbled the edge of a Ginger Thin Mrs. Leigh had fanned out on a china plate, and placed on the coffee table in front of us.

Bernice Leigh shook her head with such force that her hair, which had been so obviously a wig, dislodged itself and canted to one side. Bernice righted the wig without as much as a second thought.

"I don't know them at all really. Or didn't." She waved a dismissive hand from side to side. "Yes, I saw them around at different functions and I'd wave too them if I saw them in the yard, but no one could claim we were anything more than passing acquaintances."

"What kind of car did you see driving away, Mrs. Leigh?" I brushed the cookie crumbs from my hands onto a small plate Bernice had given each of us to hold our Ginger Thins.

"I don't have any idea. It was old and not very well maintained. That's all I can really tell you." She smiled and touched her fingers to her chest. "I don't even drive. Since my husband died, I've had to rely on friends or dirty old cabs to take me where I need to go."

My Grandmother had been the same way when my Grandpa died. After about a month, "the kindness of strangers", routine grew old and she enrolled in driving lessons. The first thing she did with Grandpa's life insurance money (which had been more than she really needed since Grandpa had been a minor financial wizard) was to pick out a brand new, black, Chevy Suburban and drive it home.

When we'd asked her why she bought a vehicle larger than she really needed, her response was, "Because if I'm going to get cracked up in one of those winter pile-ups that I read about in the paper, I want to make sure there's a few feet of American steel between me and those piled up around me."

To date, she still hasn't been in one of those winter pile-ups, though she drives like a maniac on the loose.

"What color was the car you saw?" Louise asked.

"Dirty." Bernice pursed her lips in a grimace of disgust. "Very dirty."

"A very dirty blue?" I prompted trying to jog her memory. "A very dirty green? Or black?"

"I think the paint was a dark green, dirty," she said. She tapped her temple in deep thought and then nodded her assurance. "Yes, a dirty, dark green."

"Would you be able to identify the car if we showed you a picture?"

The look of complete pissed-off-attude that crossed Mrs. Leigh's face told me without hesitation that I had over stepped the boundaries she'd set for stupidity. She crossed her left leg over her right, wrapped her arms around her knee, and pulled her back straight.

"I might be old but I'm certainly not feeble."

With any luck, I could recover before Louise laid one of her warning looks on me. The kind of look that told me my lessons in tact had failed. Perhaps I could slop enough sugar on the woman to make her believe my sincerity.

"I apologize, Mrs. Leigh, my question didn't come out at all right."

I smiled. From the softening of the sharp lines around her frown, my smile, stilted as it was, had worked.

"What I meant to say was did you get a clear view of the car? Enough to recognize a photo or did the driver speed off too quick?"

Louise who had been my Sensei of tact for the past few years cast a glance in my direction that looked vaguely like pride. A *perhaps-you-are-learning-after-all* glance. I don't think Mrs. Leigh caught the look or if she did, she didn't register anything out of the ordinary about Louise's Cheshire smile.

"Oh, no," Bernice cooed. "I got a full side and front view when the driver tore out of here. I happened to be watering the plants in my front window at the time."

Happened to be snooping out the front window at the time is more like the truth. The binoculars on the front windowsill hadn't escaped my attention when we came in, though I'm sure, if pressed, Bernice Leigh would claim to be an avid bird or squirrel watcher.

"It wasn't one of those little sporty models like the Luther's boy drives. I know that for sure, and it wasn't a pickup truck or those other ones." Bernice pressed the fingertips of her right hand to her upper lip. "Oh what are those boxy things called? STDs?"

A burbling laugh rolled out of me before I could cage the sound behind my teeth. Bernice's brows drew together in the Grand Canyon's of furrows; only on her, the change wasn't so drastic.

I let out a slow breath.

"I am so sorry, Mrs. Leigh. I think you meant to say SUV. A sport utility vehicle."

She shook her sausage of a finger at me. The last knuckle bulged out at the sides adding to the effect that someone had tied off a sausage. On the tip of her finger was a perfectly manicured red nail and the errant thought that this would be Louise in thirty-years, ran through my head.

"Are those the ones that are square? The ones that tip over all the time?"

"Yes," Louise said. "You're thinking of SUV."

"Well whatever they're called it wasn't one of those numbers. It was more of a normal sized car."

She crunched into a Ginger Thin and gave a smug satisfied smile around the crumbs as if she'd helped us crack the meaning of life.

I riffled through my purse and found my notebook. "Let me write this down."

I made a show of flipping through the pages until I found a clean sheet of paper. When I finally did, I clicked open my ballpoint and poised the tip over the page.

"Let me make sure I have everything. We have a normal sized, dirty. . .."

I paused.

"Green," Bernice provided, when she realized I was waiting for her to fill in the details again. "Definitely a dirty green."

"A normal sized, dirty green, car of unknown make and model."

Bernice smiled plaintively and nodded.

"Did you happen to see if it was a man or a woman driving the car?" Louise asked.

"A man." She rocked back on the ottoman bracing her hands on her knees to keep from tipping backward. "Well, I guess it could have been a woman. The side windows were dark like a limo."

"A normal sized, dirty green, car of unknown make and model, with tinted windows, driven by a man or possibly a woman."

I read back the details with all the enthusiasm of a drive up window cashier. The only thing missing was the phrase, "do you want fries with that?"

Bernice tilted her head as if trying to read the writing in my notebook. There was no way she could read my chicken scratch handwriting. Hell, there was times I couldn't read my own handwriting. She pointed to the page.

"Tinted *side* windows."

I scribbled a note near where she had pointed, which seemed to appease her. Louise on the other hand was not amused by my charade.

"Thank you, Mrs. Leigh," Louise said. "We'll send someone by with photographs of cars for you to look through." She reached into her pocket and drew out a business card. "If you think of anything else please call and let us know."

Bernice snatched the card from Louise's hand as if Louise were only joking and might take the rectangle of cardstock back at any moment.

"Oh, I will." She held the card close to her chest as if it were her most prized possession.

Five seconds after we left, she'd be on the phone all right, to all her biddy friends. There had been more excitement today than in all her previous days combined was my guess and now she was helping the police solve a murder. Bernice Leigh, alleged kin to Janet, would probably tell her friends how she was the Angela Lansbury character in *Murder She Wrote* and Louise and I were the bumbling detectives who couldn't find the right path with a neon-sign pointing the way.

Once outside, my entire body, which had been on point since my tact slipped, sagged with relief. Parts of me sagged more than others, and I made a mental note to buy a new bra. Soon.

"Well at least we were able to get something from her." Louise pulled her jacket closed to ward off the chilly wind that gusted down the street. "She should be of some help."

"She's lying through her teeth." I slung my purse up over my shoulder and started down the front walk toward the street.

"What?" Louise jogged up next to me. "I didn't get a sense that she was lying. What did she lie about?"

"There is no way she's related to Janet Leigh. Leigh isn't even Janet Leigh's real last name. It's Morrison or something like that."

"Catherine, try to focus on the investigation," Louise said and gave me the warning look I had artfully avoided in Bernice's house. "Did you get a sense she was lying about what she saw today?"

"Oh, that. No, she's as honest as she can be about that topic." I pointed back toward the house. "Did you see the binoculars in the front window? If someone comes home drunk and pukes in their flower bed she could give you an exact description of what they'd eaten for dinner."

Louise blanched and then looked back to where the outline of Mrs. Leigh was already in the window watching us trot away. The shadowy figure waved and we waved back.

"She saw everything," I said. "Bernice Leigh is the eagle eye of the neighborhood. She might have seen more than she knows. I say we give her a couple days to get the excitement out of her system and then pay her another visit."

"Agreed." Louise folded her arms across her chest and narrowed her eyes at me.

"What?"

"Nothing. I was just thinking that maybe we should have Gavin come in every morning and get you all worked up. You seem to function better with an edge of sexual frustration."

I tried not to smile, but she'd given a great zinger and it deserved acknowledgment. I snuffled out a laugh.

"We'd have to put him on payroll as an Investigative Boy Toy."

Louise gave a giggle. "Investigative Probe."

"That's so disgusting, Louise." I gasped in shock. "I love it! He's hired."

We shared a laugh at Gavin's expense. Of course, I would have to tell him about it later so I could watch the sexy flush that creeps into his cheeks. He can never understand all the things that women share, from chaffed nipples to sexual problems; women share everything, usually to the complete embarrassment and utter dismay of their spouse.

I had to agree with him on some levels. There's a strict two-year waiting period before I share the most intimate details of my life with other women. I'd been at parties where a complete stranger will tell me about their chaffed nipples, their tragic childhood, their sex-life, and the results of their last pap-smear in the first ten minutes of a conversation. A clear-cut case of too much information.

"Where are we heading now?" I asked.

The smile on Louise's face evaporated. "The part I'm not looking forward to."

She turned her gaze across the street to Pam Hind's house, a caravan of cruisers still parked in front. Two uniformed officers were trying valiantly to keep the press at bay, but eventually they would be gone and the news-wolves would be on her doorstep asking for any gory details they could get on an exclusive basis.

A couple of the press hounds must have scented us because they turned and looked toward where we stood. I could see their mental-wheels turning. If they were unable to breach the lines to Pam Hind and the Luther's son, they would settle for a quote from Bernice Leigh.

"The son," I said.

She nodded. "I hate talking to kids who have lost a parent. This kid lost both parents in one day."

"I wonder if he's called any relatives to be with him," I said. "He's going to need someone to help him sort out the details."

Hell, I'm thirty-three years old and I'm not sure I could deal with the stress of planning a funeral for both of my parents.

We crossed to Pam Hind's house, dodged the reporters' questions with a quick "no comment", and ducked under the barricade tape.

"How long do we need to be here?" The younger of the two uniforms complained. "My wife is making my favorite dinner tonight."

"You'd better call her and tell her to put a plate in the microwave for you," I said. "You're going to be late."

He grimaced but before he could protest a dark haired woman, wielding a mini-tape recorder ducked under the tape. The young officer intercepted her with the ease of Viking's lineman.

She struggled against his embrace without success. "Detectives! Detectives!"

She held her mini tape recorder in both hands straight in front of her as if she were waving a sword.

"Please Detectives, just one quick comment."

I stopped and whirled around. My boot heel caught in the grout of the faux-cobblestone sidewalk. I listed to the side, and stumbled two steps to the left before catching myself. "I have a comment."

"Catherine?" Louise touched my arm.

"It's okay, Louise."

She let me go.

The reporter shook out of the uniformed officers hands and straightened her jacket. She eyed him with a smug ha, ha look.

"I'll give this comment to all of you." I took my place in front of a mob of reporters jockeying for the best position.

"Here it is, and make sure you quote me accurately."

I paused for dramatic effect and to make sure the reporters had time to set their tape machines and video cameras to record.

"You should all be ashamed of yourself. A child has lost his parents and you want to pick at the remains. All of you should get on your knees, and ask for forgiveness, for the vultures that you are."

A few audible gasps rolled up from the mass in front of me. Lights blinked off and the video and audio recorders drooped. I even received a "boo" from somewhere near the back, which prompted other boos from those less intelligent to think for themselves.

There was a reason our former governor called the press media jackals. I could have cared less for the Governor's politics but him and I shared an opinion of the press that few outside of law enforcement, politics, and celebrity stardom could understand.

Before any of them could recover from their nose-tweak, and ask questions that would piss me off, I marched toward Pam Hind's house. A roar of protests erupted about halfway up the walk.

"Very concise," Louise said. "I don't think it will make them go away though."

"Nothing short of a toxic spill, from a drunk-driving tanker truck, that landed on the front law of the capitol building, and annihilated three bus loads of elementary school students, could move them from a double homicide in an affluent neighborhood," I grumbled. "It doesn't mean they don't need to hear the truth now and then. Not that a one of them has conscience enough to process the truth."

Louise shook her head and smiled. "Your dislike for the media has reached legendary proportions, Catherine. Someday you'll have to explain to me where this hatred for all things press related comes from."

Maybe I would. Someday but not today. Today she would just need to accept that I have my reasons.

Louise charged up the front stoop of Pam Hind's stone house, her shoes making a quick snick, snick, on the steps with each jog. My boots made a clop, clop, like horses hooves as I stomped up behind her. She rapped lightly on the door.

After a few moments of waiting, my impatience got the better of me and I leaned on the white doorbell. Finally, sounds of life rattled from inside the house. Pam Hind jerked open the door, bent slightly at the waist, head forward like a dog that had gone feral ready to attack. When she saw Louise and me, her expression changed from one of attack to one of complete surprise. She straightened and took a step backward.

"Oh, Detectives. I thought one of the reporters had gotten to the front door." She jerked her thumb toward the back of the house. "A few have climbed the fence in the alley and have been knocking on the back door looking for a quote."

My heartbeat thrummed in my ears. I stuck two fingers in my mouth, turned toward the street, and let out a high-pitched whistle, a talent my Father had taught me when I was young. The two uniformed officers guarding the front turned in unison.

I cupped my hands around my mouth. "Send someone around back to arrest anyone they find in the back yard. Charge them with trespassing."

The older officer gave a brief nod then pulled his radio from his belt, and made a call for help. I gave him the thumbs up sign, which he returned.

"I apologize, Mrs. Hind," Louise said. "We try but sometime the media's zeal eclipses their commonsense."

Pam nodded and tsked as if she knew this instinctively. "Come inside. Chad's in the living-room."

The two-story entryway glowed in a sun-golden color that made my entire body feel warm and I shivered off fall's chill. Three doorways and a staircase merged onto the entryway, like roads converging on a four-way stop. Through the doorway to the right was Pam Hind's living room.

Chad Luther sat wrapped in a forest-green, polar-fleece blanket in a recliner by the fireplace. The flames licked at the bricks on the surround, as if Pam were worried that a reporter would pull a Santa Claus on her to get a quote.

"Has he said anything yet?" I asked.

"No." She sighed and hugged her arms as if the chill from my body had transferred to hers. "I tried to talk to him but he just glared at me."

"Glared at you?" Louise said. "Like he's in a daze?"

Pam closed her eyes. "Maybe I'm misinterpreting, but the look was actually more like he blamed me. Maybe he's just in shock."

"Maybe," Louise agreed.

We made eye contact for a brief second. In that second, we exchanged more information than Pam Hind could have picked up.

"We need to speak with Chad," I said.

"I'm not sure you'll be able to get anything from him," she said. "But I have no right to stop you from trying."

Chad Luther turned bleary eyes toward us without seeming to register our presence. An ember snapped from the fire and he jerked his head away from us to stare at the hearth. Louise sat on the sofa across from him.

"Can I get you ladies anything to drink? I have a pot of coffee percolating."

My addiction's want sprang to life and though I didn't think I wanted anything to drink, I heard myself answer, "Yes, coffee please."

Someday I may need to confront my coffee demons but now I had other, more important problems at hand.

Louise waved off the offer and Pam ambled out of the living room to get the coffee.

"Chad?" Louise reached out and laid her hand on his forearm. "We need to ask you a few questions."

Chad Luther's eyes closed and in a deep gravelly voice he said, "Take your hand off me and don't ever touch me again."

Louise slowly drew her hand away, as if sudden movement would cause Chad to strike out like a coiled snake.

He lolled his head toward her. The greasy mop of bangs fell over his forehead and into his eyes. He didn't brush the hair away, which made me believe that's where the hair usually stayed.

"I don't like to be touched by anyone," he said to Louise then turned his gaze to me. "Especially not by some fucking cop."

Louise's earlier assessment of Chad's emotional fragility had been wide off the mark. This kid was going full on punk kid, attitude and all, which was fine by me. I could treat him like a punk if that's what he wanted.

"Did you kill your parents, Chad?" I tossed my purse on the sofa next to me and opened it as if I didn't care what his answer or reaction would be. "What? They gave you the Spyder instead of the Bugatti so you offed them?"

I located a pack of Wrigley's in the side pocket of my purse, and offered a stick to Louise, before taking one of my own.

"Fuck you, okay!" Chad strangled the edges of his blanket and shook with rage. His fingernails were tipped with peeling black nail polish. "I didn't kill my fucking parents. You fucking whore."

I balled up the gum's tinfoil wrapper and launched it at Chad. It bounced off the greasy bangs on his forehead.

"You fucking bitch!" He shook out of the blanket.

"Hey!" I slapped my palm down on the coffee table. Chad jumped with surprise.

"You be nice," I said.

"Or what?" He was now huffing breaths like a marathon runner.

"Or I'll place you under arrest for the murder of your parents."

"I didn't kill my parents," he bleated.

I pointed to my chest. "I don't care, Chad. If you don't behave, I'll haul your ass in, and make sure you get a full body cavity search before your lawyer can say police brutality."

Chad fell back in his chair, jerked the blanket edges around his shoulders, and stared at the fireplace again.

I glanced at Louise. "He's so fragile I don't know if we should question him just yet."

Louise, safely hidden behind Chad's back so she was sure he couldn't see her unprofessional behavior, flipped me the bird.

And she lectures me on tact?

"Ask me your questions," Chad said. "Just don't touch me."

"Fair enough," Louise said. "Why don't you begin by telling us exactly what happened. We'll jump in if we want to know more."

Pam Hind came in carrying two cups of coffee. She set one in front of me and then perched on the edge of the sofa next to me holding her cup cradled between her two hands.

"Is everything okay in here? I thought I heard raised voices."

"Oh no, not raised voices." Chad fanned his hand in front of his face. "We're fine and we don't need an audience."

Pam's eyes widened. Her mouth moved open, but any protest she could make muted by Chad's hard glare.

"Come on lady." He turned his face back to the fire. "Take a hint."

"What did I say about being nice," I said and considered throwing something else at him.

"No, it's okay." Pam set her cup on the table with a clatter then stood. "I have some laundry to take care of this afternoon. You go ahead and talk in private."

She left.

Louise whose normally placid expression had turned dour said, "Maybe we should do this at the station."

Chad pffed out a breath. "Whatever."

"Start talking, *Chad*."

"I came home and they were dead," he said. "I don't know what you want from me."

"When was the last time you spoke to your parents?" Louise asked before I could verbally assault him again.

"This morning, around ten, I called to let them know I'd be over for dinner."

I snapped my gum. "You don't live with your parents?"

Chad didn't have the look of a kid in shock. Instead, his features seemed frozen in the dull, bored look of a man holding his wife's purse at the mall. The look was wrong – unsettling somehow.

"No, I didn't live with my parents." He squeezed his eyes shut. "I live at the dorms at the University. My parents always wanted me to come home on the weekends for dinner. Mom would clean my clothes for me."

Too bad, she didn't wash his hair for him too. It looked like the grease that coated the strands would repel water and soap.

"Did you go in through the front door?" Louise asked.

"No, I went through the garage. I have a garage door opener."

"You went in through the garage and then where did you go first?" Louise thumb typed notes into her smartphone.

Chad cleared his throat. "I went to the kitchen. I figured that's where Mom would be, but she wasn't."

An almost imperceptible shiver ran over him.

"Then I went into the living-room to watch TV." His voice cracked and wavered. "There was a smell. It was bad."

True. After all these years, I'd learned to block out the copper smell of blood mixed with feces and urine. My brain registered the smell but the receptors in my nose shut down.

"She was on the floor."

"Did you touch her?" I said.

"I don't remember. I puked, I remember that, and the next thing I remember was running through the house yelling for my Dad. I found him in his train room."

He pinched the bridge of his nose, then leaned forward and rested his elbows on his knees.

"Did you touch him?" Louise asked.

"No." Chad spoke into his lap. "I didn't touch anything. I just ran."

"Which direction did you run?" I asked.

His head jerked up. "Why does it fucking matter? God it's not like you people will do anything about their murders anyway. My Grandma was killed and the cops never caught her killer. The fat fuck of a cop who investigated her murder just rubbed my head and said, *that's the way things crumble sometimes, cookie*. So do me a favor, and don't pretend. Just go back to your station house, eat your donuts, and collect your fat checks at the end of the week."

That explained his hostility toward cops. I'd be more than a little pissed too in the same situation.

"I'm sorry about your Grandmother," I said. "That really sucks."

Finally his tears fell.

"Yeah, it does."

"Where was she killed?" Louise asked.

Chad turned a blank expression toward her as if he didn't know about whom Louise was talking.

"Your Grandmother," Louise clarified. "Was she killed in Saint. Paul?"

"No." The tears stopped as if the floodgates closed. "She was killed up north, near Duluth. We lived in a small town up there. Her murder is why we moved to Saint Paul. My parents didn't want to live in the same town as the person who killed my Grandma. They didn't want to live with the rumors either."

"Rumors?" I asked.

"Yeah, there were rumors that the family killed her."

I leaned forward. "Did the police ever have a suspect?"

Chad's eyes went from hard onyx, to the soft orbs of a doe, like it were the first time anyone was truly interested in what he said. He gave a one-shouldered shrug.

"I don't know. I think they did, but they didn't."

I wondered if there were any relatives left to take care of him. True, Chad was old enough to be on his own, but age didn't make being alone in the world easier.

Chad pulled the blanket tighter around his shoulders. "I guess it doesn't matter now."

"That was a long time ago," I said, "and we're not small town Sheriffs, marking time until our pension kicks in. We have the best forensics guy in the state working with us. Louise and I aren't slouches either."

Louise gave him the knee-melting smile. Chad Luther tried to resist but didn't last. He finally smiled.

"Chad," Louise said. "We need to know where you went in the house, because there might be fibers, blood, or other evidence from the killer. You may have accidentally contaminated the scene."

"I didn't."

Louise held up her hand. "You don't know that for sure and neither do we. Please tell us which direction you left the house."

"The same way I went in – through the garage."

"Thank you," I said.

Louise dipped her hand into the side pocket of her jacket and came up with a business card. "Chad I want you to take this card. I'm going to write my cell phone number on the back."

She fished a pen from her purse quicker than I could have found my wallet on some days. Then again, her purse was the size of my shoe. My purse was the size of a grocery bag. Louise jotted her cell on the back of the card and handed the paper to Chad.

"If you need anything or have questions about the investigation, please call or text me. We're happy to answer your questions."

We'd be happy to answer questions, but he only had her numbers. What did she think I'd say? *Quit bugging me kid.*

"Your parent's murders are our only priority," Louise said. "We're not going to come back, rub your head, and say tough break kid."

"That's right," I agreed. "I personally don't want to touch your head."

They both stared at me in disbelief.

"Well, not until you shower."

Chad laughed, not heartily, but a healthy laugh. Maybe the shock had dissipated enough to allow him to grieve.

"We are sorry for your loss, Chad." Louise touched his arm again. I held my breath and waited for the explosion that never came.

"Thanks." Chad's shoulders slumped and the frame of his thin body seemed to float in the overstuffed recliner.

"Is there anyone you can call?" Louise asked. "Somewhere you can stay tonight, so you're not alone?"

He sniffed up a wad of snot, and then ran his hand under his nose. "My aunt, Linda. I should call her and let her know."

"We'll call her for you," I said. "One of the uniformed officers will take you to your Aunt's house."

Chad shifted to his left side, reached around behind, and pulled out his wallet. He opened the wallet and tucked Louise's business card in the money slot. In the process, he tipped the wallet enough for me to see a large stash of bills inside, beginning with a hundred dollar bill. He snapped the wallet shut, leaned to the left, and replaced it in its accustomed place, over his right butt cheek.

"Thank you." He said the words with enough sincerity to make me believe him, and then returned to staring at the fire.

Chapter Two

Louise and I found Pam Hind right where she said she'd be; ankle deep in dirty laundry. Instead of separating the clothes into piles of light and dark, Pam sorted through the layers of clothing until she found the color she wanted.

She picked up a pair of jeans, pulled off the white pair of underwear, that been shucked at the same time as the jeans, and then she tossed the jeans into the washer.

"Ms. Hind," I said.

Her whole body jerked upward and forward. She dropped the clothes and gripped the edge of the dryer like she were about to vault the machine. After a few moments, Pam caught her breath.

"Oh, Detectives." She laid her hand over her chest. "I'm sorry, I'm a bit nervous considering."

Pam pointed toward the outside wall in the direction of the Luther's house.

"Perfectly natural," Louise said and leaned against the jam of the laundry room door. "I don't think you have anything to worry about though."

Pam's brows drew together. "What do you mean? Wasn't there a robbery?"

"Not that we could tell," Louise said.

Pam turned her questioning eyes to me. I pressed my lips together and nodded my support for Louise's theory.

"Really?" Pam bent, snagged a black t-shirt, and slam-dunked it into the washer with all the grace of pro basketball player. "I just assumed they were killed in a robbery."

"All the electronics and easily pawned items are still in the house," I said. "The Luther's murder appears to be motivated by something other than robbery."

Pam dropped the lid of the washing machine into place with a hollow, metal, thunk.

"They seemed like such a nice couple. I can't believe they could be involved in anything seedy enough for murder."

A familiar refrain. Every victim's neighbor says something similar.

"Did Chad tell you anything helpful about his parent's deaths?"

"He told us what we needed to know from him." Louise side stepped the question with ease. "We'd like to ask you about what you saw today."

Pam nodded. "Of course, if I can help. Why don't we go into the kitchen? That way we won't disturb Chad again."

More like Pam Hind didn't want to incur Chad's wrath. Until he left for his aunt's house, she'd give Chad a wide birth.

Louise and I sat at the breakfast bar while Pam tidied her kitchen, which was as overrun with dirty dishes as her laundry room was with dirty clothes. Pam Hind hadn't been expecting company today, or in the near future, and it showed. A fine veil of dust, accumulated over some time, hazed her entire house.

"Sorry for the mess." Blossoms of red appeared on her cheeks. "I've been winterizing the house and cleaning up the yard so I haven't had a lot of time to work inside."

She flicked on the hot water and let the sink fill around the dirty dishes. From a drawer next to the sink she pulled a washcloth, ran it under the tap, and then swiped at the counter top in front of us.

"Ms. Hind," Louise said.

"Please call me Pam." She smiled.

"Pam, did you see or hear anything?" Louise asked. "Any loud noises? Did you notice any vehicle leaving the Luther's house?"

Pam thought for a few seconds and then shook her head. "I didn't notice any cars that were out of the ordinary, but my central-air unit is on the side of the house away from the Luther's. I wouldn't have been able to see a car pull in while I was wrapping the central-air in plastic."

She closed the hot water tap in time to keep the sink from flooding onto the floor.

"You didn't hear a gunshot?" Louise stacked a few plates on her side of the bar and pushed them toward Pam. "Anything that could be considered out of the ordinary?"

"No."

The answer was too quick.

"Please, Pam," I said. "Take your time and think. You were outside all morning. You had to have heard something."

She picked up the plates that Louise had pushed toward her, and piled them on top of the dishes in the sink, creating an impossible tower that put the Leaning Tower of Pisa to shame.

"Maybe I did." She sagged against the cupboard and covered her face with both of her hands.

I pressed on. "What is it, Pam?"

She whimpered into her hands. "I swore I'd never be one of those people who would ignore something, no matter how small."

"What?" Louise asked. "You won't be in trouble, Pam."

She dropped her hands from her face. "Maybe not legally but morally I am in trouble, because I ignored my own instincts."

Pam picked the washcloth from the counter and threw it at the sink. The dishes rattled and teetered but thankfully held their place.

"I moved here from the hood, Detectives. Where even if you were shot in front of a group of one hundred, no one would see anything. I made a promise to myself back then that I would not be one of those people."

She braced herself against the countertop and dropped her head so she wouldn't look directly at us.

"If I saw a guy beating up his girlfriend. If I saw a drug deal going down, I would call the police. I would never become so callous as to believe what was happening wasn't my problem."

Pam lifted her eyes to look at us.

"Like the old saying, *when they finally came for me there was no one to speak for me*."

I knew that proverb well. My Grandmother, a Polish immigrant, had come to America after the holocaust. Though she would never speak about what she saw, she would recite, *First They Came*, at least once every visit.

"When I moved here –" Pam raised her arms and looked around at her kitchen. "I guess I thought I had finally escaped."

"Tell us what you heard." Louise's tone was to the point.

Pam took a deep breath. "I heard the gun shots."

"More than one shot?" I asked.

"Two." She swallowed hard. "Then I heard a scream. I think it was Mrs. Luther screaming. The voice was too high pitched to be Mr. Luther."

Her account confirmed my timeline of events. Mr. Luther's murder occurred first. This was the only explanation that made sense, unless Mr. Luther had expected his wife's death, and our killer knew how to clean up his blood trail from the first floor to attic fast enough, and well enough, to escape detection.

"The scream ended so fast that I thought maybe I hadn't heard a scream at all. Maybe my over active imagination was getting the better of me. After all, things like this aren't supposed to happen here."

Things like this weren't supposed to happen anywhere, but they did. Regardless of the price you paid for your home you couldn't pick you neighbors, or the activities in which they were involved.

"But you didn't see a car in their driveway?" Louise typed a few notes in her phone then turned a questioning glance toward Pam.

"No."

"Not even in the street?" I asked.

"No. Why?"

Louise leaned back in her seat. "Mrs. Leigh across the street claims she saw a car speeding away from the house."

Pam Hind snorted a laugh. "She also claims that she's related to Janet Leigh, and that Elvis came to her in a vision to tell her that he isn't really dead."

Well, there was a small tidbit of information we didn't have yet. Surprising, since the Janet Leigh info came out in the first thirty-seconds of our conversation with Bernice.

"Mrs. Leigh likes attention."

Pam reached under the sink and came up with an industrial sized bottle of Dawn Dishwashing Liquid. She squeezed the blue liquid over the top of the dishes in a swirling pattern.

"I may not know a lot about the people who live around me, but that much I do know. Mrs. Leigh was the first person to pay me a visit when I moved in. I had barely gotten out of my car, and she told me the whole history of the people who had lived in the house before me."

All the more reason why Mrs. Leigh would know if there were a car in the neighborhood or not. There was always one neighbor who was the eagle eyes, and Mrs. Leigh was it, but then why would Pam Hind lie to us?

"When was the last time Chad visited his parents?" Louise asked.

Pam shrugged. "Last weekend, I guess. I really don't keep close tabs on his comings and goings."

From reports received from the other neighbors, everyone knew when the Spyder was in town.

"Did he seem to have any problems with his parents?"

My interest peeked. Where was Louise going with these questions? Did she really believe Chad might be involved in his parents' death? Or, did she just want Pam to think she did?

Unfortunately, her face was unreadable, and we hadn't discussed what line of questioning we would take. I would have to trust her instinct, which was next to impossible for me and my control-freak ways. I couldn't participate if I didn't know the dance, and this change in tempo had just left me up against the wall in my best party dress to tap my toe to her tune.

"I guess so." Pam's curiosity was as on point as mine. "They always seemed to be a *Leave It to Beaver* kind of family."

Pam turned a wary gaze down the hall, as if wondering if she had a killer reclining in her living room.

"You never saw them fight about anything? Girls? The car? Friends? Money?"

Pam's brows knitted together so tightly, I was sure she would develop a cramp in her forehead and be stuck that way permanently. She must have run through every day since she'd moved in and found nothing of great interest, because she shook her head and her brow smoothed.

"I can't think of anything."

"Thank you, Pam," Louise said and then smiled. "These are just routine questions in an investigation like this."

Pam made a silent "o" with her mouth and then gave a hesitant half smile.

"We'll be in touch." Louise stood.

I stood. "One of the uniformed officers will take Chad to his Aunt's house. Is it okay if he stays here until then?"

"Of course." Except the worried expression on her face didn't match the lightness in her voice.

Louise had planted a seed of doubt with Pam Hind and I was peeing myself to find out why.

What remained of the afternoon sun had disappeared from the sky. Only a soft, pink glow remained on the horizon. If it hadn't been for the spotlights of the news crews, it would have been a beautiful but chilly Minnesota evening.

Once I was certain we were out of earshot of the press and the line of gawkers who had gathered to watch, I quizzed Louise.

"Spill." I turned to face the Luther's front door so that my back was to the crowd, and any proficient lip readers in the crowd couldn't see what we were saying. "What was that all about?"

Louise turned to face the front door too.

"I don't know why, but I had to put the doubt in her mind. No one has a peachy keen, Cleaver-esque life. As long as Pam Hind believed that her neighbors were living the perfect existence she wasn't going to dig up any useful information."

"Ah." I nodded. "So even if it's not really the kid you're trying to get dirt on, Pam will now start thinking seriously about every move the Luther's have made without the rose colored glasses."

"Exactly. The, *everything here is wonderful*, attitude really does nothing to further our investigation. Pam Hind, by her own admission, came from the hood. To her, I'm sure, this neighborhood and everyone in it really is perfect, compared to what she's seen in the past."

A bracing wind cut down the tree-lined street and Louise and I both rushed to zip up our coats.

The cold from the concrete sidewalk had permeated my suede boots creating toe-cicles. I stomped in place to drive blood into my feet.

"Where to now?" I gritted between chattering teeth. "Please tell me it's somewhere indoors and warm."

She stuffed her hands into her pockets. "Standard drill. Talk to everyone who knew the Luthers, find out if there's any smoking gun evidence, and solve the case. You know – typical day at the office."

"Okay, but where do we begin?"

"Nothing really jumps out at me as the best starting place." She shrugged. "The father's work?"

I checked my watch. "That would be a tomorrow thing, because they're closed by now. What about the Grandmother's murder?"

Louise raised her eyebrows. "You think they might be connected?"

"Three murders, one family? Most families don't experience one murder in a lifetime, let alone three."

Even the best odds maker in Vegas wouldn't make book on that one.

"Maybe the family is dirty," I said. "Maybe they're part of the mob."

Louise's eyes rolled heavenward. "You and that Elliot Ness fantasy."

"What?" I splayed my arms out in front of me. "The mob used to run through Saint Paul all the time. Capone, Baby Face, even Dillinger called this town home at one time or another. Who's to say one of the modern mob families hasn't decided to follow in the footsteps of their underworld forefathers?"

"Catherine."

"What?" I tried to sound equally nonplussed.

"Go home to Gavin and get a terrible night's sleep."

I snapped to attention and saluted her.

"If you insist."

She made a shooing motion with her hands. "Give him my love."

"No way, but I will give him mine." I waggled my eyebrows, and then took off toward my car before Louise could change her mind.

"See you tomorrow," Louise called after me.

I waved my hand in the air but didn't turn back. "Bright and early."

Dinner, Gavin's special meat loaf, mashed potatoes, and green beans smothered in his secret seasoning, was cold by the time I made it through the front door of our run down old Victorian house. I found Gavin elbow deep in dishwater. KC a mutt that followed Gavin Home from vacation was nestled at his feet. Part of my brain whispered that if I didn't have Gavin my kitchen would look like Pam Hind's.

"I'm sorry I missed dinner, again." I slid my arms around Gavin's waist and kissed his cheek.

KC raised his head and gave a low growl so I toed him toward the living room. He grudgingly moved to the other side of the table and lay down but kept a close eye on me. My relationship with KC was tentative at best, but we were learning to find space for each other for Gavin's sake.

He turned his face toward me and kissed the top of my head. "At least you're home before I fell asleep on the couch, again."

I picked an apple from a bowl on the stove and felt around it for brown spots.

"It's not my fault you fall asleep. Try watching something more stimulating than the *Weather Channel*."

My thumb pushed through a soft spot and I threw the apple in the trash. Gavin let out a disgusted grunt but decided not to pursue the old argument we've had since we started dating about cutting off the brown spots. Just the thought made me nauseated.

"Nag, nag, nag." He removed the last dish from the water, rinsed it, and pulled the plug on the dirty dishwater. "You criticize the *Weather Channel* and you criticize the other shows I watch."

"Like what other shows?"

"*C.S.I.*"

"I like *C.S.I.* but it unrealistically raises the expectations of victims of real crimes. I'm good at my job but I can't solve a crime in less than forty-five minutes."

I plucked another apple from the bowl, pressed my fingers around the outside, found no soft spots, and took a bite.

"Besides," I said, through a mouth full of Honeycrisp. "Some of the stuff they do on that show you can't do in real life. Especially not with our budget."

He finished drying the last dish and put it away.

"And that's why I watch the *Weather Channel*. So don't complain."

He leaned against the cabinet. Only a few hours earlier I had been running my fingers over the dark hairs on that chest and feeling my toes curl when he kissed me. I glanced at the apple in my hand, thought about my rumbling stomach, and decided I rather devour my husband than an apple.

Hell, it wasn't the first time I'd gone without eating and it wouldn't be the last. At least this time I had a good reason. I was in desperate need of a Gavin fix.

I tossed the apple into the garbage. Gavin grunted his disapproval.

"Don't tell me that apple was bad too."

"Nope, the apple was fine."

"Then why did you throw it away?" He looked as though he were ready to dive in after the apple.

"I thought of something else I wanted more." I took a step toward him.

He still stared into the garbage as if he could resurrect the apple.

"What?"

I slid my finger under the waistband of his jeans and gave a sharp tug. The snap above his fly popped open with a satisfying click.

"You."

The look on his face went from mild surprise to complete understanding.

"Oh." He gave me a lusty smile. "Are you sure you're not biting off more than you can chew?"

"Only one way to find out."

I inched my hands from the front of his waistband to the back, then down the back of his underpants. I squeezed his bare butt cheeks, then let go.

Gavin wrapped his arms around my waist. He lifted me off the floor in a bear hug. I wrapped my legs around him in a python embrace.

"Floor, couch, or bed?" he asked. "Ladies choice."

"Hmm." I tapped my chin with my index finger. "Since I'm going to fall asleep immediately afterward, you'd better make it the bed."

He planted a huge kiss on my lips, and then walked toward the front stairway.

"Are you sure you can carry me all the way up the stairs?" I mumbled against his lips, unwilling to leave his kiss for a minute.

"If not," he mumbled back. "You'll have to sleep on the stairs."

Chapter Three

The alarm clock on my nightstand blared to life at five-thirty in the morning. I sat up half on and half under the comforter, with my t-shirt wrapped around my neck like a scarf. The rest of my body was naked and shivering.

I blinked to clear the sleep from my eyes.

"Shut up!"

I slapped my palm down on the wide button of the clock and silenced the incessant ree, ree, ree. The dog woofed at me from the foot of the bed and I shoved him off.

Gavin poked his head out from the master bathroom, which wasn't quite a master bathroom yet. At the moment, it was more of a stud-walled closet with bathroom fixtures in it.

Victorian houses didn't come equipped with master bathrooms, so my husband decided to correct this design flaw. He does after all own his own remodeling company. They renovate and remodel huge old buildings in a matter of months. A small master bathroom project, right in his own home, shouldn't take more than a few weeks to complete.

That was over eight years ago.

True, all the amenities that traditionally classify a room as a *bath* were in place. The toilet, sink, and tub were all functional but not yet in their permanent location. The walls were just studs, insulation, and vapor barrier.

An intricate network of extension cords, which had to be a huge safety no-no, supplied the power for the bathroom. The only light was a portable, metal, clamp-light clipped to a stud by the sink, and was so hot that every morning I felt like I were giving a make-up applying demonstration on stage at the Ordway Theater.

"Good morning sunshine," he chimed.

I grunted, and tugged the comforter across my legs to ward off the cold.

"I'm almost finished and then the bathroom's all yours," he said.

The only thought that kept skipping through my consciousness was, *why did I marry a morning person*? Every morning he was cheery and it pissed me off; at least until after four or twelve cups of coffee.

After a few irritating seconds of blow dryer whine, Gavin emerged. He tucked his t-shirt into his Levis and moved to his side of the bed. The sweatshirt he pulled from the nightstand drawer had his company's logo embroidered on the left side. He tugged the shirt over his head.

"I'll get the coffee started."

It was the first thing he'd said all morning that made me smile.

He braced himself on the mattress and kissed my cheek. I made a halfhearted pucker, which was the best I could manage.

Gavin left with KC close on his heel. I watched his butt as he left. A little more inspiration to start the day right.

My life could be a lot worse. I could be married to a morning person who didn't have such a nice ass. Plus, he knew how to make a hell-of-a cup of coffee.

Blinking at the wall didn't produce any results in the getting dressed department, so I snaked my way out from under the blankets, padded over to my dresser to assemble a clean outfit.

The shower did wonders to open my eyes, but the coffee that Gavin left steaming on the nightstand in my favorite Star Trek mug, pushed the trolley off the cliff. Gavin had read my bleary eyes and used an extra scoop of coffee this morning. The result was high-octane jet fuel in a cup.

I sucked down the coffee without pause and then wandered, one step above the living dead, down the stairs to get another cup.

Gavin waited for me in the kitchen, the dog sitting at his feet. He held out a plate containing a fried egg sandwich, one of his many culinary specialties.

"No, thanks." I grabbed the coffee pot off the burner. "I have all the breakfast I need right here."

"Not good enough." He stuffed the toasted bread, egg and cheese concoction between my teeth. "Bite."

I chomped down only because I knew the sandwich would remain lodged in my teeth until I did.

"You didn't eat anything last night, so you are going to eat the whole sandwich."

"But I'm in a hurry."

I topped off my mug and put the pot back.

Gavin trapped my free hand on its return and closed my fingers around the edge of the sandwich crust.

"The beauty of the sandwich design, my dear, is that it is portable. You can finish your breakfast in the car."

Breakfast really wasn't my meal. Even the little bit I had swallowed was turning flip-flops in my stomach.

"I suppose I can't convince you with the distracted driving argument?"

Gavin scrubbed at his chin.

"Maybe you're right."

He took the Star Trek mug from my hand.

"Leave the coffee; it will be too distracting for you."

I sucked in a deep, shocked breath.

"You win, Gavin James O'Brien." I opened and closed my fingers in the air like a child saying gimme, gimme. "Just don't think I'm going to forget this little incident."

"Don't worry, I know you won't. You still remember little incidents from before we were married." He kissed my cheek. "You're like an elephant."

I narrowed my eyes. "Did you just call me fat?"

Gavin put his arm around my waist and pulled me toward the front door. "Yep, that's why I'm forcing you to eat. I like my women with a little meat on them. Now go to work."

He jerked open the front door, then grabbed my purse from the banister, and hung it around my neck.

"You're in a hurry. Remember?"

"If I were a suspicious woman I'd think you were trying to get rid of me for a reason."

I leaned in and kissed Gavin. At the same time, I tossed what was left of the sandwich to KC. He snapped it out of midair and trotted away to eat in private.

"Call me later," he said. "Let me know if you'll be home for dinner."

With the new case we were working on, I had a better chance of becoming the next President of the United States. I agreed to call and left.

Although I live less than ten miles from work there were two sections of my commute that bottlenecked with commuters jostling their way into the city. Up until a few years ago, my commute had been a breeze, and then the City of Saint Paul made a big push to get businesses back into downtown. Urban renewal scoured the city of its industrial past and turned the downtown warehouses into luxury condominiums, hip, trend topping bars and restaurants.

This renewal is what had probably brought the Luther family to Saint Paul, after the murder of Chad's Grandmother, instead of one of the equally well to do suburban neighborhoods. Trying to disconnect the murder of the Grandmother from the murder of Chad's parents yesterday was like trying to shove a watermelon up your nose — it doesn't fit.

Louise was already in the office and on the phone. She waved a good morning. I toasted her with my coffee mug, which was in desperate need of a refill.

I dropped my purse on the floor, kicked it into its customary place under my desk, and then went to the break room. Once I had refueled, I returned, and dropped into my chair.

Mounds of paperwork littered the top of my desk. A delicate dance of ordered chaos, all of my own design, except for the section of newspaper displayed in the center of my blotter with a bright, red circle around one of the articles.

I leaned in to get a better look.

"Oh, shit."

"Way to go, O'Brien." Bob Shackelford leaned over my shoulder and tapped the newspaper. "Front page. I think that's a first for you. Usually your tirades are limited to interoffice email. You're really stepping up in the world."

"Thanks, Shackelford. Say, you oughta have that growth looked at."

"What growth."

I pointed to his head. "Oh, never mind, it's your face."

"Haw, haw, O'Brien. Very childish"

He was right but it was the best I could manage on limited coffee.

He lifted the paper from my desk and unfolded it in mid-air. "At least the story appears on the bottom half of the front page. Hardly anyone looks at the bottom half."

The headline read, *Saint Paul Police Defensive Over Botched Investigation.* Under the headline was a photo of me in front of Pam Hind's house. The photographer had snapped the photo while I was speaking. My lips curled back from my teeth and I was pointing into the crowd. I looked like KC when he sees the neighbor's cat on our porch.

Shackelford tweaked the edge of the paper. "It took me a whole ten seconds to skim down far enough to see this article."

I snatched the paper from his hands and began to read.

Officer Catherine O'Brien, a seven-year veteran of the Saint Paul Police Department, gave an impromptu press conference outside the house of Mr. and Mrs. Jonathan Luther who were murdered inside their Saint Paul area home Tuesday morning.

Officer O'Brien, stumbled drunkenly down the sidewalk, scolded the media, and referred to the press as "vultures" after attempts to question the officer about the path of the homicide investigation. This outburst is just the latest in what has become a pattern of denial and hostility by the Saint Paul Police Department and crime lab when questions regarding investigative procedures arise.

The story went on to outline the perceived pattern the reporter was seeing, whether real or concocted by them to sell papers. Too bad this reporter hadn't managed to convince her editors to run the story above the fold. Police corruption and incompetence always sells.

"The Chief's been on the phone all morning," Shackelford said. "He's been fielding calls from all the local stations about the story."

"Shit." I buried my face in the papers on my desk. "Why do I come here in the mornings?"

I rolled my head to the side so I wouldn't breathe in newsprint.

"I could have been a cage cleaner at the zoo."

Shackelford gave a short laugh. "With people skills like yours, O'Brien, I'm surprised you weren't a social worker."

Louise dropped her phone back onto the cradle.

"Leave her alone, Bob. Don't you have some work to do today? If not, clock out and go home. Stop wasting taxpayer's money."

"She made the whole department look bad, Montgomery." His tone changed to a bleating sound.

"The article is a lie. You should know how the media twists a story better than anyone."

Last January, Shackelford faced charges of beating a guy who was out of his mind on crystal meth. The family sued the city and the department. Unfortunately, for the drug addict, he didn't realize that all holding areas are video taped. The tape was proof that he sustained his injuries from repeated attempts to ram through the cell door with his forehead. Of course, by that time the Police Department suffered permanent damage to its reputation. The story with the truth of what had happened ran on page ten of the metro section of the paper.

"Who was the most outspoken about your innocence, Bob?" Louise touched the tips of her finger to her desktop and pushed to her feet. "Catherine defended you in private and in the press. I think you owe her better than this."

Bob hung his head like a shamed dog. "I was just giving you shit, O'Brien. You know I didn't mean anything by it, right?"

He gave my shoulder a playful punch.

I decided to let him off the hook. With the day I was having, I could use all the support I could get, even if it were born out of guilt. "Sure, Shackelford, we're cool."

Shackelford skulked away, head down, and tail firmly entrenched between his knees.

I gulped down a slug of coffee ignoring the searing hot pain in my throat as it slid toward my stomach.

"Thanks, Louise."

She perched on the edge of my desk and picked up the newspaper. "It's the least I can do, considering the onslaught you're about to face. There won't be any way to save you from the Chief."

I dropped my head back to the desktop. A stack of files I hadn't gotten around to filing yet, crashed onto the floor. I groaned.

"Oh, come on." She pushed my chair with her foot. The casters engaged and rolled the chair backward until my head came off the desk.

"You had to have known you'd get some blowback from what you said yesterday."

"Yeah."

"This story is a lie. All except the part where they directly quote you. You did call the press vultures."

"I know." I raked my fingers through my unruly curls, then snagged a rubber band from my drawer and secured my hair into a ratty ponytail. "They are vultures. It's the rest of the story that's so bad."

Louise crumpled the paper and dropped it into the wastepaper basket. "Come on, we have to talk to the Chief. We know the investigation isn't botched. We'll just tell him what really happened."

She sounded like a perky nurse trying to convince a terminal patient that everything would be fine in a day or two.

I slowly got to my feet. "Can't you just talk to him? You could just smooth things over first and then I'll go talk to him."

She picked up my mug and handed it to me. "No, I can't. He said he wanted to see you first thing. He really didn't sound that mad."

Right, and the sound of dentist's drills are only mildly annoying.

"It's better to get it out of the way anyway," she said. "We have a long day ahead of us."

There wasn't enough coffee in Colombia to make the ass chewing I was about to receive any easier to take. I gulped down what remained in my mug in three long swallows, then swept my hand out in front of me.

"Lead the way."

The chief's door was wide open like the jaws of an angry monster. Inside, the chief paced the length of his phone cord from one side of his desk to the other.

"He's busy now," I said. "We'll have to come back later."

Before I could escape, the chief spotted me, and flagged me inside.

Louise put her hands on my shoulders. "He's never too busy to talk to you, Catherine. You should know that by now."

Chief waved again, this time more emphatically.

I stepped forward and from somewhere I swore I heard TAPS playing. I looked over my shoulder and saw Shackelford tooting out the tune through his fingers.

I gave him the finger.

There were only two guest chairs in the chief's office. Neither provided easy access to the door if I needed to escape, so I chose the one near the window. Who knew, a leap from the eighth floor might be more fun than what was heading my way with all the speed of a runaway freight train.

I slumped down in the seat and tried to make myself as small as possible under the chief's dark glare.

I didn't need to know who he was talking to on the phone. His only contribution to the conversation was, *yes sir* and *I understand sir*. Finally he said, "Yes sir. We'll take care of it."

He lowered the phone so slowly it looked like a video on frame-by-frame motion. With each inch closer to the cradle the phone got, the more pain I felt. By the time he'd hung up the phone, I could have sworn I'd already received my ass chewing.

He laced his fingers together then let out a slow breath.

Hour-like seconds, ticked by without a sound. He didn't look up. He didn't move. The only sign that he was still alive was the rapid pulse at his temple.

"Tomorrow." He flattened his palms out on the desk. "Is my twenty-year anniversary with the Saint Paul Police Department."

"Congratulations," Louise said in a bright and cheery tone.

He turned his head, flattened his lips into a humorless smile, and gave her a short nod.

"Instead of celebrating my anniversary with a glass of champagne, as I had planned to do," each word measured and slow, "I'm going to be playing clean up with the press."

He turned to me and smiled. Not a happy, friendly smile; a disturbing, frightening smile.

"Sorry."

He leaned forward and cupped his hand behind his ear. "What's that? I'm sorry. I couldn't hear you, O'Brien."

"I am sorry, chief."

He waved off the apology.

"I know you are. And I know that part of the story was sensationalized. Right?"

Louise and I nodded, with our most innocent expressions, like disciplined children.

"So you will do everything in your power to correct the problem."

He nodded.

We nodded.

"Good." He held up a rumpled copy of the paper. "Tell me how this happened."

I hung my head and waited for Louise to explain my actions so I wouldn't sound like a raving lunatic. When no explanation came, I glanced at Louise from the corner of my eye and realized she was looking at me and so was the chief.

I straightened and took a deep breath. Then I took the plunge.

"I lost my temper." A good start and the truth. Not crazy yet. "The press was camped in front of the neighbor's house trying to get at the Luther's son."

So far so good. No real damage done.

Chief nodded as patiently as a therapist listening to a patient spill their guts.

"The press –"

He held up his stubby sausage shaped index finger, then lifted the well-folded newspaper.

"You mean the vultures?"

"Yes, I called them vultures. They were trying to breech the line and get to the front door. Some even jumped the fence in the alley."

He let out a heavy sigh. "So they were doing their normal thing and you went on the attack?"

"I wouldn't have but they should know better than to go after a kid."

Chief lifted a manila folder and flipped open the cover. He skimmed the page on top of the file.

"This kid you're talking about would be . . .?"

"Chad Luther," I said.

"Chad Luther?" He slid the folder around to face me. "The same Chad Luther who is nineteen years old and attending the University? Is this the *kid* you're speaking about?"

Damn Louise's clerical efficiency. I glanced at the folder. The report of the Luther's murder, neat and complete, glared up at me.

"Okay, so he's not a little kid but chief imagine being nineteen-years-old, finding both your parents murdered, and then having to have to deal with those . . .."

"Vultures," Louise filled in for me.

"Yes." I closed my eyes and prayed that the word *vulture* wouldn't follow me around for the rest of my career though I knew it would. "Thank you, Louise."

"You're welcome."

Smart-ass.

"Imagine chief."

"Okay." He sat back and held up his hands in surrender. "I understand the reasons. And they're good reasons. But how you handled the situation, good reasons or not, was wrong."

"I know." It was my turn to tuck my tail between my knees.

"Therefore, as your penance, you will give an exclusive interview regarding the case."

"What?" I shot up straight in my seat. "Come on, chief. Penance is three Hail Mary's and don't do it again. This is punishment, cruel and unusual."

He ignored my pleas and folded the newspaper so it fit in the folder.

"I suggest you avail yourself of the services of our media relations people. They can help coach you in the best way to deal with this situation."

"You're not serious," I said.

Even Louise had moved to the edge of her seat with a "*that's not a good idea*" look on her face.

"I'm very serious, O'Brien."

"But chief," Louise said. "We don't want to compromise our investigation."

"That's why you will run your responses by the media experts, and do a little research before you meet with her."

"Her?" I asked. "Her who?"

"The reporter who wrote this story." He held up the newspaper and squinted at the puny, black type. "Her name's Jane Katts."

"Are you crazy?" I tapped my index finger on my temple.

If I hadn't already committed career suicide, I had just performed the coup de grace. In for a penny, in for a pound – I pushed on.

"If I were going to give an exclusive interview about this case, it sure as hell wouldn't be to a reporter who just tried to Titanic the entire Police Department over one off-the-cuff remark and stopped short of saying I was drunk on the job."

"Chief, I have to agree with Catherine on this one," Louise said, to my great relief. "This reporter printed a story that was a complete lie."

"Except the vulture part," I said.

Louise nodded. "Except that. The rest was completely false."

"All the more reason to set her straight." He stood. "Too late to argue with me, it's been decided."

"How could you –"

"I didn't." He came around the desk and stood in front of us. "The person I was speaking with when you came in decided for us."

"Who?" Louise asked.

"The Mayor." He folded his arms over his barrel chest. "He's taken quite an interest in you, O'Brien. He's especially interested in how you'll handle this debacle next."

The Mayor is watching me now? That couldn't be good news.

"I guess, I don't have a choice," I said.

"Not really. No."

I clasped my hands together on my lap. "I'll speak with Ms. Katts, when I have the time. The investigation comes first."

Louise gave me a supportive smile.

Chief mulled over the proposal, knowing that my ground was shakier than a six-point-eight on the Richter scale.

Either I accepted the Mayor's proposal or I found a new job. What the chief was trying to decide was how long he could put the Mayor, and this Katts woman, off and still keep *his* job. He didn't like bullies any more than I did, and he sure as hell didn't like the press any more than I do.

I was gambling that the stubborn rebellious streak we shared would win out over his good judgment. Then I could fulfill the Mayor's request and still keep a small shred of dignity by not immediately bowing to Jane Katts' blackmail tactics.

A knowing grin split the chief's face. "Agreed O'Brien. You'll do the exclusive on your schedule only when it doesn't conflict with the investigation."

We shook hands.

The chief took a scrap of paper from his desk blotter and handed it to me.

"Here's Jane Katts' number, though I'm sure she'll be in touch with you. The Mayor has already spoken to her."

I stuffed the paper in my jacket pocket.

"What's your next move, ladies?" he asked.

"Jonathan Luther's office," Louise said. "None of the Luther's neighbor knew the family all that well. We'd like to talk to someone who might know who their friends were. Or if the Luther's were involved in something that got them killed."

I had to add my seven cents. "We'll be checking out the murder of Chad Luther's Grandmother as well. Maybe the local law enforcement uncovered something that might be pertinent to this investigation."

That little nugget of information was one the press would not get. The last thing we needed was for Chad to see his Grandmother's name splashed across newspapers, along with his parents, in a news story that made his family out to be the Corleones of Minnesota.

The Chief in his usual, graceful style issued the order, "get to work," as a single-word bark.

When we stepped into the bullpen area, half of the office was watching with worried eyes. The other half cast surreptitious glances over their shoulders pretending not to be watching.

"Do you still believe the Grandmother's death is connected?" Louise strode through the office, and ignored the questioning gazes.

We passed Shackelford whose brows rutted into a deep V. He followed me with his eyes as if trying to determine whether I was about to clean out my desk. He gave an almost imperceptible nod. I gave him a discreet thumbs-up and he grinned.

We gave each other a hard time but we both played on the same team, and neither of us held any real malice toward one another.

"What do we lose by asking about the Grandmother's murder?"

"Time," she said.

"One phone call, Louise. We're not talking about driving to Duluth for God's sake."

"How about information that sends you on a wild goose chase?"

Louise opened her bottom desk drawer and pulled out her slim purse. I toed my purse out from its hiding place.

"That might be helpful in dealing with Jane Katts," I said. "Maybe it would give her a project."

"Speaking of."

Louise fanned a stack of pink *While You Were Out* notes that someone had dropped on the top of the stack of papers in my *In Basket*, which no one ever used anyway. If they needed me to see something they just left whatever it was on my chair where I wouldn't mistake it as just one of the other ignored files that littered my desk.

I did a quick flick through the stack. Every single message was from Katts.

"Why didn't she just leave a message on my voicemail?"

I glanced at my phone and noticed the red light above the abbreviation MSG blinked a rapid blink that meant more than one message. I lifted the hand set, pushed the message button and then when cued punched in my pin number.

Your mailbox is full. The sweet automated voice said.

That explained why I was receiving pink message slips. I bet Arnie, who manned our main reception area, had cursed my name every time my phone rolled to the main switchboard.

The first message started to roll.

"Hi Officer O'Brien this is Jane Katts."

I hit the number nine on the keypad.

Message deleted. The sweet automation said.

The next message left a few minutes after the first began. "Hi Officer O'Brien, it's Jane Katts, again."

Nine.

Message deleted.

This process continued until the final message, the last satisfying, *message deleted*, chimed in my ear.

I slung my purse over my shoulder.

"Anyone important?" Louise smirked at me.

"I think it was a wrong number," I said. "They kept asking for an Officer O'Brien. They must not have realized they'd been transferred to *Detective* O'Brien instead."

I shrugged. "It was probably just someone wanting to renew a newspaper subscription."

"You're not interested then?" Louise asked.

"No, I've decided to get my news from reliable sources, like the *Weekly World News*."

Chapter Four

"Jonathan Luther was a saint."

Liz Trainor, Jonathan Luther's boss at Balsam Real Estate stabbed her finger toward us punctuating each word with a thrust forward. Each stab fanned the air around her and sent the heavy smell of some high-class perfume I couldn't identify wafting toward us. The smell might have been nice if Liz Trainor hadn't bathed in the perfume.

"He would have never, could have never hurt anyone."

She sat back with such force that her Dolly Parton-esque boobs rippled up and down in grotesque waves of fat. Her deep-veed, gauzy white blouse barely covered the bottoms of her breasts let alone the top.

"I have no doubt that he wouldn't hurt anyone," Louise said. "But someone did want to hurt him."

"They succeeded," I said.

"Are you the Detective I saw in the paper this morning?"

Liz Trainor looked at me with deep concentration. I squirmed in my chair.

"You are, aren't you?"

The wrinkles on her face smoothed with resolve. Her lips flattened and she nodded.

My gut twisted into knots. I had a sudden overwhelming urge to bolt from the room. Instead, I stared wide-eyed and mute.

"Yep, you are," she said. "You've botched the investigation and now you're here trying to dig up some dirt on the victim. Well you're not going to find any skeletons in Jonathan Luther's closet."

"We're not looking for skeletons." My tone was surprisingly calm and even, considering the irritation grating at my nerves. I was sure an edge of malice would lace all my conversations today. "We want to find the truth."

"Well, you just found it. Jon and his wife would give you the shirts from their backs. They were probably attacked by some junkie," she said. "Did you check for finger prints? Whoever it was probably already has a record."

Gee, why hadn't we thought of looking for fingerprints? I mentally rolled my eyes.

"Do you mind if we go through his desk?" Louise asked.

"What are you looking for?" Liz Trainor folded her chubby, fake nail-tipped fingers together. The thin-banded rings looked as if they would cut into her flesh or break in half from the pressure at any second.

"I don't know yet," Louise said. "I'm hoping we'll find something that might give us a direction."

"We'd like to speak with his co-workers too," I said.

"I think I'm going to call my lawyer first." She turned to her credenza, punched up an address book on her computer, and scrolled through the names. "I don't want you people crawling through my office trying to find a way out of the hole you've dug yourself into."

"Mrs. Trainor –"

"It's Ms. Trainor. I'm not married."

"Ms. Trainor." I corrected myself, though I couldn't care less if she were offended by my non-politically correct title. The correction was more to smooth her hackles back down, than a genuine show of courtesy. "We're not trying to dig ourselves out of a hole. We haven't had time to dig a hole yet."

Louise and Ms. Trainor exchanged raised eyebrow looks. Louise grinned and then Trainor's face split into a full smile.

"What?"

Trainor snickered and Louise laughed. I rolled back the last words out of my mouth. Understanding slapped me across the face.

"Give us a little more time and I'm sure we can really screw up the investigation." I joined their reverie.

Liz Trainor set the phone back in its cradle. "I don't mean to be a hard ass but I need to know that Jonathan's investigation isn't being handed off to someone with their head up their butt." She gestured toward the door. "Half the people in the other room were brought in here and trained by Jonathan. My business wouldn't be the success it is without Jonathan."

She sat back and studied us as if she stared long enough the answers of the universe would appear on our foreheads. Her gaze rested an extra long time on my face. She looked away for a brief moment then back at me again, this time her brow smoothed.

"I'll tell you what, Detectives. I'm going to allow you go through Jon's desk and question my employees."

I opened my mouth to utter a grateful thanks but Liz Trainor interrupted before the sounds would come out.

"Two conditions. One –" She held up both of her index fingers. "You cannot browbeat my employees into speaking to you. They must volunteer."

"Of course," Louise said. "What's the other condition?"

"The second condition." She closed her eyes. "God help me for saying this; if you find out that Jonathan was involved in something illegal, you don't embarrass this company. I want to hear about what you find first, not read about it in tomorrow's paper."

She flicked her gaze to me as if I would have some particular interest in talking to the newspaper. Probably to cover my own ass, if she still believed that I needed a fanny shield. All she had was my word and a shared laugh (not much comfort at the best of times) to tell her any different.

"Agreed," I said. "Are you sure there's nothing else you'd like to say?"

She cocked her head. "Why do you ask?"

"Because you looked at me funny a few minutes ago. Like you might know me."

"Yeah." The rolls on her neck contracted and expanded with the bobbing of her head. "I think I do know you."

I shook my head. "I don't think so. We've never met before."

"No, we haven't," she agreed. "But I do know you and not just from the paper. You're Gavin O'Brien's wife aren't you?"

A shockwave thundered through me at the sound of Gavin's name. It was the same feeling I get when Gavin runs into friends when we're shopping, or out for dinner. Gavin has a whole world away from me, and he knows people I don't. That thought disturbed me.

Of course, I knew people he didn't, too. Par for the course when you both work outside the home. I saw him every morning when I left and there he was every evening when I got home. There's a little piece of my brain that takes over from time to time—it's only purpose is to delude me and doesn't like to be confronted with reality. That section of gray matter makes me believe that Gavin sits at home hermetically sealed until my key turns in the lock to reanimate him.

Yet here was reality, in the form of an overweight, overly perfumed, real-estate agent.

"Yes, I am."

"I thought so." Liz Trainor nodded satisfied. "I usually have a good memory for faces. It helps in this job."

"Then the two of you have met?" Louise asked.

"No." Liz said.

I shook my head at the same time.

"Then how did you know she was married to Gavin?"

Thank God, Louise was there to ask all the questions I would kick myself later for not asking. Now, I was too stunned to form a complete thought.

"I saw a picture of you on his desk." She shrugged. "Well it's more of a table than a desk. Anyway, your picture is in his construction trailer."

What picture could Gavin possibly have of me? I maintained the mantra that my image didn't show up on film, so it wasn't like I'd gone down to the local *Glamour Shots* for one of those cheesy, feather boa, photos that the guys in my office had of their wives. I couldn't understand why men thought that bouffant hair, bright pink lipstick, and lots, of gauze and Vaseline over lenses made women look glamorous.

When this case was over, I'd have to take a trip down to his construction trailer. That was if I could remember where Gavin had said he was working this month.

"So you've worked with Gavin?" Louise continued to channel my questions.

Liz Trainor nodded. "I do commercial real-estate as well as private homes. I've worked with Gavin a few times in the past."

She gave a lascivious wink that made me want to punch her.

"You've got yourself one hell of a firecracker. Gavin O'Brien is a damn good business man, and darn cute if you don't mind me saying so."

She winked again.

I did mind her saying so. She was a colleague of his not a horny teenager. Liz Trainor needed to keep her eyes and mind off my husband.

"Some of the girls in the office can't wait for the days when Gavin has an appointment. They all make sure they're at their desks when he comes for a visit."

My breath hitched in my chest. The delusional part of my brain screamed, *NO! NO!* Not only did Gavin leave the house when I left for work, but other women were looking at him the way I used to look at him.

Bile crept up the back of my throat. I couldn't speak. All I could manage was a weak smile and pathetic laugh that must have sounded to Liz Trainor's ears as if I was agreeing with her. She waggled her brows up and down at me and chuckled.

"Where did Mr. Luther sit?" Louise finally broke the painful deadlock between us.

Liz pushed back from her desk and stood.

"Follow me," she said. "I'll show you."

Liz Trainor had to have been at least three hundred pounds and close to six feet tall, but she moved with the grace of a lithe dancer. She wove her way through the maze of desks and open file drawers with the ease of water flowing down an open drain. She came to a stop next to two partitioned walls tucked into a corner. Light showered through the windows and washed across the particleboard desk.

"This is Jonathan's area," Liz said.

Photos of Chad at various stages of his life, littered the credenza behind the desk. The largest showed Chad with both his Mother and Father on his graduation day. Chad swathed in cap and gown in the center with arms embracing both parents, who had the, *I just won the lottery*, smiles on their faces.

"Try not to make a mess," Liz said. "And don't remove any files unless you clear it with me first."

We weren't going to find anything in his desk. I could tell by looking at how open the area was. If Jonathan Luther had been involved in anything illegal, he wasn't talking about it on the phone in this office. Everyone within fifty feet would be able to hear his conversation no matter how quiet he tried to be.

I nodded my agreement and Liz left us.

Louise took a seat behind the desk and I sat in one of the guest chairs across from her.

"The desk isn't locked, is it?" I said it as a statement of fact instead of a question.

She pulled the drawer and it slipped open easily. "Nope. Not locked."

"Of course not," I said. "This guy is exactly what Liz Trainor said he is – honest and trustworthy."

I picked up one of the photos from the edge of the desk. Jonathan and Susan Luther smiled back at me from behind the glass, embracing one another on a tropical beach somewhere.

"Maybe it was her," I said and pointed to Susan. "We're barking up the Dad's tree but maybe Mom was the one we should be looking into."

Louise finished rifling the drawers and came up empty. No surprises. No smoking gun.

A pretty, young blonde, who couldn't have been more than a perky twenty-two, stuck her head over the wall.

"Hi," she said like a sparrow chirping out a song. "I heard Gavin's wife was here and I just had to see you."

Her eyes trailed to Louise.

"You're as beautiful as he said you are," she said. "He didn't mention that you were African-American though."

She covered her mouth with her hand. "I'm sorry, was that rude? It was, wasn't it? I'm not racist or anything like that, it's just that he only said you were pretty, he didn't describe you. You know, in detail."

She babbled like the airhead she was, and her air needed a change, quick.

Louise gave a patient smile, as if she dealt with adolescent idiots everyday of her life.

I stood and turned to face the girl.

"I am Catherine O'Brien," I said. "I'm Gavin's wife. This is my partner, Louise Montgomery."

She blinked a beady-eyed little blink like a startled rabbit caught outside its hole. Her nose even twitched to one side as if she were scenting the air to determine if I were a threat.

"Oh, sorry." She blinked again. "It's just you're not what I expected. You know – I mean – Gavin described you a little different is all."

"You mean he described me like her?" I jerked my thumb over my shoulder toward Louise.

"Well, yeah." She thought for a moment. "Well, no."

I understood the confusion well enough. My husband has the same delusional piece of his brain that I do. Only his convinces him that I am a great beauty when I'm out of his sight and sometimes when I'm in his sight. Gavin doesn't see my pale skin, my flat butt, my small boobs, or my frizzy hair. The hair was the thing that bothered me the most. My frizz chooses to stand up and be counted at the most inopportune times, usually during photos. That's why I still couldn't figure out what photo Gavin had managed to get out of the house without me knowing.

I looked at Louise over my shoulder. "Gavin's getting the two of us confused again, Louise. I'm going to have to have a talk with him."

The girl let out an uncomfortable laugh, then stuck out her hand. "Nice to meet you. I'm Madeline."

I shook her hand and Madeline looked relieved that it was only a shake and I didn't take her hand off.

"Your husband is such a darling. He's quite a flirt." She giggled.

"Is he?" Gavin and I would be having a long conversation later. "Madeline? Do you mind if we ask you a few questions about Jonathan Luther?"

The smile dropped from her face. "Sure. It's so sad what happened to him and his wife."

"Come have a seat next to me." I twisted one of the guest chairs.

Madeline stepped around the partition and she was even more petite and curvy than I had imagined. Gavin, *the flirt*, and I would have a serious conversation about Madeline.

"Ms. Liz said you'd want to talk to some of us about Jonathan."

"You call your boss Ms. Liz?" Louise shook Madeline's hand across the desk.

"Everyone calls her Ms. Liz. She likes it."

We stared at one another for several moments before Madeline squeezed her hands together and stretched her arms out in front of her.

"It feels really kinda creepy to be sitting in Jon's area like this." She shivered. "I sort of expect him to walk in at any second. He always brought donuts and coffee for the office."

She picked at the cuticles on her fingers. "He was a real decent guy to work with. I'm gonna miss him."

A single tear slipped down her cheek. Madeline flicked it away quickly and sniffed.

"Sorry. I thought I was done crying this morning."

"It's okay to cry," Louise said. "It's natural when someone you cared about is violently taken away from you."

Louise spotted a box of tissues on the edge of the credenza. She picked up the box and handed it to Madeline.

Madeline took a tissue and dabbed at the tip of her nose.

My cell phone chirped the theme from *Gilligan's Island.* I checked the caller I.D. and saw Gavin's name pop up.

"Sorry," I said. "It's my husband."

"Oh, tell Gavin, Maddie says, 'hi'."

I shut the ringer off and slipped the phone back into my pocket. Gavin would have to wait until I had a private moment to quiz him on his activities when I'm not around.

"I'll talk to him later."

Madeline frowned.

I lifted the family photo so it covered the lower half of my face.

"Did you know the family well?"

She gave a one-shouldered shrug. "I guess. How is Chad doing? Is he okay?"

She shook her head.

"That's stupid. Sorry. Of course, he's not okay. Where is he staying? Not in the house?"

She looked horrified at the thought of Chad sleeping in the house that his parents had been murdered in the day before. Then she seemed to dismiss the idea.

"Chad is with his Aunt." Louise had a way of speaking that made everything sound as if it would be alright, no matter how fucked up the situation.

"Madeline?" Louise leaned forward. The sudden shift in position drew Madeline's complete attention away from her own addled thoughts. "Did you ever hear anyone threaten Mr. Luther? Or ever hear him arguing with anyone on the phone or in person?"

Madeline let out a deep huffing breath, pouted her bottom lip, and turned her eyes toward the ceiling. Her forehead wrinkled in concentration so deep, I thought her skull might cave in at any moment. The *Final Jeopardy* theme music played in my head, only by the time I reached the *tip me over and pour me out* portion of the song, Madeline didn't have her answer ready.

Sorry, Madeline you don't win *Final Jeopardy* but we do have some lovely parting gifts for you.

She finally nodded. "He did have a fight with one of our clients. The client sued him but Jonathan won the lawsuit. The guy really wasn't happy about the whole thing."

Now we were getting somewhere. Jonathan Luther apparently did have a skeleton in his closet.

"Do you remember the client's name?" Louise removed her phone from her purse and prepared to thumb wield her notes.

"I ought to," Madeline snorted. "He called every day for over a month."

We waited but she stopped as if she'd said all that there was to say. After a few moments, I realized that Madeline wasn't going to notice why we were staring at her expectantly.

"And that name would be?"

"Oh, duh." She slapped her forehead. "Sorry. His name was Walter Wren – double-u, double-u." She drew the letters in the air. "That's why I remember so well."

Louise clicked the name into her notes.

"Anyone else?" I asked.

"No, just him. Like I said, Jonathan was a real good guy to work with. That's why double-u, double-u lost his lawsuit. Jonathan would never try to screw someone over."

We thanked Madeline and she left, promising to send in the next coworker who would be willing to speak with us. It turned out that the entire staff of Balsam Real Estate wanted to talk to us. All the employees told pretty much the same story with only minor variations. Jonathan Luther was a great guy. Oh, there was that one incident, with that one guy, but Jon was vindicated. Other than that, there was nothing new they could add.

"What a relief." Ms. Liz patted a hand over her chest. "I kept praying you wouldn't find anything dirty on Jon, but you never can tell these days. God forgive me for saying so."

"Thanks for your help." I held out my hand and she pumped it with vigor. "We'll be looking into this Walter Wren character and see if he has anything to do with the Luther's deaths."

Ms. Liz shook her finger at us. "He was extremely mad about losing the lawsuit, but I never thought he would be mad enough to do something like this."

"You'd be surprised," Louise said. "Thank you."

The blustery cold day had turned drizzly by the time we left Balsam Real Estate. Soon we'd be dealing with snow. I cinched my jacket all the way up to the neck and tried to remember if I'd had my winter coat dry-cleaned. I would have to remember to check when I got home or ask Gavin; he'd know.

I'd almost forgotten about Gavin's phone call. I checked the display on the cell phone. The message envelope glowed on the screen.

"I should call Gavin back," I said to Louise.

"You go ahead," she said. "Meet me down the street at the café."

She pointed down the block toward a coffee cup sign swinging in the rain.

"I'll call Digs and see if he found anything in the evidence we sent to him yesterday."

"Oh, we got Digs again." I grinned.

Louise ignored me, turned toward the café, and trotted away.

It seemed that Randy Ray (affectionately called The Digger – Digs for short – by those of us who knew how far he would go to find a minutia of evidence) always found a way to work our cases. Digs had a huge, and not so secret, crush on Louise and did anything he could to work her cases just to be near her. It worked in our favor, so I didn't mind. Digs was the best forensic pathologist we had, consequently we were able to resolve most of our cases with lightning speed.

I pressed speed dial one without checking the message from Gavin. His messages usually consisted of two words anyway "call me". He answered on the second ring.

"What have you done now?" He said without even a hello to lead me into the conversation.

"What are you talking about?"

"You're on the front page of the paper today, or didn't you know?"

I closed my eyes and sighed. "It's nothing."

"Really?"

I heard a door slam and the construction noise that had peppered the background of his side of the conversation ended. He either went into the trailer, or more likely, jumped into the cab of his truck.

"My mother and your mother called, Catherine. They both wanted to know what was going on."

Oh, great.

"You screwed up a double homicide?"

"No!" The defensiveness was immediate. "Why do you believe the shit the papers say? You know only one tenth of it is true. The rest is just sensation to sell papers."

"Then tell me what happened," he said. "I've got fifty people crawling up my back to find out."

Gavin had a flair for exaggeration.

A stiff breeze blew a spray of drizzle into my face and I decided to head for the warmth of the café. I could seek shelter in the doorway if I hadn't finished explaining myself to Gavin by the time I arrived.

"I lost my temper, called the reporters trying to get to the victims' kid, a bunch of vultures, and one of the reporters decided to embarrass me as repayment."

"And that's all?"

"Yep."

He didn't have to express his doubt; I could feel it worming its way from his end of the line through to mine.

"Gavin, I swear it's the truth. That's all that happened. I've spoken to the chief about it and everything's cool."

A black Jeep pulled up next to me striking the curb. I skitted sideways and shot the driver a dirty look. The woman behind the wheel backed the Jeep up, and straightened the wheel so the tire wasn't half on the sidewalk, and then got out and headed for the sidewalk.

Gavin gave a terse laugh, and I completely forgot about the idiot driver, whose staccato footfalls seemed to be heading my direction.

"So what's your punishment?"

How does he always seem to know these things?

"An exclusive interview with the bimbo who wrote the lies in this morning's paper."

"Oh, you have to be kidding."

"No, I'm not. She must be sleeping with someone in the mayor's office because he's insisting."

"When is this supposed to take place?" he asked.

It was my turn to laugh. "When I have time."

"Alright, I have to go back to work," he said. "I'll smooth things over with the moms."

He would have a devil of a time smoothing things over with my mom. She'd been on a steady diet of anxiety medications since I graduated from the police academy and donned my first uniform. She's been poised to receive the news that I'd never come home again, ever since. I'm guessing when she read that I'd botched an investigation her hopes of me quitting the police department (getting thrown off was equally good for her) and staying home to cook dinners and give birth to her first grandchild ran rabid.

Of course, I keep reminding her that my brother is older than I am, still not married, and has no children. That doesn't seem to count because he's a boy and not expected to produce for her.

"Thanks, hon. I swear, I'm going to have your babies some day."

"Yeah, right. When you're finished saving the city Super Girl."

He hung up and I smiled to myself, lost in the warm fuzzy feelings I always get from my husband. That was until I realized that there was someone standing behind me.

I glanced over my shoulder and a woman who looked vaguely familiar, smiled at me with a smug, shit-eater smile.

"What are you looking at?" I turned to face her.

"Hello, Officer O'Brien."

I recognized the voice.

"I'm Jane Katts. You know the bimbo who's sleeping with someone in the mayor's office."

My heart dropped to my feet. Could this day get any worse?

"Of course you are." I turned and walked away from her.

"You know, you're really difficult to get in touch with." She followed. "I've been trying to call you all morning."

"Yes, I know."

I stopped short of telling her I'd been deleting her messages *all morning*. That nugget of information would only prolong our conversation, and I was already finished with Miss Jane Katts.

"Is now a good time for our interview?"

"No. I'm not sure when I'll have time to speak with you, Miss Katts."

"I can understand that you're a little upset about the article in this morning's paper."

"No." I whirled around to face her. "I'm pissed as hell about your article. There's a big fucking difference."

"I'm a journalist, Officer O'Brien."

"Forgive me but you're a fiction writer, Miss Katts. If you were a journalist you'd have your facts straight. I'm *Detective* O'Brien, not officer."

We faced off like two boxers on the *Caesar's Palace* marquee. Had someone wrung a bell one of us would have thrown a punch.

"Okay look," she held up her hands in surrender. "You're going to have to give me the interview, so you might as well just get over yourself."

This girl had a lot to learn about poking the bear. Especially when the bear hadn't had enough coffee yet today.

"Miss Katts –"

"Jane."

"Jane." I smiled like a patient schoolteacher. "I will *get over myself* exactly three seconds after you print a front page retraction telling your readers what a liar you are."

Jane stepped back as if I had physically slapped her.

"I'm sorry," she said. "You just don't know how hard it is to build a reputation in my business."

"And I don't care. You didn't give a shit about destroying my reputation, so why should I give a shit about helping you build yours."

I marched to the entrance of the café and yanked the door open.

"You'll have your interview when I say."

Louise waited for me just inside the entry of the café with eyebrows raised. "Everything okay?"

"I could use a cup of coffee." I faked a smile. "And a gigantic cheese burger."

"That bad, huh?"

I waved off her concern.

One of the waitresses directed us to a booth near the window. Jane Katts stood outside talking to someone on her cell phone.

"That seemed to be a pretty heated discussion." Louise slid into the booth across from me. "Anything I should know about? Who is that?"

She jerked her head toward the window.

"That is Jane Katts." I held my coffee cup up to a passing waitress. She nodded her understanding. "She was asking if I'm ready for our interview. I told her not yet."

Louise looked out the window, and then back at me. "You're sure that's all you said."

The waitress brought the pot of coffee to our table, poured me a cup, and asked Louise if she wanted any. Louise turned her cup right side up on its saucer, and slid it to the edge for her to fill, all the while not taking her doubting eyes from me.

I thanked the waitress and turned back to Louise.

"That's not exactly what was said, but I think Miss Katts understood that's what I meant."

Louise took a sip of her coffee. "You know, Catherine, I saw a help wanted sign on the door on my way in."

I rolled my eyes toward the ceiling.

"Just something to keep in mind," she said.

Chapter Five

By the time we finished eating lunch, Jane Katts had disappeared from the sidewalk, which was just as well. The last thing I needed was another acid producing moment to ruin a perfectly good cheeseburger, French fry, and coleslaw lunch.

Louise informed me, after she was convinced that I didn't need to begin my food service career early, that Digs wanted to see us as soon as we were finished eating. He wouldn't tell her what he had, but he never did. Digs liked the dramatic reveal. That, and if he gave us information over the phone, he wouldn't be able to get his daily dose of Louise time.

Normally when we went to see Digs, we found him hunched over his desk or a microscope, or some other bit of evidence. Today he was waiting for us. We had just stepped inside the door when Digs unloaded his big news without preamble.

"The medical examiner found a diamond inside the Dad."

"You mean like a gem of a clue?" I asked.

"No, I mean a one and a half carat chunk of rock." He held up a clear plastic baggie with the diamond inside. "Your killer was very weird. He loaded his own shotgun pellets, with the standard lead and one nice sized diamond."

Louise took the baggie, held it up to the light, and shook the stone.

"Nice cut and quality," she said. "I'd say VVS1."

"Close." Digs slid his Coke-bottle glasses up on his nose. "It's not quite perfect."

Part of me wanted to pretend that I knew what they were talking about; the other part thought that whatever code they were speaking, might be important to this investigation, and I'd eventually need to show my stupidity and ask.

"Okay, De Beers gemologists, what the heck are you two talking about?"

They exchanged glances as if they couldn't believe I needed this explained. The part of me that wanted to pretend to understand flushed with embarrassment.

"There's a diamond rating system," Digs explained. "The letters indicate the quality of the cut, color, and clarity."

Louise handed me the bag so I could get a better look at the diamond. The light blazed through the stone and flashed a rainbow of colors. In the center was a small spec of dark.

"It looks like there's a piece of dirt or something in it," I said.

"Good eyes." Digs nodded. "There's a small inclusion in the stone. You could see that with your naked eye? I couldn't see that until I had the stone under a microscope."

I pointed at his thick cheaters. "No offense Digs, but I'm not surprised."

He touched the edge of his glasses. "Yeah, I guess I forget about these sometimes. Thanks for reminding me, O'Brien."

"Any time."

"So the killer shot our victim with a diamond?" Louise asked. "Why?"

"Not just shot him," Digs said. "Killed him with a diamond. The diamond pierced Jonathan Luther's heart, and liquefied it."

"Now we just have to figure out the meaning." I handed the stone to Louise who held it aloft and studied the stone.

"There's more." Digs leaned back and folded his hands behind his head. He grinned up at us.

This was the dramatic reveal I'd expected when we arrived. Digs was just dragging out the moment for his own sick and twisted pleasure.

"We give up." I shrugged. "Do tell. What's the rest of the story, Paul Harvey?"

Digs opened the tiny plastic zippered bag and dropped the diamond into a shallow glass dish. He used a tweezers to deposit the diamond under his microscope.

Louise moved closer to him. Digs began to sweat. He adjusted the magnification, with a lot of fumbling until the magnification was where he wanted it, and then he clicked a few icons on his computer's desktop. The super magnified image of the diamond filled the screen.

"We can't be that lucky." Louise whispered so close to Digs' ear that he shuttered. "Is that what I think it is?"

"Yep." Digs could barely choke the word out. "The diamond is engraved."

"So what?" I held my hands out, palms up. I still wasn't following. "They engrave diamonds with a serial number just like a VCR?"

"Not like a VCR," Digs said and shook his head as if I were the stupidest person on the planet.

Louise straightened and picked up where Digs left off, instructing me on the merits of diamonds. "Diamonds of a certain quality are sometimes engraved with a jeweler's mark and or the certificate number on the girdle to certify the quality."

"Then we can track down the jeweler who engraved this stone, and get a list of all the people he sold a stone of this size and this quality?" I asked.

"It's even better," Digs said. "The jeweler should have a record of a stone of this size, quality, and a notation of the exact quadrant of the inclusion."

I was beginning to share their excitement. "And that will narrow our search down to how many people?"

Digs and Louise both held up their index finger.

I grasped Dig's face between my hands, pulled him forward, and kissed him on the lips. He looked stunned for half a second before realizing who had kissed him. When he recovered, he wiped his sleeve across his mouth.

"You are the best, Digs." I patted his cheek. "So when will we know?"

Digs' shoulders slumped. "That's the tricky part. We don't know where the stone came from, so we'll have to do a broad search. If we can't locate the jeweler in Minnesota we'll have to branch out from there. Many stones of this quality come from off shore. We could be looking at a few weeks."

So we weren't that lucky. Damn, it would have been sweet to have the killer in the next few hours. Then I could make Jane Katts eat crow in the morning edition of the newspaper. I should have known better than to be an optimist. Optimism was a small luxury I couldn't afford these days.

"I guess it's back to the streets for you and me, my friend."

Louise nodded. "Afraid so."

"Look at it this way," Digs forced his voice to sound chipper. "The diamond will be the nail in the killer's coffin when he does go to court."

"Great," I said. "We just have to catch him first."

I turned to leave.

"Hey, O'Brien," Digs said. "I almost forgot. I bought you a gift."

If my overweening curiosity hadn't gotten the best of me, I would never have turned around, but I was like the proverbial Catherine, I needed satisfaction.

"What?"

He tossed a brown paper sack to me. I snagged it in midair before Digs' pathetic throw could go wide and hit the doorjamb next to me. The bag's contents squished and made a squeaking sound. I drew my brows together and looked at him.

"It's just a little something I saw and thought of you."

I unrolled the top of the bag and reached inside. My fingertips brushed something furry. I pinched a bunch of the fuzz between my fingers and withdrew the contents.

There was no mistaking the orange beak and the scrawny neck of the toy. Digs had found a stuffed vulture.

"I couldn't pass it up," he said. "That was classic, O'Brien."

I crumpled the brown bag and whipped it at Digs' head as hard as I could. The paper ball bounced off his head, the computer monitor, the edge of his desk, and then dropped into the wastepaper basket on the floor.

"Two points!"

I raised the stuffed vulture over my head like a trophy and victory-danced my way out of the lab.

The elevator door closed behind us. I pushed the button for the records floor and assumed the elevator wait stance, hands folded politely around my vulture, head tilted upward to watch the floor numbers on the digital display change.

"You read my mind," Louise said, assuming her own waiting stance; head bent over phone checking email. "We should be able to find Jonathan Luther's court records easy enough, and then we can swing by and talk to this Walter Wren person. Maybe we'll get lucky and find out he's a diamond broker."

The elevator stopped on a floor that wasn't ours and a man with his arms full of electronics pushed in. He managed to press the button for two floors up without spilling his armload and littering the elevator floor with busted components.

I inched over to Louise so I could whisper to her without breaking elevator etiquette for the volume of speech.

"I was going to ask records to find information regarding the Grandmother's murder."

The man with the electronics whiplashed his head toward me at the word murder.

I smiled and resumed staring at the numbers on the display over the door.

Sometimes I forgot there were people working in our building that had nothing to do with police work. This poor guy was probably some computer tech here on a temporary basis.

He finally turned back to juggling his electronics.

"You're not going to give up on that angle are you?" Louise also used her elevator whisper and stared at the display.

"No."

"There's no reason to believe the three murders are connected."

This time the man jumped so hard, he bobbled his electronics. I reached over to help catch any components before they fell to the floor. He jerked back and hugged the wires and plastic boxes to his chest. His head bumped the wall behind him.

"Sorry," he grunted.

"You okay?" I asked.

"Yep." He nodded vigorously and hugged his bounty tighter. "Fine."

The elevator hissed to a stop and the door opened much to the relief of Mr. Electronics. He hustled out the door, and nearly tripped on a cord that hung around his ankles.

The door slid shut and we were safe to discuss the case again.

"There's no reason to believe the murders aren't connected." I returned my normal speaking voice.

"You're not going to give up on this bone even if it has no marrow?"

I shook my head. "No."

We reached our floor and headed down the hall to the records office, where Rainey Harper held court like a librarian from hell. Rainey was the ultimate taskmaster, and whenever I saw the new recruits she had working for her, my heart went out to them. One slip would bring the admonishment of Rainey Harper, that maybe they should consider a career in another field.

Rainey was even tougher on the customers of the records office. If you didn't know exactly what file number, county, investigating officer, and date you were looking for (in other words if Rainey would actually need to do research), you would receive her over the glasses glare and a pinched-faced, scornful sigh.

I expected to see Rainey's glare today, but I didn't care. It was Rainey's job to roam the stacks in search of information, and if she hadn't gotten used to the idea after all these years, perhaps she'd better find a new profession.

The records office was empty except for a new clerk I'd never seen before. He looked up when we entered, smiled, and set aside the document he'd been reading.

"Can I help you, ladies?"

Louise stepped up to the counter first, showed her badge, and explained to the young man what she needed. He punched a few keys on his keyboard and nodded at the screen.

"I can get that information for you, Detective." He smiled. "It will take a few minutes."

Louise nodded, said she would wait, and took a seat on the vinyl-covered couched that had seen its better days somewhere in the mid-sixties.

I stepped up to the counter, expecting boy wonder to look up my information before retreating to find Louise's court documents. Instead, he turned, mumbled something to someone hidden in the stacks then disappeared.

Rainey Harper appeared like an apparition and I felt my chest tighten.

"How may I help you?" Her shriveled lips pursed together as if she'd sucked a few lemons before coming to work this morning.

I took my badge from my pocket and laid it on the counter. Rainey picked up the wallet, examined the photo and then me, as if trying to determine whether the badge was really mine. When finally satisfied that I was Detective Catherine O'Brien she handed the badge back.

"What do you need, Detective?"

"I need to find out who investigated a homicide near Duluth."

"What county?" Her hand poised over the keyboard and her head tilted back to look through her bifocals.

"I don't know."

Her eyes flicked at me briefly and then back at the screen. "City?"

"I'm not sure."

Rainey turned slowly and folded her hands on the counter. "What information do you have for me, Detective? How am I to help you find the information you need if you have no place to begin looking?"

"The murder has a possible connection to a current case." I justified my position to counter her crankiness. "The last name of the victims should be the same."

Or I hoped. Chad hadn't said whether it was his mother's or father's mother who'd been killed.

"There should also be an address change for our current victims that will give you the county of the first murder."

Rainey Harper studied me over the tops of her glasses. Her lemon-wrinkled lips puckered even tighter, and she glared at me for several moments. She slipped a pencil from a cup to her right and a piece of scrap paper from a tray to her left.

"What's the name?"

"The last name is Luther. Our current victim's first names are Jonathan and Susan."

She jotted the information on the paper.

"And they were somewhere near Duluth," I said.

She nodded without looking up.

"Where may I reach you if we are able to locate this information?"

I handed her my business card. Rainey took the card and paper-clipped it to the back of the scrap paper. She deposited the scrap paper into a plastic bin filled with other papers then turned back to her precious stacks.

"I am in a bit of a hurry for this information, Miss Harper. The information is relevant to an ongoing murder investigation."

"It has our top priority," Rainey called over her shoulder and then disappeared down one of the book-lined paths.

I glanced at the tiny scrap of paper languishing on top of the other more official looking requests. Top priority my ass, I'd be lucky if they'd be able to locate my scrap of paper in a few days.

Louise's helper returned, a bright smile lit his face. "Okay, Detective. I have your file."

He laid a folder on the counter and slid it across for Louise. She took the file and tucked it under her arm.

I reached into the basket and snagged my piece of scrap paper.

"Rainey said this would be top priority," I said. "I really need this information for our," I indicated both Louise and myself by rapidly pointing back and forth. "Current investigation. It's very important that we get this information A. S. A. P."

He pinched the edge of the paper between his fingers and nodded. "Of course Detective, I'll see what I can find."

I did my best to do a sexy wink. He gave a grimace that said I fell short of the mark.

"I appreciate your help," Louise said and tapped her file. "Thank you."

"You're welcome."

I winked again, and this time I think I frightened him. Whatever it took to get my information.

Louise settled in behind her desk to review the file she'd managed to retrieve from Rainey's realm. I dropped into my chair and noticed my message light flashing again.

Wasn't this day over yet? I checked my watch, two o'clock.

I picked up the phone and punched the message light. There's no time like the present to delete all messages from Jane Katts.

The automated voice came on the line.

You have one message.

One? Maybe my day just got better.

The message began. "Detective O'Brien, this is Linda Meyers, I'm Susan Luther's sister. Chad Luther's Aunt."

She added the last bit as if I wouldn't know who she was from her sister's name alone.

"When you have time, I'd like to speak with you about the investigation."

I jotted her number on the back of one of my business cards and slipped it into my pocket.

"Louise, I just got a call from Chad Luther's aunt. She wants to speak with us about the investigation."

Before she could reply, my phone rang. I answered on the second ring.

"Detective O'Brien, speaking."

"O'Brien." It was the chief and he didn't sound happy. "I want to see you in my office now. Bring Montgomery with you."

He hung up before I had the chance to let out a breath, let alone respond.

"We're wanted in the chief's office first," I said.

"Then we shouldn't keep him waiting."

The chief's door was open again, but this time there was a woman in his office. He smiled politely at her and chatted as if she were an old friend he hadn't seen in awhile. When he reached the punch line of his story, the woman laughed and turned her head to the side.

"Shit." I turned away and felt a wave of nausea roll through my stomach.

"What?" Louise asked.

"It's Jane Katts. What the hell is she doing here? We don't have time for her right now."

I checked over my shoulder. The chief hadn't yet spotted us.

"Let's just go see this Walter Wren character," I whispered. "She'll be gone by the time we get back."

"O'Brien!" Tension crept up my back, stiffening my spine.

"Too late." Louise pinched my cheek. "Big smile now. You don't know what he knows yet. If he sees the guilt on your face, he'll know everything."

Without hesitation, I plastered on a pleasant smile and marched the final feet toward certain doom. Jane Katts watched me over her shoulder.

I locked eyes with her and wished, not for the first time in my life, that I had telekinetic abilities. If I had, I could mentally disembowel Jane Katts. That's probably why God never blessed me with that particular gift.

"Hello Detective." Jane Katts' tone was overly pleasant. She must have trumped me in some way and now she's was just waiting for me to concede the trick.

"Close the door behind you, O'Brien." The chief rocked back in his chair and smiled.

There was nothing in his smile except pleasantry, which made me more nervous than the one Jane Katts had given me. A broad smile was so alien on the Chief's face that I was certain that Jane Katts had managed to pull a switcheroo and replace the chief with a pod person of her own design; one who is not hard-edged and sand-papery as I have come to expect but instead soft, with as much grit as a nail file.

"I'm afraid there's not enough chairs so one of you will have to stand." The smiley version of our chief of police said.

I braced my feet a shoulder width apart and crossed my arms over my chest, I preferred to stand for whatever nasty surprise Jane Katts had in store for me.

Louise sat and introduced herself to Jane. They exchanged a handshake.

"Ms. Katts is the reporter who asked for the exclusive interview."

He glossed over the detail about her being the reporter who had engaged in a calculated smear campaign against the department.

"She would like to change the angle of her story to get more of an inside view." The chief's eyes cut to my face and I saw a hint of the real chief behind whatever hoodoo Jane Katts had performed on him.

'Uh-huh' was the best I could manage from my anger-constricted throat.

"What does that mean?" Louise asked, and turned toward Jane Katts for the answer.

Jane smiled and crossed her right leg over her left so she angled toward Louise.

"I'd like to follow you through the investigation," she said.

"No."

The clipped, one-word response was the best I could manage. I would give her an exclusive interview, that included all my darkest secrets and fears, before I would let her follow me around during an investigation.

"It's already been decided, O'Brien."

In the chief's eyes, I saw something I never thought I'd see – sympathy. This dictate had come down from a higher power and he didn't like to bend this far over backward either.

"Ms. Katts feels that she may have been a little hasty in her portrayal of the department."

"Yes," Jane jumped in. "I'd like a chance to show our readers what a murder investigation is really like, start to finish. Not just the initial news flash and then the final outcome of the investigation."

"The mayor feels that it's a good idea," chief said in a slow, make-sure-they-understand-what's-really-going-on way.

"No offense, Ms. Katts." Louise turned to her and smiled. "But I hate this idea. You've already written –"

Louise waved her fingers around as if she could Houdini the right words from thin air.

"Let's call what you wrote half-truths about our department and this investigation."

"As I said, I was hasty."

The corners of my lips turned up slightly. Jane Katts miscalculated again. She poked the bear this morning when she challenged me, but compared to Louise, I'm a cub. She was about to feel the strike of a full on Kodiak.

"You were deceitful, not hasty, Ms. Katts. Now you have used whatever influence you have in the Mayor's office, to force us into allowing you to tag along as we do our work."

The smarmy smile that had been a mainstay on Jane Katts' face since we walked in the door disappeared.

Louise continued without pause. "I'm only saying this because, you're going to be underfoot during this investigation, there will need to be guidelines for you to follow."

"I'm sorry but I don't believe in censorship. I believe Andrew has been instructed to give me all access."

Icy fingers squeezed my heart and heat boiled into my cheeks.

Now she's on a first name basis with the chief?

This day had slid so far down into hell Satan would need a shovel to find us.

Louise leaned forward within inches of Jane's face. "You will be given all access, but you will not have access to the victim's family. You will also not go to press until either Detective O'Brien or I have read and approved your story."

"That's censorship."

"Call it what you want but we cannot allow you to jeopardize an ongoing investigation by publishing sensitive information. You want a story on the inner workings of an investigation, then that's what the content of your stories will be limited to."

Jane Katts stood, fumbled for, and finally found, her cell phone.

"We'll see," she said, and then stormed out of the room.

My eyes had gone panorama-wide. I waited for the chief to turn various shades of red and then progress into purple. He looked as stunned as I felt.

"Detective Montgomery?" He found his voice after a few minutes. "Have you gone completely mental?"

Louise smiled and shook her head.

"Not at all, chief. When I found out that Ms. Katts was using her influence at the Mayor's office, to arm twist the department into giving her an exclusive on this case, I called a friend of mine at the Mayor's office."

Louise looked over her shoulder to where Jane Katts was furiously gesturing while barking into the phone.

"Jane is about to learn that my friend is higher up on the political food chain than her friend."

Check and mate.

"Louise swiveled toward the chief. "The Mayor has agreed that we have full discretion on which areas we allow her to see and the information we feel is fit for publication."

"But you can't force the paper to censor her," I said. "I don't think they'll go for us having final approval on the story."

"Actually, I already spoke to another friend of mine who sits on the board of directors at the paper. I simply explained the situation to him."

"That can't be it," I said and turned to watch Jane Katts have a complete meltdown. She was learning a valuable lesson on how to run with the big dogs.

"The blood-suckers at the paper couldn't care less about our investigation. What else did you promise him?"

Louise stood and crossed to me. She laid a reassuring hand on my shoulder.

"I promised him, that when the investigation was over, we would both sit down for an exclusive. He scoops all the other news agencies in the Twin Cities and we have final say during the investigation."

"Thanks for having my back on this one, Louise."

"When do I not have your back, Catherine?"

We watched Jane's meltdown like spectators at a fireworks display.

"This was fun," Louise said.

"You have a mean streak two trucks wide." Chief stepped up behind us. "I never thought you had it in you, Louise."

"I guess I've been hanging out with Catherine too long."

"No." I shook my head and patted Louise on the back. "You have surpassed the master on this one."

She pressed the palms of her hands together and bowed to me. I returned the gesture.

"She's your puppet now, Catherine. Ms. Jane Katts can only go where you want her to, when you want her to, and see what you want her to." Louise crossed to the door, opened it, and stood back. "Let's go pull her strings."

Jane finished whining to whomever she thought could help her out of the bind, and snapped her cell phone closed. A pronounced pout affixed to her face and for an instant, she looked like she must have as a spoiled child who always got her way.

"If you're done jaw jacking, Ms. Katts, we have work to do." I strode past her without a glance in her direction. "You're wasting time."

I didn't turn back to see if she followed and frankly I didn't care. Jane Katts could throw herself on the ground in a full-blown tantrum and I wouldn't care. She gambled and lost, but that didn't mean she would lie down and accept defeat.

No, Jane Katts was too dangerous. We were able to push back her line, but the battle was far from the finale.

The first stop on Ms. Katts' whirlwind tour of a murder investigation was our desks to retrieve Louise's file on Walter Wren.

As I picked up my purse, the phone on my desk rang. I debated over answering then I caught a glimpse of Jane Katts from the corner of my eye. She'd been the reason I didn't want to answer my phone in the first place. Whoever was calling couldn't be that bad, after all the boogey man was standing right behind me.

I lifted the receiver just before the ring that would throw the call into voicemail. "Detective O'Brien speaking."

"Yes, Detective O'Brien." A male voice said. The person on the other end cleared his throat. "Sorry. This is Stephen Hathaway in records."

He said it as if he wasn't sure that was his name.

"Oh yeah," I said. "What did you find out? Anything?"

"Actually, yes." He sounded full of pride, which made me believe he hadn't been in records very long. If he had, Rainey Harper would have squashed his pride by now. "I have the phone number for the Sheriff of McCann County. His name is William Rose. He's listed as the lead investigator on the Marion Luther murder investigation."

"You are the best, Stephen." I found a pen and dug the business card I had written Linda Meyers's phone number on, from my pocket. "Hit me with the phone number."

I jotted the number and then tucked the card back into my pocket.

"Was that phone call relevant to this investigation?" Jane had taken out a mini-tape recorder. She shoved the mic end toward my face.

"If it was, I guess you'll find out soon enough."

She pulled the recorder away from me and held it under her chin.

"Officer—"

I shot a warning glance her direction.

"Sorry. *Detective* O'Brien's desk is messy and disorganized. Very apt considering the state of the investigation so far."

She pressed stop and smiled.

"Too bad you won't be able to print any of that." I gestured toward the tape recorder. "It would have made a sensational story: messy cop the reason the investigation is botched. You should think of moving to tabloid journalism. Oh, never mind. I forgot which paper you worked for."

Her face blanched slightly.

"You driving, Louise?" I heard keys rattle behind me.

Louise's car is a pewter Toyota Prius. The Prius is a safe car, however, when Louise is behind the wheel, her Prius becomes what I affectionately call the Chariot of Death. An experience I think Jane Katts should live for herself. For someone who likes to believe she's in complete control of all situations, the terror of riding with Louise should fry the balance of her resolve to follow us around.

"Shot gun!" I called when we were halfway to the car.

There was no way I would ride with Louise without a shoulder strap and an airbag for protection.

"Where are we going?" Jane got in the compact backseat, but failed to buckle her seatbelt, understandable since a seatbelt wasn't required in the back seat in Minnesota. This would be her second huge mistake of the day. One I felt no urgent need to correct.

"We're going to interview a client of Jonathan Luther," I said. "You will wait in the car."

She slid to the center of the back seat, what my brother and I called riding on the hump.

"Detective, I'm not going to sit in the car waiting for you like a dog in a grocery store parking lot."

Louise glanced into the rearview mirror. "Don't worry, Ms. Katts, we'll crack the window."

She careened around the exit ramp and out of the parking garage. Jane tumbled across the back seat and slammed against the driver's side rear window.

If it had been anyone other than Louise driving I would have found the move malicious, but there's a reason I hold tight to the chicken-bar when exiting the parking ramp.

"Jesus." Jane righted herself. "Take it easy, Detective."

"I'd buckle my seatbelt if I were you," I said and gripped the chicken-bar extra tight as we approached the loop down to the main level.

Jane took my advice and braced herself against the back of the driver's seat.

"This isn't some sick initiation right, Ms. Katts. Louise really does drive like she's being chased by the devil."

I doubt if she believed me. We were, after all, the enemy and not to be trusted.

"Why can't I sit in on your interview?"

By the time we reached the street, Jane had fallen into rhythm with Louise's driving, which was akin to getting your sea legs during a raging storm.

"Maybe I can help," she said. "I'm a veteran interviewer and I know a lie when I hear one."

I bet. Liars probably gave off a special pheromone that only other liars could smell.

"I'm sure you can," I said. "But this guy might be hesitant to speak if he thinks his words will be plastered all over the front page tomorrow morning."

Hell, if I had known my words would grace the front page, *I* would have thought better about speaking.

"We'll fill you in when we're done."

"Edited of course." She tucked her hands under her thighs and slouched against the seat. The spoiled child had returned.

Louise jerked into the left lane and around a slow moving truck. Jane flopped against the door.

"Ouch!"

A piece of me thought that maneuver was malicious. The idea came to me when I saw the wicked little smile twist Louise's lips as she jerked the car back into the right lane.

"We will limit the scope of the information we share with you to procedural," Louise said. "You said you wanted to slant your story to the procedures of an investigation."

She glanced up in the rearview mirror again. "Right?"

If Jane Katts dared to tell the truth, that this was just a ploy to get the scoop on the Luther murder, she would be out on the sidewalk.

I held my breath waiting to see if Jane would roll the dice.

She stared hard at Louise's reflection trying to decide if she could afford to be a high roller, or if the deck were stacked against her. She settled against the leather of the back seat. "Of course, Detective. I'd be grateful for any information you could share with me on the ins and outs of an investigation."

She drew her mini-tape recorder from her pocket and held it out.

"For instance. How did you know where to begin on this case?"

Was that a procedural question, or a sneaky back door attempt to get information out of us? Damn, having her with us would be stressful. Every question, no matter how innocuous it seemed on the surface, seethed with poisonous barbs beneath.

I prayed that Louise would know. I waited, pretending to be wildly interested in the passing scenery.

"We always begin with those closest to the victim," Louise said after a few moments. "Spouses, children, brothers, sisters, friends, coworkers."

"You said, children. Does that mean you consider Chad Luther a suspect?"

"What that means, Ms. Katts, is that we follow the same procedure for all investigations."

"Okay." She thought for a moment. "And what if none of those suspects pan out? Then where do you look?"

"There's a progression," I said. "From immediate family, to friends, and coworkers, to any one who might have had a grudge against the victim."

I held up my fingers, one for each progression. She nodded.

"And if none of those leads pan out?"

"Pray for a miracle." I laughed.

Louise moved her head slowly from side to side.

"What? I was joking."

Jane had clicked off her tape recorder by the time I admitted to having a sense of humor. She was now writing something in a small, spiral bound, notebook.

"Oh come on," I said and crooked my arm over the seat. "You had to know I was kidding."

"What does it matter, Catherine?" Louise wheeled around another slow-moving vehicle causing Jane to smear whatever she was writing. "It's not like we'll let her print that comment."

"Maybe I'll take this story to another paper," Jane chimed.

"And violate your non-compete?" Louise said. "You're smarter than that, Ms. Katts."

Jane snapped the notebook closed. "You've got me by the short-hairs, so you might as well use my first name."

"Alright, Jane," Louise said. "Was there anything you wanted to know about our procedures?"

"How do you know it wasn't a professional hit?"

"We didn't say anything about this not being a professional hit," I said.

She waved off my protest. "Not just this case – any case. When you walk into a crime scene, how can you tell that you're not dealing with a mob hit of some kind?"

"You and Catherine have something in common," Louise said. "She's always looking for mob connections too. I think both of you have seen too many movies."

There are times I envy Louise and times I wouldn't want to be her for the world. Times like these were the latter. Louise didn't see enough movies growing up. I made her watch *The Untouchables* at my house one weekend to try to educate her on the thrill of Elliot Ness, but the whole concept was lost on poor Louise.

"So you've never been involved with any mob cases."

My lips turned down involuntarily and I shook my head.

"Not one," I said.

"No gang hits either?"

"Plenty of those." Louise wheeled us off the freeway and onto a frontage road. "Believe me this wasn't a gang hit."

"How do you know?"

I glanced at what Jane jotted in her notebook. She was writing directions to where we were going.

Perhaps we were underestimating Jane. She knew she could only print what we gave her authorization to run, yet she was still mapping the route. She was up to something. Quizzing us on procedures and gangs was only an attempt to disguise what she was really doing.

"Gangs are particularly bloody," Louise said and looked down at the directions on her Post-It-Note. "They also usually kill in public places – while their victim is walking down the street, driving in a car, or standing in front of their house. Gang hits are more of opportunity than planning."

"So you believe the Luther's murder was premeditated?" Excitement burbled in Jane's voice.

I became fascinated with the suburban landscape rolling by my window, and waited for Louise to pick up the reigns – she didn't. Instead, she was more concerned with finding the address listed on her pink Post-It-Note.

"You're leaving me to infer a lot from your silence, Detectives."

"Infer whatever you choose." Louise pulled up to the curb on a tree-lined street, and jammed the car into park. "We're here."

"Wait." Jane Katts unbuckled her belt, slid to the center again, and put a hand on each of our shoulders. "Please let me go in with you."

I opened my door. Jane tightened her grip.

"Please." Her gaze morphed from one of pure cunning to pleading. "We don't have to tell them that I'm a reporter. I won't use my tape recorder, or my notebook. We can tell them I'm an observer from the P.D."

Here to make sure the story in this morning's paper wasn't true no doubt.

"You said it yourself, I can't print the story. My editor says you'll be giving us an exclusive on the case when it's over anyway."

She took her hands from our shoulders.

"You'll just be giving me a head start on the background information."

Louise and I looked at each other trying to perform some sort of telepathic communication across the front seat of the Toyota. After a few moments, I realized that I had zero telepathic ability.

I pointed to Jane Katts. "You wait here."

Then pointed to Louise. "You, conference."

I pointed to the roof of the Toyota. Louise understood.

We stepped outside, closed the front doors, and spoke across the roof of the car.

"What do we do with her?" I asked.

"I told you at the office, you are the puppet master." She splayed her hands as if to say, nothing up my sleeve. "Whatever you say goes."

I drummed my fingers on the roof. "Part of me wants to be mean to her."

Louise nodded. "Understandable."

"Then again, the image of her waiting in the car like a dog at a supermarket makes me feel bad."

"Understandable as well."

"So what do we do?"

"No." She shook her head. "What do *you* do?"

I grimaced, reached down, and opened the back door.

"Come on out, Fido."

Louise pointed at me across the roof. "You are such a softy."

"I must be." I tapped my temple. "Soft in the head."

She bounded from the back seat and onto Walter Wren's front lawn. Envy gnawed at the edges of my consciousness to see her enthusiasm. I couldn't recall, from the dusty recesses of my mind, if I had ever been so eager at the beginning of an investigation. Of course I must have been.

"All right, settle down," I said. "Try to remember you're supposed to be an observer. Observers are never happy to be anywhere. They're usually bored."

"Got it." She aimed her finger like a gun and hammered her thumb down.

"No, you don't *got it*," I said. "Look bored, right now."

Jane opened her mouth to speak but I preempted any protests.

"If Mr. Wren is watching us from a window –" I snagged her wrist and tugged her forward before she could turn toward the windows in Walter Wren's home.

"He would see you out here bouncing around on your toes and know you're lying. In this job, it's not good enough to spot a liar. You also have to be a good liar."

I gave her a sly grin.

"It shouldn't be that hard for you."

Jane stopped fidgeting and her enthusiasm changed into cold flint. "How authentic do you think it would look if he saw you holding my arm like that? You wouldn't do that to a real observer."

"You could just wait in the car." I parroted her snotty voice and let go of her arm.

She feigned boredom.

"Perfect." I looked at Louise. "I think we have an Oscar winner on our hands."

"At least a Golden Globe winner," Louise said. "Now can we get going? Mr. Wren has taken note of our arrival."

The front door was open. Behind a rusted out screen door, hung on a crooked wooden frame that could have been, and probably was, original to the house, stood a silver-haired, hulk of a man.

He waved us toward the porch.

"Are you coming in or not?"

He opened the screen door partially as we strolled up the sidewalk.

"No, just take your time. I enjoy heating the outside."

We hit the porch double time.

"Mr. Wren?" Louise asked.

"Yes, come in."

He shooed her through the door, then shoved Jane and me inside. The three of us huddled in the four by four entryway. We pressed ourselves flat against the wall to allow Mr. Wren to close the door.

"Take your shoes off and come inside." He locked the door. "Normally I wouldn't make you take your shoes off. It's not like I have new carpet or anything. But the lawn is wet from the frost this morning, and I hate to step on wet spots in my stocking feet."

He shuffled past us. His time hunched back made every step look painful.

Louise had stuck the pink Post-It-Note with Walter Wren's address to the flap of her purse. I ripped the note off and examined the address. It was the correct address.

Maybe there was a Walter Wren Junior, because the Walter Wren who slithered away from us in his moth eaten socks didn't look like he could lift a fork, let alone a shotgun or a knife.

"Mr. Wren," Louise said. "We're with the Saint Paul Police Department."

She held up her badge. Wren didn't turn back; he stayed the course toward a nubbly, plaid recliner in the corner.

"I figured that's who you were." Either the chair or Walter Wren's bone creaked as he eased himself into a reclined position. "I don't get many visitors these days, and I never get any unannounced visitors any more."

"You're not surprised that we're here?" I kicked my shoes into the corner and moved into the living room. I sat on a sofa whose cushions had seen the better part of the nineteen-sixties.

Wren shook his head. "Naw. When I saw the news last night, I figured you'd be around to see me eventually. Frankly, I thought you'd show yesterday. I even made coffee for you, Detective O'Brien."

He jerked a thumb toward the kitchen. "I could re-heat some in the microwave but it won't be as good as last night."

I stopped trying to pull myself out of the two sofa cushions that sucked down my ass.

"How do you know my name, Mr. Wren?"

His laugh sounded like the ember snaps from a roaring fire somewhere in his chest. "Your name was the top news story on the ten o'clock news, and every half hour this morning until the game shows came on."

By this time, Louise and Jane had removed their shoes and neatly stacked them by the door. Both were smarter than I had been and took a seat in two wooden chairs opposite the sofa.

"Was I indeed."

He crackled out another laugh. "You sure were. You are what in my day we used to call a spitfire."

He winked then slapped his hands together.

"You're full of fire. That's why the good Lord gave you red hair." He leaned forward as if he were sharing a secret. "To warn others."

Jane and Louise shared a knowing laugh with Wren at my expense. I had the feeling that after our publishing ban on Jane Katts ended, Walter Wren and his commentaries would appear in the paper as a follow up to the original story.

"Mr. Wren." It was time for a change of subject. "You threatened Jonathan Luther's life."

His laugh trailed away and then ended in a hard swallow. He nodded slowly.

"I did. I'm not proud of that fact, and I didn't kill him, Detective O'Brien."

"Why did you threaten him?" Louise asked.

"'Cause I'm cranky." He thumped his chest like an ape and gummed his lips together. "I'm a curmudgeon who got his nose out of joint."

"Being a curmudgeon doesn't give you the right to threaten someone, Mr. Wren."

I tried to sound as authoritative as I could but grilling him was like trying to interrogate my grandfather. Walter Wren even wore the same two-pocket, flannel shirts as my granddad. I could hear my mother scold me and tell me not to speak to grandpa that way.

"No, it isn't." He nodded. "But we were like two cocks in the hen house. I said things that I'm not proud of, and if Jonathan were still alive, he'd say the same. I was mad at him, that's for certain, but I respected him."

"Why did you file suit against Mr. Luther?" Louise asked.

He turned his gaze toward her and smiled. "Aren't you the pretty one, but that doesn't mean you can pull one over on me. I'm old, not blind."

He jabbed a gnarled finger toward the floor.

"Isn't that folder under your purse holding all the details of what went on between the two of us?"

Louise glanced at the folder and then back at Wren.

"If your memory is so short, pick up the damn file and check."

He rocked back in the recliner and looked at me. "Are you going to play games with me too, Detective O'Brien?"

He winked.

"Come on, firecracker. I saw you last night. You're more direct than that." He looked at me through half-closed lids. "I respect the direct approach more than this pussy-footing around."

"Fine." I gave one final heave and succeeded in extracting myself from the cushions. I moved to the edge of the couch. "We know that you claimed Luther cheated you on an investment property. The court ruled against you and my theory, just by looking around this place, is that you lost your retirement nest egg. So, you killed him."

The ember snap laugh returned, and he slapped his knee. "I knew she was a firecracker. You're all hell-fired-up, but you're wrong, Detective O'Brien."

Of course I was.

"I have more money than my children will be able to spend when I'm gone – though they'll try."

I glanced around the dusty, sun-faded living room. "Are you sure about that, Mr. Wren."

"Oh yes. The one thing my Father always told me was to love rich and live poor. It kept him in good stead for more than ninety years, and it's done me the same.

I loved one woman for over fifty years, until she died last year from the cancer. For all those years, we owned six cars, four dogs, no cats, and one house. We didn't chase what the neighbors had and we never bought on credit."

"Then why the lawsuit?" I asked.

"Cause I was mad, damn it." He pushed the chair to a sitting position and locked eyes on me. "As I said, the only woman I loved, the one I had been with for over fifty years, died. Then this young, real estate punk comes and tries to rip me off, and that's what he did with the courts blessing.

Luther knew how much I would lower the price on my property, because he was supposed to be working for me. I found out later that he'd told the buyers what I'd let the property go for, because they'd gone to college together.

Jonathan Luther should have lost his real estate license for what he done to me. When they wouldn't take his license, I threatened him. It was a heat-of-the-moment sort of thing. I wasn't serious at all. I was real, real sorry when I heard he was killed."

"Where were you yesterday afternoon, Mr. Wren," Louise said.

"Right here watching *TV Land*." He nodded to a big-screened television in the corner. "There was an *I Love Lucy* marathon on. I wouldn't have missed it for the world."

"Not a great alibi, Mr. Wren," I said. "You don't have anyone who can vouch for you?"

"Nope, but I haven't been able to drive, or had a car, for over three years." He tapped the side of his head. "I keep blacking out and the state won't give me a driving card anymore."

"We can check that you know, Mr. Wren," I said.

"You know firecracker." He smiled. "I thought you would have checked that before you got here."

"What about diamonds?" Louise said.

Walter Wren's brow wrinkled. "What about diamonds?"

"Do you have any diamond investments?" Louise rolled her hand in the air. "Ownership in a jewelry store? A diamond mining operation?"

"Diamond mining operations?" He gave her the thumbs down. "Do you know how many tons of earth they need to move to find just one decent stone? Not to mention the number of people they need to employ to move that earth. Not to mention the civil wars and other conflicts."

He shook his head and wagged his finger at the same time.

"Bad investment those. Land is the only thing I invest in and it hasn't let me down yet. I don't need to do a thing to it and it doubles and triples in value the longer you sit and do nothing."

He had a point. We paid one hundred and fifty thousand for our house over ten years ago. The people who lived down the street just sold theirs for over three hundred thousand even after the dip in the housing market. I'd told Gavin that if we stayed in the house until we died we'd die rich. Of course, we wouldn't be able to enjoy our wealth.

"I think that's all we have for you Mr. Wren." Louise stood, followed by our surprisingly silent observer.

"Are you sure?" His face lined with worry. "I don't mean to chase you off. I can make some coffee and in the freezer I have some of them Girl Scout cookies that the neighbor girls sell."

His watery, old, gray eyes pleaded with us not to leave just yet and my heart broke. I hadn't gone to see my grandfather the week before he died, and the last time I'd left him, he had the same look on his face. Never, will I forget that lonely, pleading look.

"It's such a cold day, I'd love some coffee," I said. "As long as it's fresh."

Louise's head snapped toward me. I nodded that she should sit and she did. Jane Katts however stayed standing and gawked at me.

"I can make fresh coffee." He pushed himself out of the chair with great effort. "It won't take a minute if you have the time."

"We have plenty of time," I said and let myself get sucked in by the sofa cushions again.

When we had downed a cup of coffee and more than a few *Thin Mints* and *Do Se Does,* we said our good-byes to Mr. Wren. He grabbed my arm before the screen door closed behind me. He crooked his gnarled finger and waved me closer to him as if he wanted to share a secret with me.

"Hey, firecracker." He grinned a yellow-toothed grin. "I'm glad it's you investigating the Luther murders. Jonathan Luther was a good man and he deserved to have someone with your spirit, investigating his death."

He gave my arm a reassuring pat. "You give 'em hell, firecracker."

"I will, Mr. Wren." I laid my hand over his. "Thank you, for the coffee."

He tipped his head down, gave a short wave, and then closed the door.

For the first time since I woke up this morning, I forgave myself for being me. I may be a firecracker, but not everyone was afraid of blowing their hands off when handling explosives. Some people enjoyed the random, unexpected detonations.

I made a metal note to call my grandmother when I got home tonight and tell her how much I loved and missed her. Like Mr. Wren, Grandma Gimse appreciated a good firecracker when she saw one.

I slid into the passenger seat of Louise's car.

"What was that all about?" Jane Katts rolled her eyes. "Did you need to do your community service for the day or something?"

"No, I thought I'd do my human service." I clicked my seatbelt into place, something Jane had once again forgotten. "Maybe you should look that word up when you get back to your office. Its spelled h-u-m-a-n."

"Whatever. The old guy wasn't lying though. I can tell. What was all the questioning about diamonds, Detective Montgomery? Did you find a diamond, diamond dust, or diamond certificates at the scene?"

Louise looked at me and I gave a small shake of my head. The diamond was something that only we, and the killer, knew about and that's how it should stay. The last thing we needed was Jane Katts accidentally giving away our most vital evidence in some passing conversation.

Apparently, our telepathy was functioning this time because Louise nodded.

"No," she said. "I was just curious. He seemed like a savvy investor and I've been debating over adding diamond stocks to my retirement portfolio."

"Right. You know the funny thing is you two really believe I can't read the little signals you give each other. I'm going to note that for my future article. Especially, if you underestimate your suspects as much as you underestimate me."

Jane rifled through her purse and found her spiral bound notebook. She poised her pen over the page just as Louise tore away from the curb.

Jane ricocheted against the back wall of the Prius.

"Jesus, you really drive like crap, Detective Montgomery."

"I'm going to tell you the same thing I tell, Catherine." She glanced in the mirror to make sure Jane was paying attention. "Take your *Xanax*, look out the window, and hope for a miracle."

I nodded. "It's true. I just close my eyes and hope for a miracle. It's much less stressful on my heart than looking out the window."

I gave my chest a good thump.

Jane shifted into position and buckled her seatbelt. "Now where are we going?"

"Back to the office?" I turned to Louise for confirmation.

She shook her head. "You were going to call Chad's aunt. As long as we're out we might as well stop by for a visit."

My cell phone, and the card I had written the aunt's number on, were in the same pocket. I took them out and dialed the number.

"I'll have to call for the address."

Louise reached into her purse. The car swerved to the right, dangerously close to the embankment. I braced my feet on the dashboard and held my breath. Louise came up with a blue scrap of paper.

"No need, I got the address from the uniforms who dropped Chad off last night." Louise swerved back into the center of the lane. "Catherine, get your feet off my dash."

My heart dropped back to a samba and I returned my feet to the floor. I pinched the piece of paper between my thumb and index finger, and checked the address. Chad Luther's Aunt was less than two miles from Walter Wren.

"You're good, Louise."

"I know."

She wheeled us onto the freeway again, and within a few minutes, we had reached the home of Linda Meyers. The colonial revival, with its neatly trimmed and freshly raked lawn, belied the turmoil of the family inside.

I rang the doorbell. From the other side came the baritone bark of a large dog. Probably one of those shorthaired, menacing models, that was taller than I am, and could take an intruder's face off in one large chomp.

The muffled sound of a male voice issued commands to the dog to get in the garage. The dog's voice became more distant and then nearly disappeared as a door thumped shut. Then the front door opened.

A tall broad shouldered man, who would be in shape if he hadn't been carrying the standard middle-aged ten pounds around his middle stared at us from behind the screen.

"Yes?" His tone was clipped and impatient. "What do you want?"

My Mother had instilled the idea of good manners in me as a child. Instilled isn't quite the word; she drilled the idea into my head, and good manners dictated that you call before dropping in on anyone other than immediate family members. I'd managed to overcome most of what she'd taught me through the years, but a few flashbacks struck me now and again.

"Mr. Meyers?" I asked.

"Yes." His eyes fixed on me with a mixture of boredom and anger. "I don't want whatever you're selling, and I've already accepted Jesus Christ as my Lord and Savior, so I don't need to share a bible passage with you. Thanks."

I looked down at my jeans and T-shirt and wondered what sect of Jehovah Witnesses were visiting this neighborhood.

Before he could slam the door in my face, I pulled my badge from the pocket of my jacket.

"Mr. Meyers, I'm Detective O'Brien from the Saint Paul Police Department."

He pulled the door open again, and scrutinized my badge, as if he were an expert in forged documents. Once satisfied, he nodded but didn't step back to allow us inside.

"Do you have an update for us?" He asked and leaned his shoulder on the jamb as if the walls were holding up his bulk.

"No," I said. "Your wife called, she needed to speak with us about something."

He tilted his head up as if to say, ah. He turned and yelled over his shoulder.

"Linda!"

He closed the door as he turned away. I glanced at Louise. She furrowed her brows at me.

Only people who had something to hide kept the police at bay when they showed up at the door. My natural curiosity wanted to know what Mr. Meyers considered important enough to conceal from us.

"Mr. Meyers, it's very cold out here." I shivered for effect. "May we come inside to wait for your wife?"

The deer in headlight stare was expected as Meyers tried to decide if allowing us to stand in the entryway could hurt. He hesitated a little too long.

"Yeah, come on in," he said. "Linda!"

He stood back enough for Louise, Jane, and I to step inside the entry. He made no effort to take our coats and no offer of refreshments.

"I'll be right down," a voice called from the second floor.

Meyers folded his arms and cast his gaze to the floor. Then he began an uncomfortable shuffle dance of impatience from foot to foot.

"Is there a problem, Mr. Meyers?" Louise asked.

His lips pressed flat. "No. Why?"

"You seem –" She paused a moment to think. "Distracted. Is there something on your mind?"

"We've had a stressful twenty-four hours or so." He splayed his arms wide. "I'm sure you can understand."

There was a slight, but distinct, sneer in his voice. Even if Mr. Meyers had nothing to hide, he certainly had no love for the police.

"Who is it Jack?"

The top of the stairs wrapped around to the opposite side of the entry so a person at the top couldn't see anyone at the bottom until they rounded the first half flight of steps. Jack stepped back a few paces and cocked his head toward the second floor landing.

"There are some police officers here to see you, Linda."

Slipper clad feet appeared first, then gray sweatpants and sweatshirt. When Linda Meyers turned to face us on the landing between floors, her face was as ashen gray as her sweat suit. Dark crescents framed her tear puffed eyes. Clumps of hair had worked their way out of a ponytail holder and hung around her face.

"Detective O'Brien, right?"

I nodded.

She descended the last length of steps.

"I saw you on the news last night." She reached out her hand to me. "Thank you for coming. I didn't expect you to stop by."

I shook her hand and introduced her to Louise and our observer, Jane. Linda Meyers didn't appear to notice that Jane was the only one who didn't produce a badge.

"Thank you for coming." She held out her arm toward the living room. "Please come in. I'd like to speak with you if you have time."

"That's why we're here," I said and removed my shoes.

Jack Meyers stared at his wife with a mild look of astonishment, though she didn't seem to notice or care. Linda Meyers had other more important things running through her mind, than whether or not her husband approved of her houseguests.

"I saw you on the news last night, and I heard how you tried to protect Chad. Thank you. I'm sure you caught hell for what you said, but he needed someone to watch over him last night."

"Is Chad here?" I asked.

"No. He went back to his dorm today. I guess he wanted to be with his friends."

She rocked slowly on the couch and rubbed her hands together as if trying to drive warmth into them, which probably wasn't far from the truth. She had been through a terrible shock and her entire circulatory system had more than likely gone into slow motion.

"What is it, Mrs. Meyers?" I asked. "You sounded troubled on the phone."

Her eyebrows shot up and a hysterical laugh brayed from her. "You could say that I'm feeling a little troubled too."

"I'm sorry. I know you're going through a hard time. I meant you sounded like you had something urgent."

The rocking started again and she closed her eyes. Her lips moved silently. Linda Meyers twisted her hands together so hard that her knuckles went white.

"Not urgent anymore," she said. "It would have been, and should have been, urgent two days ago."

Tears streamed from her puffed eyes. Linda didn't try to hide or wipe the large salty drops away. She just stared with glassy, void, eyes at nothing on the wall behind me.

"My sister confided in me and I didn't take her seriously." Her hoarse voice was close to inaudible. "I told her that she was being silly and that everything would be fine, if she just forgot about it."

Jane Katts moved to the edge of her seat. Her hand twitched toward her purse where her mini-tape recorder and notebook were hiding. I gave her a sharp glare that told her not to even try. Jane clasped her hands together on her lap and grimaced at me.

"Forget about what?" Louise asked.

"Our cousin, who's not well mentally, had threatened Linda."

"Why did she threaten her?" I said.

Linda plucked two tissues from a box on the end table and blew her nose. "Susan promised my uncle that, when he died, she would keep our cousin Katie's inheritance in trust for her. He was afraid that Katie would spend it all, or lose it, or give it away to some man."

"How old is your cousin?" Louise asked.

"Thirty-five."

My brows lifted in surprise. I had expected her to say late teens or early twenties but not mid-thirties.

"At what age was your cousin supposed to come into the full inheritance?" I said.

"Katie is to have an allowance, adjusted annually for inflation, for the rest of her life. She'll never inherit the full amount. If, when Katie dies, she has any children of her own, they would split what was left, after a large chunk went to charities designated in the trust."

I could see why a thirty-five year old woman would be upset about her father giving her an allowance even after his death. Money was always enough motive for murder.

"My Uncle was right not to trust Katie. Her allowance for this year should have been more than enough to live comfortably, even for someone used to having a lot of money. She received a lump-sum payment for the year in January. It's October and she's broke."

Linda plucked two more tissues from the box. She dabbed at her eyes, which seemed to stream tears non-stop now.

"According to the trust she doesn't get her next lump sum until next January."

"No exceptions?" Jane piped in. She flinched as if Louise and I might pounce on her for asking a question.

"No," Linda said. "Katie thought there was a loophole though. She kept calling Susan. Katie would say things like Susan was trying to cheat her out of her money. Katie called Susan last week and told her that if she didn't give her more money, she would hurt Susan."

Linda's voice broke with grief and a shiver ran over her shoulders.

"Susan said she thought Katie was serious." Linda took a deep shuddering breath. "I told her that Katie was just mad. I told her Katie would calm down. I told her to ignore the threats. Now Susan and Jonathan are dead."

"Mrs. Meyers," Jane said. "You can't believe any of this is your fault."

Jane had made the mistake only a rookie, or a reporter, could make. She had dismissed the power of survivor guilt.

"It is my fault! I told her to ignore the threats and now she's dead."

"But you didn't kill her." Jane Katts was digging herself a deep hole, and if she didn't stop digging soon she'd find herself at the planet's core.

Louise jumped in to rescue Jane as she had done many times for me in the past.

"Mrs. Meyers." She laid her hand on Linda's shoulder. "We'll need information on your cousin. Could you get her address and her phone number for us?"

The question of what diamonds could mean to her cousin would have to wait for another time. If we asked Linda about diamonds now Jane Katts would know we were hiding something from her. She already suspected, but there was no need to spell out our deception for her.

Linda Meyers blinked at Louise for several seconds before nodding. "Yes, of course. I'll get the address."

She left the room.

I pressed my fingertips to my temples and rubbed in a circular motion.

"What on earth were you thinking, Katts?" The question came out as more of an accusation than an inquiry.

Her eyes went wide. "What are you talking about? I'm trying to help her. She's blaming herself for something that she had no control over."

I leaned forward and braced my elbows on my knees. "Yeah, and your job, as an observer, is not to play amateur grief counselor. Telling a survivor that their guilt is wrong, when they're not ready to hear it, is the worst thing you can do."

Jane shrank back in her seat, as if she hoped the chair could swallow her whole.

"I'm sorry. I didn't know." Her lip pouted again. "I was trying to help."

There was a lot Jane Katts didn't know. Suddenly, I realized that having her with us on this investigation might be the best thing in the world. She had received her first lesson in the aftermath of people unraveling, that the media helped create, but didn't care to stick around to see – unless of course the aftermath meant better ratings or sold more newspapers.

In our line of work, Louise and I had to deal with the worst of human nature on a day-to-day basis. If we didn't turn off our feelings for the victims, we'd go insane.

However, Jane Katts, as a member of the average human race, doesn't get the luxury of a callus over her compassion. The rest of this investigation she would learn the true price victims paid, and not the scrubbed up, sanitized Cliff Notes version available daily at five, six, and ten. Usually sandwiched between the weather and a feature about a lost dog that traveled forty-miles to find his way home unharmed.

Linda Meyers returned carrying a blue leather address book.

"I can't find a piece of paper." She lifted a stack of magazines from the end table and peeked under them. "You don't happen to have any paper?"

Louise took out her phone and took a picture of the address while Linda looked on.

"Mrs. Meyers, I really hope that, after we visit your cousin, we'll be able to come back to you with some good news." Louise patted her hand.

"Me too." Linda covered Louise's hand with hers. "It's really hard for me to accept that someone I grew up with could have done something so terrible."

No more needed saying. We stood and told her we would be in contact as soon as we had any information on the investigation.

She thanked us but her expression of despair never changed, as if Linda Meyers had lost all dare to hope. Someday she might smile again but, in the near future, hope might be a sparse commodity.

On our way out the door, Mr. Meyers approached us. This time he didn't look away, or fidget like a man left holding the duffle after a bank heist.

"I'll walk you ladies to your car." He held open the door.

Outside he made sure the door closed tightly.

"Detectives, I have some information regarding the murders of my brother-and-sister-in-law." He checked over his shoulder as if his wife may have opened the door without him hearing. "I think my nephew might have had something to do with the murders."

"Really?" Jane sounded too gleeful for an observer and I gave her a rib-poke to remind her of her place. She frowned and rubbed the spot on her side.

"Chad?" Louise asked. "Why?"

"I don't know." Jack produced a cigarette from a crumpled pack in the front pocket of his jeans. He fished a lighter from his other pocket and lit the cigarette. "It's just a feeling I get. The kid's just so different."

He took a long drag from the cigarette and released the smoke through his nose.

"A year or so ago Chad started to wear what I call trash clothes. Everything was baggy and dark. Half the shit looks like he dug it out of a dumpster."

He jerked his thumb toward the front door.

"My wife thinks Chad's an angel. She says it's just a phase that all kids go through but I'm not so sure."

"Did the change in Chad coincide with anything significant?" I asked. "Like his first day of college or anything like that?"

"Yeah, it was right after the murder of his, Grandmother."

An audible gasp escaped our impartial observer. Jane looked as if she were about to bolt for the nearest phone to call in the breaking news flash. I gave another rib jab, which she shrugged away from without a second glance at me. Jane was wrapped up in the Luther family story, and how to spin the tale for the morning news.

Stopping her from telling this story would be like trying to reign in a tornado.

"After she was killed, Chad went from a clean cut kid to a kid who looked homeless, or like some fucking junkie. Chad is frightening now." He tapped his chest with his cigarette-entwined fingers. "At least to me he is. I'm not sure if his Mother felt that way, probably not. She probably thought of him as the same saint my wife thinks he is, but I know Jonathan's feelings."

Jane Katts bounced on the balls of her feet again, on the verge of doing the pee-pee-dance of excitement.

"What were his feelings, Mr. Meyers?" Louise ignored the maniacal gleam in Jane's eyes.

"He was worried." He flicked the cigarette ash into the bushes next to the door, where a collection of butts had been disposed of behind an overgrown juniper bush. "Jonathan said that Chad was like one of those kids you hear about on the news. The ones who just decide to go on a killing spree."

Linda Meyers peaked through the living room curtains. No doubt wondering why we hadn't pulled away yet. I flicked my eyes her direction several times, to alert Jack. He glanced over his shoulder and waved at her. She didn't wave back.

"I should go inside," he said. "Anyway, I just had to let you know my feelings. What you do with the information is up to you."

He stubbed out the cigarette under his shoe, and then went inside without saying another word. Through the front window, Mrs. Meyers gestured wildly in our direction. Jack put his arm around her shoulder and drew her out of our sight.

"When were you going to share that little tidbit of background information with me?" Jane took her notebook from her purse and scratched out a few words.

"I was thinking never," I said.

Her response was momentarily, and blissfully, blocked out as I closed the door. My happiness died a quick death when Jane popped her head in the back door.

"The public has the right to know." A protest older than Methuselah.

She crawled into the car and hugged herself up against the back of my seat. I could feel her breath creating dew on the side of my face.

"You can't sensor this information," she brayed into my left ear. "The public has the right to know."

I turned my head to the left until I could see her from the corner of my eye.

"Why?"

She blinked, and then moved back from me as if I had flicked her between the eyes.

"What do you mean?"

"I mean, why?"

Jane's eyes were blank as if she genuinely didn't understand the question.

"Why does the public need to know anything about a murder that took place so many years ago? The only people who were affected by that murder already know what happened."

Jane turned toward the window and smirked. "The murders could be connected or hadn't you thought of that?"

Still she thought she had all the answers to any question the world could present. She was too young to sense that there were questions in the ether waiting to spring on her, that she hadn't even dreamt of yet.

Louise started the engine of the car. I crossed my seatbelt over my chest and locked it in place. From the back seat, I could hear the click of Jane's seatbelt. At least she had learned something in the past few hours.

"Yes, I had thought of the possibility, and I have the phone number of the sheriff who investigated the murder."

That got her attention. Her head snapped forward again.

"Have you called him? What did he say? Is there a connection to this murder?"

She rapid fired the questions at me, leaning forward again as far as she could until the seat belt stopped her progress.

"Where are we headed?" Louise asked. "To interview the cousin?"

"The medical examiner's office," I said. "He's cutting Susan Luther this afternoon and I think we need to be there for this one."

Louise squinted at me over the top of her sunglasses, which were unnecessary in the overcast gloom of the day, but Louise wore them anyway. One of her more eccentric affectations.

"Why?" she asked.

I glanced at Jane Katts' eager little face. "Because the public has the right to know."

Chapter Six

Digs stood outside autopsy room eight, suited from head to toe in scrubs as if he would be the one cutting this afternoon. He did a double take when he spotted us, as if his imagination had willed us there and not for the first time. His mouse-dark eyes gleamed at us in disbelief.

"Hey, Digs." I passed my hand through the air once in greeting. "Did we miss it?"

He blinked and shook his head. "No. Are you sitting in?"

"Yep."

His eyes trailed to Louise. He smiled, and then noticed we weren't alone.

"This is Jane Katts," Louise said. "Jane wrote the story in the paper this morning."

Digs went still, and a vaguely panicked look crossed his face as if he was suddenly on trial.

Jane stuck out her hand and waited for him to return the gesture. "I've been given permission to follow the investigation with the detectives."

He looked to Louise for confirmation and got it with a curt nod. Reluctantly, he raised his hand and shook.

"It's nice to meet you." Digs' voice had dropped two registers to a more authoritative tone. "I'm Randy Ray. I'm a forensic pathologist."

Jane pointed at me. "What did she call you when we walked up?"

"Digs," I said. "That's what we call him."

"It's a nickname." He shrugged. "You can call me Digs, but I prefer Randy."

I wanted to laugh and shout, "Since when" but I held back. Digs was thinking about seeing his name in the paper for the first time, a thrill to be sure, if the reporter wasn't going to crucify you.

Dave Goldwin, the Medical Examiner assigned to our case, shuffled down the hall toward us in his paper-covered shoes. He cut a more convincing figure in his scrubs than Digs ever could.

In Dave's right hand he held a sandwich and in the left a Styrofoam coffee cup. He chomped into the sandwich and then lifted his cup and slurped his coffee, before he'd even chewed the chunk of bread and meat he'd gnawed off. He toasted us with his coffee cup.

"Jesus, there's going to be quite an audience today," he said through a sloppy mouth full of food. He gave two perfunctory chews and then swallowed. "I didn't realize that autopsies were now a spectator sport."

"Do you mind?" Louise asked.

Dave took another bite and drink, and then shook his head. "Nope. The more the merrier."

He used his pinky to punch in the security code on the keypad door lock. The green light beeped on and Dave gestured to Digs.

"Help out a guy would ya' Digs?"

Digs turned the knob and Dave shoved the door open with his shoulder.

"School's in," he said and trotted across the sterile room to a counter that ran across one wall. He set his cup and sandwich on a tray that I prayed had never been used to hold anything other than clean and disinfected instruments. Even then, the thought grossed me out.

The room was cold for obvious reasons. Susan Luther lay on a table in the center of the room, her body covered with a white, cloth sheet. Growing up Catholic, I had a strong urge to cross myself and say a quick *Our Father*. No matter how many times I sat in on an autopsy, the urge to cross myself and pray remained as strong as the first time.

Louise ushered Jane Katts through the door. Jane's face had gone pale. I wondered briefly, what she had expected to find when we got here. What had she thought an autopsy was all about?

Then I decided that Jane Katts must have believed that I was trying to outwit her. That coming to the medical examiner's office had been an elaborate joke at her expense, but she'd never expected to see a body.

Dave riffled through drawers collecting the various paraphernalia that he'd need.

"Sorry, I didn't get to this one sooner," he said. "Yesterday was crazy and your murders were late in the day. Must have been a full moon or something, because we had a line of bodies waiting to get in like we were the best restaurant in town."

He unleashed a hearty laugh.

Jane Katts gave a grunt of disgust at Dave's humor. When I was new to the job, I was also shocked and surprised at the irreverence of the medical examiners. After a few months, I learned it was how they coped.

"I was able to slice the gunshot guy though," he said. "I figured you'd want the bullet from that one. You can imagine my surprise when I pulled –"

"Dave." Louise interrupted him before he could reveal our ace. "I didn't have the chance to introduce you to Jane Katts. She's with the Saint Paul newspaper."

Dave Goldwin's expression changed from placid to furrowed. He gave Jane a hard stare.

"Nice to meet you, Ms. Katts. You're the one who wrote that crap I read in the paper this morning aren't you."

The pressure that throbbed in my heart since Jane had joined us ebbed for a moment. I silently blessed Dave for his irreverence and honesty.

Digs' eyes went wide enough to pop out of his skull and he shuffled from side to side with a nervous laugh. Louise placed her hand firmly on his right shoulder to keep him from doing the Daffy-Duck-bounce off the walls.

Jane jerked up slightly at the stinging jab. "It wasn't crap."

"Sure it was." Dave turned back toward his drawer rummaging. "Sounded like spoiled grapes when I read it."

"What's your name?" Jane took her notebook from her purse, the threat in her question far from veiled.

"Goldwin." He approached her and leaned over her notebook. "G–o-l-d-w-i-n and don't spell it wrong when you write your crap about me."

Dave looked at me and jerked his thumb toward her rolling his eyes as if to say, "Get her". After all what would she print?

"You done passing notes, Ms. Katts? Because I remember saying that class was in."

Jane clicked her pen closed and dropped it neatly into the side pocket of her purse along with the notebook. She sucked her cheeks in like a fish mugging against the side of a tank.

Doctor Dave Goldwin snapped on his rubber gloves and fixed an icy gaze on her. He reached up, opened a cupboard door, and pulled out a handful of surgical masks. He dangled a mask from the end of his chubby index finger and held it out to Jane. She took the pale, green, square of fabric, and tied it around her face.

Louise, Digs, and I took our masks and followed suit.

Dave wheeled a tall table with a silver tray on the top, littered with various mean-looking, stainless steel instruments, across the room, and stationed it next to the body on the table. The neatly laid out tools looked like some grisly Thanksgiving carving tray.

He drew the sheet away from Susan Luther's bloodless, blue-tinged face, and then looked up at Louise and me. His eye danced from us to Jane as if to ask if we were sure.

For my part, I was more than sure. I wanted Jane to see what she had only previously imagined in a detached manner.

Dave folded the sheet down past her naked breasts, then again at about her knees. Finally, he drew the sheet away and Susan Luther lay naked on the table in front of us, arms at her side and legs at a hips width apart.

Digs briefly made eye contact with Jane Katts. He shifted uncomfortably in place and turned bright red. I didn't believe it was the first time Digs had seen a naked woman, but part of me wondered if it was the first time, he'd seen a naked woman with a live woman in the same room. Judging from his reaction it was quite possible that Digs was the world's oldest living virgin.

Dave switched on the microphone above the table to record his observations during the autopsy.

"The victim is Susan Luther, a forty-six year old female."

Dave ran his fingers down Susan's neck, and rolled her head toward him. He checked her teeth, then ran his hands down her arms.

"Victim appears to be in good physical condition."

A dark, slightly purple puncture marred the skin on her left side about an inch below her left breast. Dave used a magnifying glass to examine the area for trace evidence. He used a tweezers and removed a few fibers that were most likely from Susan Luther's shirt. Digs handed him an evidence bag and Dave deposited the string in the baggy.

"Preliminary cause of death appears to be stabbing," he said.

I looked across to Jane whose color hadn't returned to her face. "You okay over there?"

She dismissed my concern with a brusque, "I'm fine, thank you."

Dave probed the four stab wounds on the front of Susan Luther's body, then put one hand under her shoulder and one under her hip. He rolled Susan onto her side exposing her bare bottom to us. Jane turned away for a moment, then recovered and turned back.

Dave counted nine more stab wounds, thirteen total. We were definitely dealing with a crime of passion.

"I'm ready to cut." He took a scalpel from the tray and made a Y-incision on her chest. Dave glanced up at Jane. "You still doing alright there, Ms. Katts?"

"Yes, and I wish everyone would quit asking. I've seen blood and gore before."

"Okay," Dave said and peeled Susan Luther's skin from her rib cage.

I turned away. I could never watch him open someone. The rest of the autopsy I could cope with, but actually opening the skin bothered me. It made my hair bristle and my stomach flip-flop.

"You can look now, Catherine," Dave called and I turned back.

"Are you okay, Detective?" Jane's voice was snide and contemptible.

"I will be now," I said.

Dave picked up what I referred to as the branch cutters. That's essentially what they were; only these cutters cut bone instead of tree limbs.

He cut through the first rib. From somewhere to my right I heard a whomp, followed closely by a thud. Jane Katts lay sprawled on the floor, mouth open, arms, and legs twisted like a rag doll.

"See now, I would have bet she'd puke," Dave said and gave a wicked, short laugh. He flicked a finger toward Digs. "You know where the smelling salts are."

Digs nodded and crossed to a cabinet on the other side of the room.

Then Dave forked two fingers at Louise and me. "You two get that lying, pile of garbage out of here, and wake her up. In that order."

"Why are you so hostile toward her, Dave?" Louise didn't move toward Jane. "She didn't do anything to you."

"Yes she did." He turned back to Susan's ribcage and released some anger by crunching through another rib bone with more force than needed. "My wife is one of those conspiracy theory buffs and that woman, crumpled on the floor, made my wife mad at me before I'd even had a chance to scratch my balls this morning. My wife cornered me while I was still in bed and gave a high-holy sermon about police corruption. Then she told me I had to go into private practice."

Another crunch popped off another rib.

"I don't want to work with the living, that's why I'm here. Now I'm going to be lectured, and nagged, until my wife finds some other bug nestled in her ass. And that –" He jabbed the branch cutters toward Jane, "Woman is the reason."

"Enough said." I reached down, took Jane by the wrists, and dragged her toward the door.

Louise opened the door for me and took the smelling salts from Digs. I slid Jane into the hallway and then dropped her wrists letting them hit the floor. A tiny piece of satisfaction rippled through me at the childish behavior.

Louise knelt down next to Jane. "I'm assuming we're done with the autopsy, and that you've accomplished what you came here for?"

I nodded. “Yep, you can judge me if you want to, but she needed to see the Luthers as human, not as the topic sentence of some news story.”

Louise cracked open the ampoule, and waved the foul smelling concoction under Jane’s nose. She choked awake, sat up, and rubbed at the back of her head.

“You weren’t exactly alright were you, Jane?” Louise asked.

Jane tossed her head from side to side, still massaging the back of her skull.

“Why didn’t you say something?” Louise slid her hand under Jane’s arm and helped her to her feet.

“I don’t know.” She focused on the floor. “I thought I’d be fine, if I’d just breathed through it. Then I felt dizzy.”

“You were probably breathing too heavy,” I said. “You hyperventilated.”

Jane parked her butt on the wall and bent at the waist, and braced her hands on her knees. “I must have.”

“Next time you’re feeling sick you should tell us,” Louise said. “You could have been seriously hurt.”

“I will.” Jane straightened. “Let’s get back in there.”

I put my fingertips on her chest just below the well of her neck. “Hold up, eager beaver. We’ll skip the rest of the autopsy. The Chief will kill me if you pass out again and whack your head on something sharper than the floor.”

“I’ll be fine.”

“Yes.” I nodded. “I’ve heard that mantra before, but we have other things to accomplish today. We don’t need to send you to the emergency room to get our work done.”

“Besides,” Louise said. “Doctor Goldwin doesn’t like you much.”

Jane’s eyes went wide. “Why not?”

“You apparently got him in trouble with his wife,” Louise said.

Her face drew into a puzzled expression.

"Never mind," I said. "It's enough to know you should avoid the autopsy rooms for a few weeks."

I checked my watch. If I wanted to catch the McCann County Sheriff in his office and quiz him about Chad Luther's Grandmother, I'd have to call in the next couple of hours.

"Let's check in at the office and then we'll visit the cousin."

"I'd like to check in with my office too," Jane said, and then gave a hesitant smile. "And maybe get a drink of water."

Good. If she were distracted, she wouldn't hear my conversation with the Sheriff. Maybe her fainting spell had shaken the memory of the first murder in the Luther family out of her head. Then I remembered her little note pad. I should have stolen the notebook and her tape recorder while she was unconscious.

We left Jane in a small conference room where she could call her office in private. I wanted to lock her in an interrogation room. That way she couldn't sneak up on me while I was on the phone. Unfortunately, all the interrogation rooms were occupied.

Louise left to pull the court records on the Cousin's trust before we left. I picked up the phone and dialed the McCann County Sheriff's Department.

"Sheriff's Office." A perky female voice said.

"May I speak with Sheriff Rose, please?" I confirmed the name on the business card.

"Who's calling, please?"

"Detective O'Brien. I'm calling from the Saint Paul Police Department's homicide division."

"One moment please."

She clicked me over to the on-hold music and I was lost grooving to *Play That Funky Music White Boy* by *Wild Cherry* when the Sheriff picked up.

"Sheriff Rose speaking."

"Sheriff, my name is Catherine O'Brien. I'm a Detective with the Saint Paul Police Department's homicide division."

"Yes, Detective." His tone was friendly but impatient. "How can I help the S.P.P.D.?"

I fingered a statue of the Archangel Michael, which my Mother had given me, holding his flaming sword over his head. As the patron saint of police, mom considered Michael to be my personal guardian angel.

"I wanted some information on a murder investigation."

"Marion Luther?"

"Yeah, how did you know?"

"We do get the Twin Cities' papers up here. I read about the death of Jonathan and Susan."

I don't know why but I imagined McCann as some secluded mining town isolated from the rest of Minnesota. Of course, they had newspapers; their local papers probably covered the Luther's deaths. Especially if they still had family in the area.

"I was sorry to hear they'd died."

"Sheriff, I'm wondering if the murders could be connected."

There was no point in beating around the bush. Sheriff Rose had probably already guessed why I was calling. Anyone with any investigative background could make the leap easily enough, and I didn't want to insult his intelligence.

"They could be." He let out a heavy breath. "Marion's death is unsolved."

"Chad mentioned that yesterday. Did you have any suspects?"

"Of course we did, Detective."

He sounded disgusted by the question and I couldn't blame him. I wouldn't appreciate someone calling my investigative skills into question either.

"Unfortunately, we couldn't make anything stick. We brought the forensic team in from Duluth, and the only evidence they could come up with was circumstantial."

"Who was the main suspect?" I tapped the end of Michael's sword, which was sharper than it looked.

"That was the tricky part," he said. "We narrowed it down to a member of the immediate family."

My statue of Michael tipped over as I scrambled for a pen and a piece of paper.

"A family member? What brought you to that conclusion?"

"All the windows were locked and the doors were all dead-bolted when the killer left, which meant they had to have had a key. The only prints we found belonged to the family members. I don't know about the crime scenes you've encounter in your time, Detective, but I've never seen one where the killer didn't make some mistake."

Not many. Murders either were a spur of the moment crime of opportunity or premeditated, but even the criminals that had planned their murders to the last detail, usually overlooked something.

"There hadn't been any attempt to clean finger prints or anything?" I asked.

"Nope."

Which meant the killer knew their fingerprints would be expected to be there.

"Detective . . ." I heard a paper crinkle on the other end of the line as he searched for my name. "O'Brien, I don't have a whole lot of time to go over the details with you right now. Why don't I fax you the case file and you can look at it?"

"That would be a big help. Thank you for your time, Sheriff Rose."

I gave him my fax and my telephone number, in case he remembered anything that he thought might be helpful. He took the numbers but said there wouldn't be anything that wasn't already noted in the case file.

A nice way of saying, don't call us and we won't call you.

Louise returned from the records department as I finished my preliminary scan of Sheriff Rose's report.

"The sheriff in McCann County sent me Marion Luther's case file." I held up the pages for her to see.

"Anything relevant?"

"He believes the murders were committed by a family member." I tapped the edge of the pages. "Apparently, Jonathan Luther's family had trouble with the law prior to this. His Mother had called the police because she felt threatened by Jonathan's brother."

Louise winced. "Jonathan and Susan were a match made in hell."

"What do you mean?"

She handed me the file she'd gotten from Rainey Harper.

"Susan Luther had filed charges against her cousin for terroristic threats right after her uncle's death."

Louise eased into her chair.

"Rainey found additional information when she searched Susan Luther's maiden name. Apparently, her family has a history of violence due to mental illness. Her Mother beat her Father so bad, he went into a coma. Susan was listed on the commitment papers along with her sister Linda."

"Wow!" I pored over the pages. "Maybe these two were drawn together because of their hardships."

Louise's eyebrows rose as if she hadn't considered the possibility. "I suppose they could relate to each other's pain."

"Now we have to figure out which crooked branch of the family tree decided to drop a few leaves."

"Chad." A voice said from behind me.

Silent as a butterfly, Jane had managed to creep up on us.

"Jack Meyers indicated that he thought Chad might be involved," she said.

"We have no evidence to support his theory," Louise motioned Jane into a chair.

Jane rolled a vacant chair up next to me.

"I did some checking on Chad," she said. "It seems that it wasn't just his appearance that went downhill after his Grandmother was murdered."

Well, there went the hope that she would have hit her head hard enough to forget all about the Grandmother.

"I had a friend of mine at the paper do a little checking. Chad's grades went downhill when he moved to Saint Paul and he's been in several fights at school. One so bad that he sent the other kid to the hospital."

I checked my watch again. "You got all that in fifteen minutes? How?"

"Can't tell you." She shook her head. "I promised not to reveal my sources."

"Oh, God." I rolled my eyes toward the ceiling. "We're not falling back on that old cliché are we?"

"Yep." She swiveled her chair in my direction. "Of course, Detective, I'll show you mine if you show me yours."

Jane inclined her head toward the paper I held in my hand. Before I'd had a microsecond to consider the proposal, Jane rescinded the offer.

"On second thought, I think I'll play my cards close to my chest, and only dole out the information when it becomes necessary to help you along the path."

"Ms. Katts," Louise said in an even measured tone that told me she was pissed as hell. "If you have information relevant to this investigation, I suggest you spill your guts before I throw you in jail for obstruction of justice."

"Now how would that look? You arrest the reporter who gave you bad press?"

"Frankly, I could give a rat's rectum," Louise said. "If you impede this investigation in any way, the deal I made with the paper is off. I will call my friend on the board of directors and let him know that you're withholding evidence. I don't think the Mayor's office or your bosses at the paper will stand behind you on this one."

Never had I heard Louise utter a phrase as crass as, rat's rectum. This girl's skill for irritation far surpassed mine.

I hunkered down in my seat and waited for these two to come to a head. Louise's capacity for stubbornness would take her through to the end; that much I knew for sure. What I couldn't calculate was Jane Katts' stupidity, and if she had the need to get her one-upance right now, or if she could wait to strike.

Jane opened her notebook, clipped the pen to the metal spiral, and handed the notebook to me. Louise ruffled with irritation but held her tongue; she had after all won the battle.

"Chad was arrested for a school yard fight. The kid he brawled with lost a tooth and received two stitches in his cheek. Charges were dropped."

I handed the notebook back to her.

"That's a pretty anemic card," Louise said. "That's like bluffing with a pair of twos."

Jane shrugged. "I had to try."

Louise smiled, and in it, I saw a genuine admiration for Ms. Katts' moxie. That's the word my Grandfather used to use, moxie. I had the inkling that moxie was why Louise liked me too. Maybe that's why Jane and I rubbed each other the wrong way. We were too much alike. The thought annoyed me.

"I'm surprised you didn't run Chad's arrest record," Jane said. "Chad has been violent in the past. His Father and his Uncle had a point."

"Except!" I held up my finger. "We only have the Uncle's word when it comes to what Jonathan Luther thought of his son's change. From the candid snapshots on Jonathan's desk, some very recent, he not only wasn't afraid of his son, but he loved him and was very proud of Chad."

"Well, he can't tell us that for himself," Jane said. "We have to rely on hearsay."

"That might work in the newspaper world but we need a little more to go on." I jabbed at her for no real reason except that I was beginning to like her. "Before we slap the cuffs on Chad, we'd need confirmation from a few more people. Anyway, I thought you were good at spotting lies."

Jane looked at me with confusion.

"Didn't you notice Jack Meyers' behavior when we arrived?"

Louise leaned forward. "I did. He looked nervous. Like he was hiding something."

"That's what I thought too," I said. "I wouldn't trust anything Jack had to say at this point."

"Maybe he was just nervous," Jane said. "People get nervous when the police show up at their door. At least I would."

I nodded my agreement and then changed directions and shook my head no.

"What?" Jane asked. "People don't get nervous around cops?"

"They do," Louise said. "Usually, nervous people explain too much."

I returned to my up and down head motion. "People who are just nervous, invite the police in to prove there's nothing to hide and then jabber nonstop."

I opened and closed my fingers in front of Jane's face like operating a sock puppet. Then I pressed my fingers tightly together.

"Jack Meyers was way too tight lipped," I said.

"At least until we left." The expression on Jane's face changed to one of enlightenment. "Then he had plenty to say."

"Maybe it took him that long to think of a lie," Louise said. "His explanation did point us to Chad and away from any other direction."

Which left us, half-a-step ahead of where we'd been this morning. Forward progress at last.

Katie Dolan screamed in our faces, when we introduced ourselves, and called us tools.

"I'll fucking kill you if you come near me."

She launched a chunk of spit in the air. The juicy wad arched through the air and landed on Jane Katts' cheek. Jane sucked in a deep breath and tensed, frozen by disgust.

"That fucking bitch deserved what she got!" Katie slammed the door.

The slam of the door brought Jane out of her disgust-induced catatonia.

"Oh my God," she whined and used her shirtsleeve to clean the retaliatory loogey from her face. "She'd better not have given me some damned disease."

"You'll live," Louise said.

We retreated to the safe distance of the car parked in the street. Louise took out her cell phone and called for a warrant to bring Katie Dolan in for questioning.

"And I'm pressing assault charges." Jane rubbed her cheek like Katie Dolan's spit had been laced with acid.

"Then we can arrest her now," I said. "We don't need a warrant, we witnessed the assault. Let's just go in and get her."

Louise twisted around in her seat to look at Jane. "Are you sure?"

Jane nodded and pulled at her cheek with the heel of her hand.

Louise took her Glock from the leather holster she kept attached to her belt. I did the same with mine. Adrenaline surged through me. My heart pounded in my ears.

We approached the front door, guns drawn but pointed at the ground at arm's length.

"Excuse me!" A shrill voice called from the porch next door. "Don't do that!"

I glanced over my shoulder and saw a fat woman with stringy, salt and pepper, hair hanging in her face.

"Wait!" She waved and jogged toward us with her limp wrists flopping at breast level as she chugged toward us. "Wait, please!"

With the effort of a champion weight lifter, the fat woman huffed up the steps. She gulped for air, as if she was on the verge of a heart attack.

"Ma'am you should go back to your house," I said. "This is none of your business."

"You don't need to do this." She wheezed and braced her arms on the porch rail. "Let me talk to her. She'll come out."

"Ma'am, please." I put my hand on her shoulder to lead her away. It was like trying to move Gibraltar.

"What do you have to lose? Just let me try."

She turned her eyes to Louise.

"Please, I've been living next door to Katie for the past ten years. I know she's not well but she will listen to reason."

Louise, who had been in a ready crouch, straightened. "I'd rather have Miss Dolan come out on her own, if you think you can talk her out."

"I'm not making any promises, but it can't hurt."

The woman raked her stringy hair away from her face and approached the door. She took a deep breath, plastered a smile on her lips, and gave three short raps.

"Go away," Katie screamed from behind the door. "I swear to God I'll kill you if you fucking touch me."

"Katie," the woman sing-songed in a clear high voice. "It's Cheryl Patton from next door."

She sounded like she was asking to borrow a cup of sugar.

"Go away." Katie wasn't shouting and her voice had moved closer to the door. "Go away, Cheryl."

"Katie, you're being unreasonable," she said.

I cringed waiting for the screaming. It didn't come, only a piteous, muffled crying. No, more like weeping than crying.

"Katie, please come out," Cheryl soothed. "No one will hurt you."

Cheryl's eyes turned up to me for confirmation and I shook my head. We didn't mean to harm Katie. Of course, we were still going to arrest her, but I didn't think that Cheryl needed that little detail.

"Do you promise?" Katie wept.

Cheryl nodded. Then, as if she just remembered Katie couldn't see her through the solid oak door, Cheryl added, "I promise."

The deadbolt clicked back and the door jerked open. Katie Dolan peeked out like a frightened rabbit peeking out from its hole. She glimpsed Cheryl Patton first and then me. Her eyes dropped to my gun and she whimpered.

"Come out, Katie." Cheryl glared at me.

I slipped my gun back into its holster and covered the offensive iron with my jacket. On the other side of the porch, Louise did the same.

Katie took Cheryl's offered hand and slipped through the doorway like a dog that had been kicked one too many times. She folded into Cheryl's arms; the embrace was as sweet as a mother comforting a child scared by thunder.

Katie sobbed against the ample bosom of Cheryl Patton who petted her hair.

I took out my handcuffs, but Louise shook her head. She nodded to the street where a uniformed officer in a cruiser had parked next to the curb.

"Mrs. Patton," Louise said. "Are you willing to accompany Miss Dolan to the police station for questioning?"

"Do you want me to go with you, Katie?"

Katie nodded.

"Sure," Cheryl said. "I'll go."

The patrol officer helped the two women into the back seat and drove away. A large crowd of people gathered around the front yard and their questioning eyes locked on us.

We assured the assembled mass that we were only questioning Katie and that Cheryl was only accompanying Katie and was not under arrest. They would be home before dinner was on the table.

We crawled into Louise's car Jane still rubbed and tugged at her cheek, in the back seat. I wondered if she had a germ phobia of some kind.

"Don't go through with the assault charges," Louise said.

"What? No way, that woman spit on me."

I held up my finger. "Actually, she spit out the door. You happened to be standing where the loogey landed."

"That's still assault," Jane said. "Who knows what kinds of diseases she has. The human mouth has all sorts of disgusting bacteria."

I turned to Louise. "I was looking the other direction when all of this happened. Did you see this alleged assault?"

Louise turned toward the windshield and revved the engine of the Toyota, sending the neighbors assembled around the car scurrying for safety.

"No, I was distracted."

Instead of tearing away from the curb as I had expected, and had braced myself for, Louise slowly pulled out and ambled down the street. We passed a playground at the end of the road with a large group of children running about and shouting at one another. Louise waved at one little boy who was standing on the sidewalk waving to us.

"Come on you guys," Jane said. "What if she had spit on either one of you?"

"It's disgusting, I'll grant you that, but you're not injured," Louise said. "If we go in to interrogate her and tell her she's charged with assault, she won't tell us anything."

I picked up for Louise. "On the other hand if we tell her that she can go home as soon as she answers our questions, she might be less reticent to tell us what we want to know."

"I'm pressing charges." Jane gazed out the back window.

I bent at the waist, opened my purse, and took out a manila file. One of the advantages of carrying a purse that was slightly smaller than a large diaper bag was that you could carry more than just your wallet. Times like this vindicated my choice despite the purse's lack of fashionability.

I waved the file over the back seat.

"What's that?" Jane asked.

"The file from the Sheriff of McCann County." I glanced at her over my shoulder.

Jane's brows drew together. "And that means what to me?"

I sighed, pulled the file back, and held it in my lap. "This is a full account of Chad's Grandmother's murder."

I held up the file again. "If you agree to not press charges against Katie Dolan, I'll let you read the file."

Jane's dark eyes lit with excitement for about ten seconds, then dimmed.

"What good would it do me, Detective?" she asked and bent toward me.

"It's not like I can print anything I read anyway."

Louise glanced at me and lifted a perfectly arched eyebrow as if to ask, what now. I pressed my eyes closed, took a deep breath and resigned myself to what I was about to do.

"If you agree to not press charges, I will let you read the file. I will also work with you to come up with an acceptable story about the Grandmother's murder."

Jane cackled with laughter. "I can just see what you'd allow me to publish. No way."

I was not at all qualified to negotiate with this woman. My favorite line from *Born Yesterday* (the Judy Holiday version not the sucky remake), "do what I'm telling you" kept running through my brain. I wanted to shout at Jane, *just do what I'm telling you* – a far from diplomatic response.

"Okay." I rubbed my hands together like a miser about to dive into his booty. "Let's be reasonable here."

From the corner of my eyes, I saw a grin split Louise's face. She knew that *let's be reasonable* was code for, please do things my way.

"What exactly will it take to get you to forget the spit shower?"

Jane unlocked her seatbelt and slid forward to speak directly into my ear.

"I want access to that file and I want to be allowed to publish the story I want to write."

"Alright, a counter offer. This is what negotiating is really all about. Now it's my turn to make another offer." I smiled. "Okay, try this one on for size. You don't press charges. You get to read the file."

Jane and Louise nodded in unison.

"You get to write the story as you want to write the story."

Jane nodded.

Louise cast a look of doubt in my direction.

"Then I get to edit the story."

I nodded.

Louise nodded.

Jane cast a look of doubt in my direction.

"Take it or leave it," I said. "It's either that or your paper goes to press without a Jane Katts exclusive."

Jane flopped back against the seat.

"Take the deal Jane," Louise said. "There won't be any more counter offers."

Jane stewed in the back seat for several minutes, likely trying to decide how much she could get away with before I would start to wield my veto power. The smug smile on Louise's face told me that I was about to win the negotiation.

"Deal." Her hand snaked between the seats palm up. "Let's see the file."

I tucked the file back into my purse. "After Katie Dolan has answered our questions and is safely on her way home."

"You think I'll welch?" Jane's tone was incredulous.

I considered the question for a long moment. "I think anyone who would bluff with a pair of twos, just might welch."

Jane Katts fell silent and stayed silent for the remainder of the trip. From the glimpses I caught of her in the visor mirror, she looked like she was already writing her story.

Cheryl Patton rocked Katie Dolan back and forth like a mother comforting her child. Katie's sobs trailed down to soft snuffling and coos.

"Miss Dolan," Louise said. "Have you contacted your attorney?"

Katie's wide eyes turned to Louise's face. "No. That cop I rode in with said I wasn't under arrest. He said I was only here for questioning."

"That's correct," Louise said. "You do know that we're here to ask you about the murder of your cousin?"

Huge, glassy, tears rolled down Katie's cheeks. She nodded, and then sniffed up a huge wad of snot.

I prepared myself to dodge another loogey assault. This time however she swallowed and went on weeping. I slid a box of tissues toward her. Katie eyed me suspiciously then pulled two tissues from the box.

Louise turned on the tape recorder.

"We'd like to ask you some questions about Susan and Jonathan's murder," She repeated for the benefit of the tape.

"I don't know anything except she got what she deserved." Katie wiped her nose up toward her hairline the way a small child would, turning her nose into a snout as she did.

"Katie," Cheryl Patton interrupted before we could clarify what Katie had meant. "You can't say such things. These police officers will think that you hurt your cousin."

She spoke as if she were talking to a three-year-old. I wondered how far from the truth that assessment really was. Even if Katie had something to do with the murders of Jonathan and Susan Luther, from the dull-eyed stare Katie gave Cheryl Patton, we might be looking at a valid diminished capacity plea. It would certainly explain why Katie's father had put all her money in a trust administered by her cousin.

"Miss Dolan," Louise continued. "You threatened your cousin's life. She filed charges against you for terroristic threats."

"She was being a big baby," Katie said. "I didn't hurt her. But Susan said I had to learn not to talk to people that way, so she had me arrested."

Tears welled in her eyes again at the thought of her arrest. Cheryl put her arm around her and soothed her like a small child.

"You have to understand," Cheryl Patton said. "Katie has threatened everyone, but she doesn't mean anything by it. She's harmless."

"She spit at us," I said.

Jane Katts watched from behind the two-way glass since we forbid her from attending the interrogation. I might regret reminding Jane about the spitting, but it was relevant to the questioning.

"But she didn't hurt anyone." Cheryl chuckled as if people went around spitting on each other every day. "Katie couldn't hurt anyone. She doesn't have the strength or the malice. She threatens people, yes, but she could never follow through. She doesn't even drive. To commit a crime she would have to get to the scene and leave again. How would she have done that? By cab?"

"It's my understanding, Miss Dolan, that you were left a large sum of money by your father. Is that correct?" I asked.

Katie nodded. "Over two hundred million."

Cheryl sucked in a deep breath and her eyes went wide. Evidently, Cheryl had been under the impression that poor Katie Dolan was, in fact, poor.

"Your cousin was the head of the trust for your inheritance?" Louise lifted one of the pages in the file she held before her as if to confirm this information.

Again, Katie nodded.

"Katie," I said. "Did you hire someone to kill your cousin and her husband?"

Cheryl Patton stiffened. A flicker of concern creased her brow. She moved a half an inch away from Katie, as the reality of what I said sank through to her brain.

"I need to use the ladies," Cheryl stood. "Could you please direct me?"

I pointed her toward the toilet, but Cheryl Patton headed in the opposite direction toward the elevators instead. Katie had no idea that her support had just caved. I didn't feel the need to mention the sudden departure and upset her again.

"Katie?" Louise said. "Do you want your lawyer now?"

"No." She stuck her thumb in her mouth and started to gnaw on the skin around her fingernail. "I didn't do anything to Susan or Jonathan. It was Susan who did to me."

"Pretty little, Suzie." Her tone changed to a sarcastic mewling. "Suzie Q always had everything. She was everyone's perfect little girl. She had everything but she still had to take from me."

Katie beat one fist against her chest and the other against her temple. Her lips curled away from her teeth and she squeezed her eyes shut.

"Ahhhh!" She growled from her throat. "Because I can't think right. They let her steal from me because my head doesn't work."

Katie put a hand on either side of her head, raked her fingers through her hair, and squeezed her temples. Tears shimmered from the point of her chin, and then plunked to the front of her blouse like the drip of a faucet.

"Suzie Q had it all." Katie's voice quaked with pain. "Why did she need mine?"

Her eyes pleaded with us for an answer.

"I don't know," Louise said. "Some people just never have enough, I guess."

"Exactly." Katie's whole body bobbed up and down as she nodded. "That's exactly right. They just want more and they don't care who they hurt."

With one sentence, Louise had gained Katie's trust. Katie adjusted herself so her back touched the chair and her hand rested on the tabletop.

"Did you hurt Susan, because she hurt you?" I asked. "No one could blame you if you did."

"No," Katie shook her head. "I didn't hurt her. I wanted to, because she kept making me mad. Then she had me locked up. When I got out she said she would have me locked up for good if I didn't leave her alone."

Her thumb went back between her teeth, and she gnawed, wide eyes darting from my face to Louise's.

"So I did," she said.

"Did what?" I asked.

"Left her alone." She shook her head. "I don't want to be locked up. My parents put me in one of those homes because they said it would be best for me, but I really hated it. Anyway, I do fine on my own, they didn't need to worry about me."

"Katie," Louise said. "You promise that you didn't hurt Susan or Jonathan."

Katie's fingers splayed straight out and she pressed her palms to the side of her head.

"No! I said no. Why won't you believe me?"

"I'm sorry." Louise edged back until she were safely out of Katie's reach. "Don't be upset, I just had to ask one more time. I believe you."

One of Katie's hands slumped to her shoulder; the other stayed firmly at her temple. She narrowed her eyes as if she had x-ray vision, and could see into Louise's head to find the truth, if only she could squint tight enough.

"You believe me?"

"I do, Katie," Louise said.

Her other hand dropped to her shoulder and she nodded. "Okay."

Louise stood and indicated that I should do the same with a quick flick of her wrist. She instructed Katie to wait in this room for a little bit and promised her we would find Cheryl Patton and send her back in, a promise we couldn't keep. We'd just make up some lie about Cheryl checking her messages and being called away on an emergency. Anything to keep Katie from making a scene.

I closed the door to the interrogation room behind me. "That girl is cracked down the middle."

"I'm not sure I really do believe her," Louise said. "We need to get a psych evaluation for her. She might believe that she had nothing to do with the murder, but that doesn't mean she didn't have some help."

Help wouldn't be too hard to find with over two hundred million and change on the line. Katie Dolan could probably find half a dozen people willing to help.

"Does the trust name anyone to succeed Susan Luther if she should happen to die before Katie?" I asked.

Louise combed through a few pages, and then nodded. "In the unlikely event that Susan Luther should precede Katie in death, sole responsibility for management of the trust falls to the First National Bank and Trust."

"So she wouldn't get the money anyway."

I leaned against the wall and lifted my left foot. For the past three hours, I could feel a sore spot forming on the ball of my foot where a strange knot had worked its way into my sock. Now what I felt wasn't just a sore, it was a full-fledged blister, the size of a pillow, poking out of my skin.

"But Katie might not know that," Louise said. "Or if she did at one time, she might not remember. That's why we need a psych profile on her, to find out who we're dealing with."

I agreed and Louise left to call for a doctor. My job was to make the excuses for Cheryl Patton. I decided my original idea was the soundest, and I told Katie that Cheryl had been called away on some trumped up emergency. Cheryl could deal with the repercussions of her abandonment when Katie got home.

I had the idea that Cheryl believed she wouldn't need to deal with the truth; that her neighbor wouldn't be coming home any time soon. So, after all her protests and defense of Katie, deep down Cheryl believed this woman capable of murder or at least hiring a murderer.

Katie took the lie better than I thought. She seemed momentarily surprised then accepted the idea with a distracted, "I hope everything is okay."

She was too consumed with what was about to happen in her own world to care about her neighbor's concerns. I decided that unless what her neighbors were doing, directly involved Katie, she didn't care much about them at all.

I went to find Jane. She was holed up in the room behind the one-way mirror scribbling notes.

"I thought you had forgotten about me." She looked up without lifting her head. "And our deal."

"I haven't forgotten." I turned out my empty pockets. "I don't seem to have the file on me at the moment."

"Convenient."

"Don't worry, Jane, I'm not going to run off with the file. My word is good." I dropped into a chair next to her, and then gestured toward her notebook. "What are you working on there?"

Her pen lifted from the page, returned to its position, and then she wrote a few more words.

"Just some observations about your interview."

"Oh." I leaned over to get a look at what she was writing. "Like what?"

"Like that woman is playing you."

"What do you mean?"

Jane gestured toward the mirror, and Katie beyond, with her chin. "She's not as mentally ill as she's trying to make you believe."

I turned my gaze toward the glass. I scrutinized Katie's face and tried to see something that would support Jane's theory. Katie's slumped shoulder posture and nail chewing, while she stared dull eyed at the tabletop, did nothing to bolster Jane's claim.

"How do you know?"

"Because when you and Detective Montgomery left the room her entire demeanor changed. She stretched her back, stopped chewing on her fingers, and her expression changed."

"Changed how?"

Jane shrugged. "She didn't have that little lost girl look on her face anymore. She looked impatient like someone waiting for a bus that's twenty-minutes late."

I watched Katie and still didn't see anything except the frail child-woman we'd left a few minutes before.

"Then why is she sitting like that now."

Jane closed her notebook and clicked her pen closed. "I can explain if you want me to."

I rolled one hand over the other. "Proceed."

She pointed with the tip of her pen toward the interview room. "The door to the room has a window. She watched the window until you two were no longer visible."

"Well we're not standing in the window now, so why put on an act?"

Jane trailed the tip of her pen in the air around the frame of the mirror. "I don't know who built this place, but they must have put this glass in with bubble gum, at five o'clock, on a Friday afternoon."

"What?"

"Little Miss in there, did her Jekyll and Hyde thing as soon as you opened the door to this room. The rush of outgoing air made the mirror suck into the room and then released. As soon as the glass rattled she went child-like again."

I gave her a doubtful, narrow-eyed look.

"Give me some credit, Detective. I know you videotape the interrogation room. Review the tape. You'll see what I'm saying."

She was right. The department taped all interrogations, for our protection and the protection of the interviewees. The last thing the department wanted were accusations of police brutality in a locked interrogation room. The tape ensured that good cops weren't fired without merit. They also ensured that bad cops went home for good.

"Okay, let's go check."

I brought Jane to the control room and we reviewed the tapes. Jekyll and Hyde was an understatement. She couldn't have played us any finer if she were the lead violinist in the Saint Paul Chamber Orchestra.

"Nice, huh Detective O'Brien."

I swiveled in my chair to face her. "Call me, Catherine."

"Ooo." She smirked. "Progress. Does this mean I'm free to print my story as I write it?"

"No, but it does mean I won't ditch you at the next available opportunity."

She stuck out her hand. "Fair enough, Catherine."

I shook it. "Thanks for the insight, Jane."

Doctor Sergei Xavier watched the tape along with Louise, who looked as pissed as I felt when I had viewed the tape the first time.

"It looks to me like Miss Dolan has Antisocial Personality Disorder or APD," Sergei said. "Some of the symptoms are deceitfulness, aggressiveness, irritability, irresponsibility, impulsivity, and a lack of remorse."

"Well, slam dunk," I said. "You are the best, Doc!"

He gave me a tolerant, patronizing, smile that only doctors, and mothers of sick children, can manage with any authenticity.

"Perhaps you're right." Doctor Xavier rocked back on his heels. "However, if Miss Dolan has been hospitalized, or put in a home, as she claimed, I would like to speak with her doctors to find out what their diagnosis was before committing to APD."

"I'll call her cousin and find out who her doctor was during her hospitalization," I said.

Xavier gave a quick nod. "I don't think she'll change her act in the next few minutes, but I'll go in and speak with her. Maybe she'll give us something we can review and compare on the tape later."

"Thank you," Louise said. "I appreciate you coming down here."

Xavier smiled. Not the tolerant, patronizing smile he had given me but a warm and lusty smile. The expression was the first time since I'd known him that I had seen him look anything close to human. Normally he remained cool and detached from any situation or person. He'd fallen under Louise's siren spell. It was nothing she laid out willingly, but something she exuded through her pores and sashayed out with every step. Sergei Xavier was human after all.

"Always a pleasure, Detective Montgomery." He gave a regal bow, and then turned to me. "And Detective O'Brien. Nice to meet you, Miss Katts."

He left and I dialed Linda Meyers number on my cell phone. Jane nudged me mid-dial.

"I think Doctor Xavier has a crush on Detective Montgomery."

She giggled like a schoolgirl who had taunted a friend with thc chant k, i, s, s, i, n, g – first comes love, then comes marriage, then comes Louise with a baby carriage. This is the place where I normally check out of girl talk. I've never been interested in giggling, make up, or who was screwing who.

"All men have a crush on Louise," I said and pressed the send button on my phone. As an afterthought I added, "And some women."

Jane raised her eyebrows at Louise. "Really?"

Louise held up her index finger. "One woman. And that one was mostly Catherine's imagination."

I pouted my bottom lip and shook my head.

Jack Meyers answered the phone in time to save me from Louise's reprisal. "Hello?"

"Mr. Meyers, it's Detective O'Brien. May I speak to your wife, please?"

"What's this about? Do you have something on the murders?"

My feathers ruffled at his gruff response.

"Not yet. I need additional information from Mrs. Meyers."

"What more could you need?" His words dripped with disgust. "I told you, you need to look at Chad. Wasn't that clear to you?"

"Mr. Meyers, I need to speak with your wife. If you don't put her on the phone, I'll have to come to your house, and if I come to your house, I'll be bringing a warrant."

"What? Why?"

"Because Chad went directly from the crime scene to your home. If he wanted to hide the murder weapon, he probably ditched it in your house. We'll need to search your place. Just to be sure no evidence is hidden on your premises."

I didn't know what Jack Meyers wanted to keep from us, but his suspicious behavior had tattled on him. There was no way he wanted us anywhere near his house for a visit let alone toting a search warrant.

"Just a minute." The thud of the phone, as he dropped it onto the table, sent shockwaves through my ear as loud as a rock drum solo. Through the reverberation, I heard him yell for his wife.

A still groggy Linda picked up the phone. "Hello?"

"Mrs. Meyers," I said. "It's Detective O'Brien."

"Yes." Her voice went instantly awake. "Have you made an arrest?"

"Sorry. No," I said. "I need more information from you. We've brought your Cousin Katie in for questioning."

"You did?" Her voice was a combination of surprise and excitement. "That's great."

"Who was Katie's doctor when she was hospitalized?"

"Oh, that. Her name was Doctor Meredith."

I jotted the name in my notebook.

"She worked at the clinic off of Lexington Avenue," Linda said. The exhaustion returned like a boomerang. "Was that all you needed?"

"Yes."

I reiterated my promise to call if we had any new information for her and hung up.

Doctor Xavier knew of Doctor Meredith by reputation only. From what he said, Meredith's reputation was as solid as a rubber diving board.

"That explains why, Miss Dolan was allowed to leave the hospital without meds," Xavier said. "I'll transfer Katie Dolan's medical records to my office. I doubt there will be anything useful in them if Doctor Meredith's reputation holds true. I'm convinced that Miss Dolan suffers from APD."

From the satisfied look on Katie Dolan's face on the videotape, she wasn't suffering from her disorder at all. She believed, with great joy, that we believed she was as slow as a turtle in the road.

Too bad, she hadn't thought about the video cameras. In truth we might never have reviewed them since her act was so convincing. She could have RainMan-ed her way back home and we wouldn't have been any wiser. If she had only known about Jane.

Chapter Seven

By the time Jane finished her story for the paper, and we negotiated through the changes, it was well past dinner and the sun had disappeared from the sky.

I pulled up outside our old Victorian. The lights in the front room were off and the flickering in the window told me that Gavin was on the couch watching television. I glanced at my watch. Ten-eighteen. He was probably asleep by now.

He'd earned his rest if he had smoothed the newspaper incident over with the Moms. After sorting and soothing such tumult, Gavin qualified for sainthood in at least six different religions.

Gavin lay stretched across the sofa with KC curled next to his chest but to my great surprise, his eyes were open, alert and focused on me.

"You're awake?"

"How could I sleep before getting the low down on the article?"

He propped himself up on one arm and waited. KC raised his head as if to say, "Yeah spill it lady."

"I told you, I lost my temper."

I braced myself on the doorjamb and slipped off my boots one at a time. Some days removing my shoes felt better than arresting a serial murderer after hunting him for months. I kicked the shoes out of my way and moved to sit next to Gavin's feet. As I approached, he jerked his feet away.

"I wasn't going to tickle you. I just want to sit down."

"Yeah, right." He pushed to a full upright position. KC leapt down and disappeared into the kitchen "I've been burned by that one before."

I leaned over to kiss him, but stopped with my lips hovering less than a whisker hair away from his cheek.

"By the way, *Miz Liz* says 'hi'."

I gave him a swift tickle in the side. He jumped and squirmed as if someone had dropped ice down the front of his Levis. He grunted and shoved me away.

"You didn't see that one coming did you?" I grinned.

He rubbed his side. "No, but it hurt more than tickled."

"I'm sorry, sweetie. I didn't mean to hurt you." I slid down the couch toward him and rubbed his side gently. He put a forgiving arm around me and pulled me to him, and I stretched against the length of him.

"So, you saw Miz Liz today?"

I nodded. "And her little blonde friend who thinks you're, 'such a flirt'."

My voice pitched up in the classic, bubble-headed bimbo speak. I tipped my head from side to side so my ears touched my shoulders each time.

"Oh, please she's just a little girl," he said.

"With huge tits."

"Catherine Margaret O'Brien, you know I don't look at other women's tits." He tweaked the edge of my right boob. "Not when I have the best tits in the forty-eight contiguous states."

"That's what I like about you." I snuggled closer under his arm. "You're the best liar in the contiguous forty-eight."

He tweaked my boob again.

"Why didn't you tell me you knew Jonathan Luther?" I picked at the fraying edge of the navy polar fleece blanket we left on the couch to wrap up in on cold winter days. In Minnesota the cold days came unexpectedly even in mid-July, so the blanket was a year round fixture.

Gavin Shrugged. "I didn't know who the victim was until I read it in the newspaper this morning. If you remember you didn't give me much time to ask you about your case last night."

I slid my hands around his hips and gripped his butt cheeks. "Oh, yeah. I remember. So why didn't you tell me after you read the paper."

"Well, according the paper you were two pimples on a bugs ass away from being moved off the Luther case." He trapped my hand before I could poke him in the ribs again. "At that moment it didn't seem important."

"What do you know about Jonathan Luther?"

He leaned away and looked down at me with his clear green eyes. "Am I being interrogated, Detective O'Brien?"

"Yes. Don't make me torture you for the answers."

I gave his cheeks another squeeze.

"Did you know him, Gavin? What kind a man was he?"

"I didn't really know him that well. I'd met him a few times, while I was doing business with Liz but I really didn't know much about him. He always seemed like a happy man."

"What do you mean?"

"Shit, I don't know." He reached over to the coffee table and snagged a bottle of Summit Extra Pale Ale with one swallow left. He drank the remainder then put the bottle back on the table. "He looked happy."

"Overly happy?" I asked. "Like it was an act?"

Gavin ran a finger across my forehead, following the line of my hair. Shivers ran up my spine.

"No," he said. "Just happy, like the kind of guy who would never end up on the front page of the paper, unless he was rescuing kids from a burning building, kind of happy."

"Yeah," I said. "Unfortunately that's what everyone is saying about him."

"And that disappoints you?"

"It sure doesn't help my investigation."

"I know what will help."

He slid his arms under me and pushed me up to a sitting position. I groaned my displeasure. I was just getting comfortable and could have stayed curled up on the couch all night.

"You go upstairs and get your jammies on." He shoved me off the couch. "I'll make sure everything is locked up down here, and all the lights are off."

"And then what?" I asked.

"And then, after I'm finished down here, I'll come upstairs and give you a foot massage you will never forget."

I bolted for the stairs.

"Hurry up," I called over my shoulder. "And don't forget the light over the stove in the kitchen."

I vaulted the stairs two at a time, had my clothes changed, got ready for bed, and snuggled under the blankets before Gavin could change his mind about my foot massage. Moments after Gavin began to rub my feet, I don't remember much of anything, but before I fell asleep, I remembered the most pressing question I'd had all day. I sat up.

"Gavin?"

"What?"

He stopped rubbing my feet and his eyes went wide as if he were afraid he'd pressed to hard on a particularly tender spot on my foot.

"What picture of me do you have on your desk?"

The next morning Jane Katts was waiting for me in the lobby of the P.D. Shoulders slumped forward over a notebook and she was scribbling furiously. I wondered what she had heard that had set her scribbling again.

Her eagerness from the day before hadn't dissipated, but her shoes had become more sensible, as well as her clothing. The uniform she'd donned this morning looked suspiciously like the one I gravitated to every morning, jeans, t-shirt, suit coat, and boots. She stood when she saw me.

"Good morning, Jane," I said with more than a little suspicion. "What are you doing out here?"

"Morning, Catherine. I'm waiting for you."

She turned back to the row of chairs behind her and picked up a bag of donuts from the bakery down the street.

"I brought breakfast."

"Donuts. How cliché."

I fixed a hard stare on her and waited to see if she was making a joke at my expense. She smirked and rattled the bag toward me.

"They're cherry filled," she said.

I snatched the bag from her hand.

"I'd slap your mother across the face for a fresh, cherry filled," I said and wondered who had clued her in. "Why didn't you call for Louise?"

"I was early."

"So, Louise should be here."

I dug into the bag and pulled out a donut.

"Louise is always here," I murmured through my mouth full of donut.

I trotted off down the hall toward our office area and Jane followed. She attempted to steal one of the donuts by executing an ill-advised reach around. I knocked her arm away and quickened my pace.

"I paid for them," she mewled.

"You gave them to me." I blocked her advance like a goalie blocking a shot on net.

"I brought the donuts for all of us."

Louise exited the ladies-room as we passed by. She grabbed the donut bag from my hand, then hip checked me into the wall.

"Then you shouldn't have given the bag to Catherine. She'll descend on a jelly donut like a locust descending on a field of wheat."

"Thank you, Louise, for that relevant observation." I tried for the bag but she pulled it away, and held it over my head, just out of reach.

With her height, and my lack there of, it wasn't too difficult for her. The bag trick frustrated the hell out of me, and gave me flashbacks to my all-girl Catholic school days. Mary Kowalski used to do the same thing with my school tam; that was until I caught Mary stuffing her bra in the bathroom one morning. Mary Kowalski and I came to an understanding after that day.

"May I say, Louise that you're looking particularly bloated and puffy, this fine morning?"

She held up a perfectly manicured, pink lacquered, middle finger. Her usual mature response to my verbal jabs.

"I can see you're in prime form today," I said and made another attempt for the bag of bakery goodies. Once again, Louise held the bag just out of reach and I wondered if Louise had been stuffing all these years.

Louise retrieved her own donut and clenched it in her teeth, then handed one to Jane.

"What's on the agenda today," Jane said through a mouth full of donut.

"Digs has some test results for Mrs. Luther," Louise said. "He texted me this morning. After that we need to speak to Chad."

The firefly light in Jane Katts blazed like a beacon. Since the first day we'd met, she'd wanted to speak to Chad Luther. Now she would be within a few feet of him.

"Rein it in, Jane," I said. "You're not going to have free access to him. Remember that you're here as an observer to learn our procedure, not to harass the victims."

"We're not past this yet?" Jane's voice tipped up at the end. "You get final approval over what I print anyway. Do we have to keep pretending?"

Louise tossed the donut bag on my desk. I dove for the bag and tore into another.

"Jane," Louise said. "I appreciate you finally admitting to your sneaky ploy, and we might have an agreement, but that doesn't mean we want to ride roughshod over Chad. He needs to trust us, to remain as calm as possible so he can answer questions."

Louise turned to me as if seeking support for what she was saying. My mouth was crammed with donut so the best I could manage was a pathetic nod.

"The last thing we need is for you to freak him out by bombarding him with questions and innuendo."

"Innuendo?"

I had chewed away enough of the fluffy donut to mumble. "Yeah, like your theory that he killed his parents."

Jane sat in the side chair next to my desk, crossed her legs, and considered Louise and then me.

"What about the neighbor's account of the car that raced away from the scene?"

Oh, shit. I had forgotten that she'd seen us speak to Bernice Leigh, the binocular woman who lived across the street from the Luther's. Jane must have spoken to Bernice right after I'd had my tirade yesterday.

"Doesn't the car she described sound like a kid's?"

I swallowed the rest of the donut. "Maybe, but it wasn't Chad Luther's car. He drives a red Spyder."

"True." She nodded and then uncrossed her legs. "But that doesn't mean he didn't hire one of his college buddies to off his parents. Depending on how much money his parents had, he could pay someone to kill them. Just like you thought Katie Dolan could have."

I considered the possibility and then dismissed the idea.

"No way," I said. "Chad Luther was shell shocked when we saw him yesterday. If he had killed his parents there's no way he would be as upset as he was."

Across the desk, I saw Louise mull over my answer. She must have come to the same conclusion, because she shook her head and dismissed the idea.

"He could have been acting." Jane was perfectly comfortable with her role of devil's advocate and she played it well. "He could have left the scene, cleaned up, gone into the house, and then turned on the water works. Or, if he had his parents killed by a friend, he may not have known how brutal his friend would be. Then when he saw his Mother he freaked."

Both theories had merit and possibilities. Before I could come up with a counter to Jane's proposal the Chief strolled up. A wide grin split his face. It was so unlike him that I wasn't sure it was him at first.

"Good morning, ladies. I wanted to thank you for the gift." He fingered an elegant gold tie tack, accented with black onyx. "It's beautiful."

"You're very welcome," Louise said. "Happy anniversary."

Shit, I had forgotten about the Chief's anniversary. From the smile he gave, Louise had covered me (again) on the gift front.

I smiled back at him. "Happy anniversary, chief."

I didn't feel right saying, "*You're welcome*" when I had nothing to do with the gift. Of course, I didn't feel guilty enough to admit that I had forgotten his anniversary all together. No, I would just smile and nod, and later write Louise a check for my half of the tie tack.

"Ms. Katts." He turned to Jane. "I read your story in the paper this morning. I thought it was good."

"Thank you." She gave me an irked smile. "I'm surprised you could find it buried on page twelve."

I may have been ready to trust Jane more than I had when we started yesterday, but that didn't mean I was willing to compromise the investigation. When we were finally ready to make an arrest, she would have the scoop of her career. Jane knew it and so did we, so I didn't feel the least amount of pity for her page twelve exclusive.

"Are you any closer to solving this one?" The chief asked.

"We have a few solid leads," Louise said.

"Good. Keep me posted." He touched the tie tack again. "And thank you for the gift. You really shouldn't have."

"It was nothing," I said and grinned at Louise.

Digs was in his accustomed place, hunched over a microscope, when we came to visit this time.

"Knock, knock," I said and pounded on his desktop.

He looked up and blinked rapidly as if trying to clear his vision. He must have finally realized that without his glasses clearing his vision was hopeless. His glasses were in a plastic tray next to his microscope. He slid his cheaters on and blinked up at me again.

"What do you know, Digs?"

He frowned and shook his head. "Unfortunately, not a lot more than we did yesterday."

He nodded toward Jane. "Morning Ms. Katts. I see you're still with us after your impromptu fainting spell yesterday."

"Yes, Mr. Ray. I appreciate your heartfelt concern."

"Children," I said. "Don't make me turn this lab around and take you both home."

Digs retrieved a file from the middle of a stack of papers that wobbled like Jello but didn't fall. Digs was even more of a file, pile master than I am. He handed the file to me and I flicked the cover open with my thumb, inside were the autopsy results for Susan Luther.

"Susan Luther was killed almost instantaneously. Doctor Goldwin says after the first or second puncture she was gone."

"So the rest of the stab wounds were some serious overkill." I scanned the details in the report.

"Major over kill," he said.

"That destroys the theory that Chad Luther hired a killer," Louise said. "Stabbing is personal. To continue to stab someone after they're already dead takes malice. A hired killer, even an amateur killer, would stop once their target was dead."

"Besides," I said. "I doubt some friend of Chad's could stomach a stabbing. Unless he was a complete sociopath."

"That still doesn't rule out Chad Luther," Jane said.

She had a point, but I wasn't about to tell her so. From the look on her face, neither was Louise.

"Whatever," Jane said. "You know I'm right."

She glanced around.

"Is there a bathroom around here somewhere? I had a lot of coffee this morning."

"Down the hall and to your left," I said.

Once Jane had departed to relieve her bladder, I tossed the file into Digs' lap.

"What's not in the report, Digs? You wouldn't have called us down here for something as mundane as Susan Luther dying on the second stab wound."

A sly grin split his face. He slid open the top desk drawer and pulled out a clear, plastic baggie.

Louise put on a pair of rubber gloves and then took the bag. She opened the seal and dumped the contents into the palm of her hand.

A small gold circle with prongs.

"It's a ring," Louise said.

"Well, the setting for one," Digs said.

"Where did you find it?" I asked.

"Embedded in Susan Luther's throat."

Louise pinched the ring between her thumb and index finger, and held it up.

"She swallowed it?"

"No." Digs held up his index finger. "It was shoved down her throat post mortem."

He pretended to stick his finger down his throat.

"Ick," I said.

"Wait, there's more."

He took the setting from Louise and nestled it into a piece of Styrofoam with a slice cut in the center. He opened another plastic baggie and deposited a diamond into the plastic tray that had held his glasses.

"This is the diamond extracted from Jonathan Luther's chest." Digs located a long tweezers, picked up the stone by the edge, and nestled the diamond into the setting.

"My God," Louise said. "Someone was trying to say something with these murders. Are we any further ahead on identifying the serial number on the stone?"

"I've put in a few calls. I should hear something by the end of today one way or the other."

"I don't understand the message here." I leaned in close to the setting. "Did you find anything that could help point us towards an answer, Digs?"

He shrugged and wrinkled his nose. "I'm not sure how helpful it would be, but the setting is engraved."

Digs took the ring from the foam and read the inscription.

"True love lasts 4-ever," he read aloud. "The for is engraved as a number four."

My mind drifted back to Walter Wren. *I loved one woman for over fifty years until she died last year from the cancer.*

Digs re-bagged the evidence and tucked it back inside an evidence box, just as Jane Katts strode back through the door. The timing was uncanny as if he'd had a premonition.

"What did I miss?" Jane smiled.

"Nothing," Digs said.

"We should go," I said. "Unless you have more questions for Digs?"

Louise shook her head. "None that I can think of."

"Great," Jane picked her purse off the floor and slung it over her shoulder. "Then it's time to interview Chad Luther."

If Chad Luther had paid to have his parents killed for the inheritance, he sure wasn't acting like it. After asking every person we came across in his dorm, we finally found Chad in the library studying for finals.

"My parents would want me to do well on the exam," he said.

"Is there somewhere we could talk?" Louise whispered.

Chad spoke privately to the librarian who offered to let us use one of the audiovisual rooms. The A.V. room was five by five with a table a TV, VCR, DVD player, and a small stereo set up.

There were two folding chairs in the room, Chad sat in one and Louise in the other. Jane and I stood pressed against the wall.

A claustrophobic feeling drifted through me but I shoved it aside. It wasn't like we were trapped in the room. No one locked the door behind us. If I needed to, I could get out of the room, and into the safe openness of the library.

"Chad," Louise said. "Tell us what you did the day of your parent's death."

"Like what?"

Chad's eyes darted from Louise to me to Jane. He looked like a trapped animal. Louise gave a comforting smile and his eyes fixed on her, clinging to her assurance.

"Just start at the beginning," I said. "Then tell us everything. No matter how small you think what you did is tell us anyway, step by step."

He took a deep breath and plunged in. "I got up. Had breakfast at the union. I called my parents."

"Why?" I asked.

"To make sure they'd be home that afternoon when I got there. Mom thought they might have somewhere to go that afternoon, so I called."

Too bad they didn't have an appointment, I thought. *They might both be alive today.*

"Between breakfast and that afternoon when you went to see your parents," Louise said. "Where did you go?"

"To visit a buddy of mine."

"His name?"

"V."

Louise leaned forward and rested her elbows on her knees. "I'm sorry?"

"His name is Marcus Vincent. Everyone just calls him, V."

Chad held up his fingers in a peace sign, to illustrate what he was saying.

"Does V live here on campus?" I asked.

"No, he has an apartment two or three blocks off campus."

Chad's eyes shifted away from mine.

"What did the two of you do until afternoon?" I asked.

My mind had already started to build a sinister scenario.

"We just, uh –" His eyes shifted away from me again. "We just hung out. You know just shooting the shit."

"Chad." I pushed myself off the wall and looked down at him with my best police look. "Don't lie to me. What were you and Mister V doing?"

His eyes refused to meet mine. Chad' shifted left and right, then left and right again as if he had a wicked case of hemorrhoids.

"Chad? Did you hear me?"

"Yes, I heard you."

"Well? What were you two doing?" I demanded. "Did you two take a trip to your parent's house?"

Chad's head jerked up. "No."

"I think so," I said. "That's why you can't tell us what you were doing."

"No." His head waved from side to side. "Jesus."

He covered his eyes with his hands.

"Christ this is a fucking nightmare." He dropped his hands into his lap. He looked up at me and held eye contact. "We did some weed, okay?"

The anticlimactic revelation was a total let down, but I believed what he'd said was the truth. He and V had been smoking pot.

Jane, who had moved to a position behind Chad Luther's shoulder, rolled her eyes skyward and circled her finger in the air as if to say, *whoopty-fucking-do*. Obviously not enough for a front page exclusive.

"You're not going to fucking bust us are you?"

"We're homicide detectives," Louise said. "Not narcotics."

Chad sagged against his chair with palpable relief. "It isn't like I do it all the time, just every once in a while when the pressure is on at school. With finals coming up I've been doing a lot of studying. I just needed to blow off steam."

"So you and V smoked pot and then what?" I asked.

Chad's trail looked more and more like a dead end and I just wanted to get to its conclusion.

"I went back to the dorms, picked up some of my laundry, and drove to my parent's house." He gave a one-shoulder shrug. "You know the rest."

"Tell me about your uncle, Jack." Louise folded her hands together and cocked her head to one side.

Chad ran his fingers through his greasy dark hair.

"Jack is a total dickwad." He pointed to his chest. "In my opinion. But I'm sure he thinks I'm a dickwad too. I know he thinks I'm a colossal fuck-up."

He shook his head and let out a breathy, "haw."

"Like he even fucking knows anything about me."

"We visited your aunt and uncle yesterday," Louise said. "Your uncle looked like he might have something to hide. Do you know what that could be?"

"Hell, I don't know. He could be a drug king pin for all I know. Dealing cocaine to all his label-wearing, money-whoring buddies."

"We also met with your aunt, Katie," Louise said.

"Jesus, you've found all the loons nesting around my family tree."

"Did she threaten your Mother?" Louise asked.

He pressed his lips flat and then sighed through his nose. "Yeah, she's threatened just about everyone, I think. She's completely crazy and not just in my opinion."

"I spoke to the Sheriff in McCann County yesterday," I said. "About your Grandmother's murder."

He sat up so straight I thought he might lunge at me. "Why did you call him?"

"I wanted to see if the murder could be connected. Sheriff Rose said that they thought a family member committed the murder. Do you think what he said could be true?"

Chad's eyes went glossy and fixed on the floor again. This time his stare wasn't one of nervousness but one of someone remembering. From the contorted expression on his face, the memory was exceptionally painful.

"How could it be true if they never arrested anyone for the murders?"

"Chad, do you know who killed your Grandmother?"

He didn't look up, but tears covered his eyes. He shook his head.

"Were you at your Grandmother's house the day she was murdered?"

His eyes closed and tears rolled down his cheek. Chad's head drooped to his chest.

"Yes. I found her."

Jane Katts went for her notebook. Chad Luther had, in his nineteen short years, lost three loved-ones to a violent death, and had the unfortunate luck to be the one to find all three. A corral of psychiatrists would pay real money to follow Chad around for the next thirty years or so, to find out how he might cope (or fail to cope) with the trauma of this situation.

"I am so sorry, Chad." I put my hand on his shoulder.

His body shuddered with sobs beneath my hand. My gaze went immediately to Louise. I am not good at handling emotional situations, especially when I've hurt someone. In my years on the force, I had never inflicted the pain I had put Chad Luther through, not even with a gun.

Louise leaned forward and touched Chad's hand. Tears dripped over her knuckles and between the spaces of her fingers.

"Chad, I'd like to put you in touch with a Doctor to talk about what has happened. You can't keep this bottled inside."

From behind me, I heard the scritch, scritch of Jane's pen on her notepad. I turned and slapped my hand on the page.

"Please," I whispered and then gave her a fierce warning glance.

"Why is this happening?" Chad raised his head. "It's like there's a fucking curse following me and no matter what I do, I can't get away. I just want out of this, out of my life."

I escorted Jane out of the audiovisual room to allow Louise time to get Chad calmed and put him in touch with Doctor Xavier. After examining the aunt and Chad, plus the family history of both sides of Chad's family, Xavier would have a lifetime worth of research papers.

"You can't sensor this, Catherine."

"Call me Detective O'Brien. Especially if you feel that allowing you to use my first name means we're friends."

A harsh shush came from one of the student librarians. I fanned my hand in her direction.

"Chad Luther discovers both his Grandmother and his parent's bodies," Jane said in a harsh whisper. "This is too good to be true. I could win the Minnesota Journalism Award for breaking this story. It could make my career."

Jane rambled on about how great her bosses, and peers would think she was when this came out. Anger flared through me and my cheeks flushed with heat. I wanted to reach out and strangle her.

"This is exactly the behavior I was talking about when I called you guys vultures yesterday."

She stopped chattering.

"What?"

"What?" I mimicked the stupid expression on her face. "Are you serious? Can you not hear what you're saying?"

"I know what I'm saying. Why are you getting so pissed off all of a sudden?"

The librarian interceded before I could answer. "Ladies, please. You will have to leave if you can't keep your voices down."

I was ready to bark and snap and there was no way I was going to wait until we were outside. I swiveled my head from side to side until I saw an empty A.V. room. I gripped

Jane by the arm, dragged her along with me, and closed the door.

"What is wrong with you?" Jane said and pushed my hand away.

"Your ignorance. Didn't you hear yourself talk? The only person you were talking about was you."

I pointed to the door.

"What about him? What about Chad Luther? I, I, I, I – that's all you can say. Me, me, me – only your stories don't just affect you. Your stories are not about you at all, they're about other people. Real people."

Jane Katts reached into her purse and took out her tape recorder, and shoved it into my face. The little, red recording eye blinked at me. With each pulse of the red light, my blood pressure inched up.

Finally, I wrenched the tape recorder out of her hand and threw it to the ground.

"Jesus Christ, Catherine. What the fuck do you think you're doing? That tape recorder cost a lot of money."

She knelt and scooped the pieces of plastic into her hands.

"You saw Susan Luther lying on that autopsy table yesterday, but you didn't see her, did you? You just saw a body, not a person. And you don't see her son now."

Jane stared up at me with a blank, confused, expression.

"Maybe I wasn't right about you being a vulture, but you're certainly not a human being."

I stormed out of the A.V. room, out of the Library and onto the campus grounds. A walk would cool me down and the frigid air chapping against my cheeks and forehead was exactly what I needed. I half walked, half ran, until my heart thudded against my ribs. A mild euphoria washed over me and I felt dizzy from the blood pumping to my head.

An empty park bench nestled between two gigantic maple trees appeared on my left and I collapsed on the thick wood slats. I gulped in panting breaths. The crimson leaves drifting down from the fall branches of the maples onto my lap, looked like embers floating through the air.

After about ten minutes or so, I could no longer feel my nose or my toes. A few minutes more, despite the fact that my hands were jammed as far down in my jean pockets as they could get, I could no longer feel my fingertips. I stamped my feet on the ground in a pointless attempt to drive blood into my toes.

"Maybe you should get in the car where it's warm."

I looked over my shoulder. Louise stood behind me with more than a little concern on her face. She had parked her car on the far side of the parkway.

Jane Katts sat in the back seat still fumbling with her tape recorder.

"I'm not ready yet. I might say something really stupid and I'd like to keep my job."

Louise stepped around the maple on my right and sat next to me. She handed me her winter gloves.

"Thank you."

We sat in quiet, except for the rustling of leaves, for a few minutes. An orange leaf skipped and skidded down the street in front of us. Louise and I watched it like two old people in front of the general store watching cars go by.

"Talk to me, Catherine. What's going on? I know this is more than a general dislike of the press like the rest of the department has."

Part of me had wanted to tell Louise for years, and on a couple occasions, I'd actually tried to tell her. Somehow the words wouldn't come.

"I won't push you if you're not ready, Catherine."

"No," I said. "You have a right to know. Since you've put up with me all these years."

I couldn't make eye contact with her. Instead I folded my hands together and lowered my head like I were about to pray instead of confess.

"When I first started in homicide, I was assigned to a case where a woman was found shot to death in her bubble bath."

Louise nodded but didn't interrupt.

"Someone came in and blew her brains out with a handgun. The press went wild. Reporters were crawling all over themselves to get a quote, or some tidbit of information on the case.

My partner at the time was Spencer Trent."

She nodded again. Louise had known I partnered with Spence, before she transferred to Saint Paul P.D., so this news was no great surprise.

"He and I did what you and I do. We speculated on who we thought killed the victim. Her husband's alibi was airtight. We discovered that she'd had an affair. Her sixteen-year-old son had found out about it, so naturally we speculated that he could have killed his mother in a fit of rage."

I filled my lungs with cold air and let it out slowly.

"Somehow this theory got out. We never did learn how the press got wind of the idea, but they ran it as a front-page headline.

We found the boy hanging, in nothing but his underwear, from the banister in the family's entryway. They had one of those high cathedral numbers."

Nothing could clear the image from my head. I closed my eyes and I was there again, standing in the entryway, with a hard rock in my stomach.

"He was holding a copy of the newspaper that proclaimed him a murder when he jumped over."

"How do you know?" Louise asked.

"We found the paper on the entry floor and news print on his fingers."

"Catherine, I am so sorry." Louise put her hand on my back – a comforting gesture that didn't comfort me at all.

"We found out later that the father's alibi was fake. He had murdered his wife."

I jerked my thumb toward the Chariot of Death parked against the curb. "He confessed to killing the mother. It was people like Jane Katts who killed the kid."

Louise let silence pass between us for a few minutes. Anything she could have said to me in that space would have been lost in my anger.

"Jane wasn't the reporter who wrote that story," Louise said. "She's too young. She was probably in college when that story ran, and we have her on a short leash."

"I guess. But, you should have seen the glee in her face when she heard that Chad had found his grandmother's body. It was like she'd gotten the pony she'd always wanted for Christmas."

"Jane can be as excited as she wants to be. She's not allowed to print any of it."

I turned toward her. "What do we really have to prevent the paper from printing the story? Their word? Based on a promised exclusive interview? When they get wind of a juicy bit of fodder, our deal with them would be broken faster than a teenage pop star's vow of chastity."

Louise considered what I'd said for less than a second.

"My friend at the mayor's office owes me. BIG." A smirk that I couldn't quite read crossed her face. "He'll keep his word. He has no choice."

I considered pressing her for more information, but the numbness in my toes had progressed to pain. If I didn't get out of the cold soon I'd be dealing with an achy pain in my feet for days – a problem I'd had since I was a kid and had actually frozen my feet, because I didn't want to stop playing long enough to go inside and warm up.

I stood.

"Okay, I think I can contain my temper. Let's get back to our impartial observer."

Jane was still fiddling with her tape player. I slid into the passenger seat, reached over flicked the heat to high, and then adjusted all the dash vents so they pointed toward me. I pushed my feet as high up as I could under the dash where heat poured over my feet. I cupped my hands over the vent near the window, like a camper huddled around a fire.

Louise got in and turned the fan down a couple notches.

"You're buying me a new tape recorder." Jane shook the plastic pieces in the air between the front seats. "This one is broke all to hell."

I transferred the pieces of plastic from her hand to mine.

"Let me see what I can do," I said. "I have a knack for fixing mechanical things."

Louise pulled away from the curb and we were on our way. At this point, I didn't care where we were going.

I twisted, shoved, and pressed the pieces of the tape recorder together, mashed them until finally, success. There was a loud click of the major two pieces. After that, the smaller pieces of the recorder puzzle snapped into place with ease.

"Viola!" I pronounced the word like my Grandmother always did, vi-ola. I held up the reassembled recorder so Jane could see it. "All better."

"Great. Give it to me, please," Jane said.

"Just a second." I pulled it back before she could take it from me. "Let's make sure it's functioning. If not, then we can stop at Target and get you a new one."

I pressed the rewind button. After a few seconds, I clicked stop.

"I'm sure it's fine." Jane shoved her hand out and wiggled her fingers. "Give it to me."

"Hold your pony."

Annoyance rippled through me at Jane's insistence. I was trying to help, and I was prepared to make good on my word. If the tape player didn't work then I would have Louise stop at the nearest Target Superstore, and I would buy her a new recorder. My guilt was so great, I would have purchased one that was four times nicer.

I pressed play. The tape slowly whirred to life, the voices at first too slow.

"It works," Jane said. "Give it to me."

I slapped the player against my palm. The tape wound up to normal speed. A good smack worked every time. Any electronic equipment could be righted with a slap as long as you followed the golden rule of electronic repair, once is maintenance; twice is abuse.

Suddenly I recognized Louise's voice. *"It's a ring."* Then Digs said, *"Well, the setting for one."* Then my own voice. *"Where did you find it?"* Digs again. *"Embedded in Susan Luther's throat."*

My mouth dropped open. Our conversation from the lab. The one that took place *after* Jane had left the room.

I turned toward Jane. She shrank back against the seat and made no effort to explain herself.

"You baited us," I said. "You knew Digs had more to say but he wouldn't talk in front of you."

Jane turned her eyes to the roof of the car, but didn't say a word.

"So you baited us with your convenient bathroom break."

"Of course I knew." Jane smirked at me. "I told you, I know when people are lying. Your friend Digs isn't exactly a professional actor."

"We had a deal," I said.

Jane scoffed and leaned forward. "Which you broke."

"We broke?" Louise said. "How do you figure?"

"When were you going to tell me about the ring found in Susan's throat?"

Louise looked at me and I shrugged.

"We weren't," I said.

"Exactly, you broke the deal. I was supposed to have all access. You've already got editorial approval over what I publish, so you had no reason to keep anything from me."

"Yes, we did," Louise said and wheeled her car to the curb. She jammed the transmission into park and then turned toward Jane as much as her seatbelt would allow.

"What you don't seem to understand, Ms. Katts is that we're conducting a murder investigation. There is some information that we have to keep close to our chest."

"Why? It's not like you'll let me publish the information."

"But you'd still have it," I said. "You might have no intention of publishing the information, but let's say you're having drinks with a few friends tonight. Alcohol loosens lips. You tell two friends, and they tell two friends," I mimicked the old shampoo commercial. "And so on, and so on, and so on."

"I wouldn't," Jane protested. "Confidentiality is part of my job too."

A laugh burbled out before I could stop it. Even Louise smiled at Jane's denial.

"No offense, Ms. Katts," Louise said. "But your job is to tell people everything, not hold back."

"Yeah, wasn't it you who said, the public has the right to know?" I shook the recorder. "We could check the tape."

"Fine. Whatever you say." A flush rose high on her cheeks. "Let's just go."

"No," I said. "Let's have this out, because I don't want to keep running up against this topic."

A yellow school bus passed us with lights flashing and stopped a half a block up the road. The doors folded open. Five kids hopped down the stairs, happily released from school for at least another day. Four of the kids went up the block away from us but one young girl, maybe fourteen or fifteen years old, headed down the sidewalk toward Louise's car.

"Take her for instance." I nodded toward the girl.

Jane turned to watch her. "What about her?"

The girl noticed the three of us watching. Her pace slowed and she clutched her books close to her chest. Her wary eyes darted between the sidewalk and our car.

"Why does she need to know all the gory details of a murder?" I asked. "Look at how she carries herself and watches us. That girl knows the world is a bad place, and that murders happen. Her parents have probably drilled that fact into her since the first day she rode the bus to school alone."

I placed my left hand on the back of Louise's seat and looked over my arm.

"Tell me Jane, why does she need to know the details of a murder that doesn't directly affect her? Isn't it enough for her to know that there was a murder? Isn't she frightened enough of the world?"

Jane glanced at me and then back toward the young girl. The girl gave the three of us a wide birth, walking on the edge of the far side of the sidewalk.

"She probably doesn't even read the paper," Jane said. "*Teen Beat* or *Tiger Beat* maybe, but not the legit press."

I wondered what made her brand any more legit than the stuff printed in celebrity gossip magazines. Apparently a masthead that read, *Proudly Serving the Community Since 1898*, was all one needed to legitimize trash.

"Say her parents read the legit press." Louise had detected where I was going. "Why do they need to know what horrors could await that little girl every time she steps outside the door?"

"Or, say her parents are reading the paper and she happens to see a news story with a sensational headline that is even more interesting than one of her teen magazines. Sort of like one of the headlines your paper prints every day."

I waited for some sort of revelation to hit Jane, but I'd watched one too many Jimmy Stewart movies as a kid. Hardened by the demands of her career, there would be no redemption for Jane Katts today, or possibly ever. Not even three ghosts or Clarence the wingless angel could soften her.

"Are we done with the maudlin stuff for today? Or do you want to show me some puppies that could see a story about a runaway dog because their owners happened to leave the paper lining their kennels open to the story."

Louise shrugged at me. "Well, we tried."

"Maybe we could find some puppies," I said.

Jane shoved her hand forward again. "Give me the damn tape recorder."

"Sure." I popped the tape out and handed her the device.

"What are you doing?" She made a vain attempt to snatch the cassette from my hand.

"You asked for the recorder back and that I'm giving you. The tape is confidential and will be locked up until the investigation is over."

Jane grunted her disgust and fished through her purse, which was slightly less diaper-bagish than mine, but still large enough to hide anything she needed to find quickly. She finally came up with a small case with a fresh tape.

"I'll be talking to my boss when I get back to the paper tonight."

In the vanity mirror, I saw her push her pointy little chin forward in defiance.

"I think our deal is void and I'll be filling him in on everything that's happened so far."

A shift of unease in my gut verged on the edge of panic. I wondered what chief would do to me if Jane Katts made good on her threat. The paper would slaughter us in the morning edition and I'd be on the hook. The part of me that wasn't wading into panic mode, my Rhett Butler side, won the battle, and finally declared, *'Frankly my dear, I don't give a damn'*.

My Rhett side usually dominated my personality, gratefully. I couldn't imagine stumbling through life worried what people would think of me at every turn. Sounded like a recipe for schizophrenia to me.

Maybe Rhett was feeling so confident because of the look on Louise's sphinx-like face. She betrayed no hint of concern with Jane's threat.

We drove in grudging silence for a long while, leaving the campus but staying close to the outskirts, still in college country. Coffee houses tucked into old storefronts, cafés, sandwich shops, and books stores. Louise slowed at every building to read the street numbers.

She stopped in front of an old, three-story brownstone. What used to be respectable family housing some time in the early nineteen twenties were now run down college apartments that the landlord barely bothered to keep up to code. Gavin would come home furious when some slumlord would hire him to remodel one of these places, and wouldn't allow him to do a proper job, claiming it wasn't worth the money.

He'd quit taking the jobs near campus all together after one house burned down, and the contractor, as well as the owner, were sued by the families of the four victims who didn't make it out.

Each unit in this particular brownstone had a bay window, and a balcony off the side, which gave the building more character than most.

My curiosity finally got the better of me. "Who lives here?"

"Marcus Vincent."

Louise headed up the steps to the secure entry of the brownstone. Jane and I followed.

"Who?"

"V."

She scanned the names on the tin mailboxes inset on the wall in the entry. Louise pushed the call button below a large V written in black marker. Apartment 302.

Several seconds passed before my angry, adrenaline filled brain put together who V was and why we needed to meet with him.

The security latch on the front door buzzed open. So much for all the parents who believed their children were safe just because there was a secured front door.

I yanked open the door and stepped in front of the jamb, holding the door with my back so Louise and Jane could enter.

Curled in the corner of the entry, facing the wall, was a shaggy man in dirty clothes. He glanced over his shoulder at us and grumbled something under his breath about cold air.

I fished a ten-dollar bill from my wallet.

"Hey." I tapped him on the shoulder. "Go get yourself a warm meal."

He snatched the bill as if afraid I would take it back, like a tease. He grunted thanks.

I nodded.

Louise and Jane reached the second-floor landing before me. At the top of the third-floor steps, leaning on the rail and gazing down at us, was a gangly, zit covered man in his early twenties. His eyes fixed on me.

"You gave that skid money?"

"Skid?" I said.

"That human trash in the entry. We keep throwing him out but he keeps getting back in somehow."

Considering he buzzed us in without inquiry, it didn't take Sherlock Holmes to solve the mystery of his reappearances.

"What I do with my money is my business."

"True." He stuck his thumbs in his belt loops and hiked up his droopy pants. "Step inside my parlor."

The apartment was everything you could possibly want from a cliché bachelor pad. A ragged plaid couch. Milk crates with a board over the top for a coffee table. Vincent even had a small wire-spool set up as an end table, a sight I hadn't seen since I married Gavin.

Gavin and his three roommates had lived in a two room, brownstone apartment eerily similar to this. Markus Vincent even had a two-by-four nailed to the wall next to the door to hold keys and an oversized leather coat like Gavin did, though Gavin's coat had leather fringe dripping from the sleeves, like Bon Jovi.

The apartment had the vague air of a recent trashing. Stale beer and cigarette smells permeated the room. Empty Summit, vodka, and whisky bottles littered any surface that would hold them. Cheese Doodles were ground into the worn area rug, covering the hardwood floor of the living area, in wide orange spots every few feet.

The only new piece of furniture in the room, which stuck out like a pig in a beauty pageant, was a large flat screen television mounted to the wall. The TV probably cost more than all of Markus Vincent's furniture and his clothing combined.

"Well what can I do for you ladies? You need blow? Pot? E? You don't look like the type for Crystal Meth."

He sprawled across the couch and spread his arms wide.

"But I have it if you wanted to explore the darker side."

I leaned against the wall. "Well, you've got a regular smorgasbord here, don't you?"

"I've got it, if you need it." He leaned forward. "If you have the cash. I don't give credit. Even to pretty ladies."

He turned his gaze toward Jane and dragged his tongue over his upper lip.

"But I have been known to take trade, if the goods are primo."

Jane pulled her jacket tight around her chest. Her jaw clenched with disgust.

"Mr. Vincent," Louise said. "We came to ask you a few questions about a friend of yours."

"Ladies, I don't answer questions. If you're not here for business, there's the door, and I could give a shit if it hits you in the ass on the way out or not."

Louise and I both badged him at the same time. The look on his face went from the poker ace, holding-all-the-cards, to a guilty child.

"You can either answer our questions about your friend here," I said. "Or we can take you to our office and you can answer the DEA's questions."

He was on his feet in a flash.

"Don't you have to identify yourself or something? Isn't that some rule or something?"

Funny how those who actively disregarded the law wanted the Police to play by the rules, like good little boys and girls.

"Only if you asked if we're cops."

I took a seat in a straight-backed, wooden, kitchen chair to his left and Louise moved to his right. If he decided to bolt, we had him covered.

"You didn't ask," I said. "You were too worried about whether or not I'd given money to the gentleman in the lobby. Then you invited us in just as sweet as you could be, and then read us what was on the menu."

His gaze jumped between Louise and me.

"Sit down, Mr. Vincent," Louise said. "We're not here to ask about where you get your lunch money. As I said, we have questions about a friend of yours."

Markus glanced at the door. The muscles in my arms and legs tensed in anticipation of the chase.

Jane, who was still protecting herself as if she were concealing the crown jewels somewhere on her body, stood in the direct path between Markus Vincent and the door. I tried to will her out of the way, but she wouldn't budge. If Vincent sprang for the door, she would take a full-on body check, and that I couldn't stop.

Finally, he sagged in resignation. His brain must have calculated the distance between him and the door and between him and me. He had even calculated the *X-factor*, which was could I take him down if given the chance. Even though Markus Vincent stood a full foot or more, taller than I, he must have decided I could.

I had trained for this situation and Markus Vincent had trained to be a world-class burn out.

He returned to the couch, and retrieved a cigarette from a small pencil box on the coffee table. V dug thru his pocket and pulled out a Zippo.

"I'm not rolling on my suppliers so if that's who you're asking about you can just forget it."

His punk-ass attitude had returned in force. He ran the Zippo over his pant leg, producing a flame, lit the cigarette, and glared at us through the smoke, ala James Dean only not as cool.

Louise settled into a ratty, old recliner. Her perfectly tailored designer clothing was startlingly out of place against the nineteen-seventies, burnt orange plaid, polyester fabric of the chair.

"Was Chad Luther here yesterday?"

Markus Vincent twitched.

"That stick? Why are you asking about him?"

"Was he here?" Louise repeated the question slowly as if Markus had suddenly turned soft in the head.

"Yeah, he was." His reply was as slow and deliberate as her question. "Why?"

"What did you do when he was here, Mister Vincent?" I asked.

"No." He held his palm out to me and shook it back and forth like a Dairy Princess in the Holidazzle Parade. "No more, Mister Vincent. It's V or I won't answer any more questions."

He returned to his sprawl position with his arm draped across the back of the couch. His half smile on his face said check and mate. There he was wrong. Frankly, I didn't care if he wanted us to call him the Sultan of Brunei, as long as he answered the questions.

"Fine. What did you do when Chad was here, *V*?"

"Can't tell you."

He adjusted the crotch of his low hanging pants as if his package needed more room and eyed Jane suggestively. He got the reaction he was looking for. Jane let out a disgusted grunt and turned away from him.

I snapped my fingers in the air to return his attention to me.

His half smile returned. "I can't answer your questions on the grounds that it may incriminate me."

Louise reached into the pocket of her coat and pulled out a pair of handcuffs.

"That's fine. Let's go to the station. Then you can call your lawyer," she said. "I'm sure our DEA guys would like to get their hands on you."

"You said you weren't here for me." He mewled as Louise took his right wrist and locked the first metal shackle on him.

"As long as you were cooperating we weren't." Louise pulled his left arm behind his back and locked the second cuff in place.

"I'm going to the press," he whined. "I'm going to tell them you set me up and abused me."

He craned his skinny neck around so he could see Louise.

"They'll believe me too. The press already hates the police." He laughed. "Then I'll sue."

Jane Katts finally snapped out of the trance of disgust she'd wrapped herself in, and stepped toward V. She pulled her press pass from her bag.

"I am the press," she said. "And the only thing going in the morning edition will be a story about how you were so chicken shit about going to jail, you rolled over on your suppliers and their suppliers. I might throw in a sentence or two about how you wet yourself and cried like a baby when the officers handcuffed you."

His face went pale and he narrowed his eyes at her.

"You can't print that. It's a lie."

"It's as true as the story you were going to feed to the press." Jane shrugged. "I see no harm and no foul."

Jane might be more useful than I initially thought. The struggle in my mind liking Jane for who she was, and hating her for what she is, took a slight lean in Jane's favor.

V pulled at the cuffs with no success. His face wrinkled and twisted, like there were worms squiggling for freedom under his skin. Then tears puddled on his bottom lid.

"You can't." His voice cracked. "They'll kill me if you print that."

Jane gave a one-shouldered shrug. "That's your problem not mine."

Tears rolled down his face. "Lady, I'm not lying. They will kill me."

His words didn't seem to penetrate Jane's icy shell. She turned her back to him, clearly enjoying the torment. Payback truly is a bitch.

"Lady, I'm serious. They'd fucking cut my balls off if you print that story."

Jane slid her gaze up and down him in the same lewd manner he had used on her. Her eyes finally came to rest on his crotch.

"From what I can see, it would be no big loss." She looked up at him and grinned. "Of course, my silence can be bought."

V's entire body moved at once. His arms went one way his legs the other.

"You name it sweetheart. I got cash stashed everywhere. How much do you want?"

"I'd be afraid to touch your money." Jane's lips turned down in disgust. "God only knows what kind of diseases your clients carry on their cash."

V stepped toward her. "You name it. Smack? Blow? What?"

"Information on Chad Luther," she said. "You tell these officers everything, and I won't even remember who you are when we leave here."

Relief rippled through him. "I'll tell you everything you wanna know."

He lifted his arms behind him and turned his wrists toward Louise.

"Little help here."

Louise pushed his hand back down.

"I think we'll leave those in place until the interview is over," she said. "Just so you don't forget any of the good pieces. Get comfortable, V."

Louise placed a hand on his shoulder and pushed him onto the couch. With his wrists bound behind his back, he had to lean over his knees at an awkward angle.

"What were you and Chad Luther doing yesterday?" Louise asked.

He shook his head back and forth, frustration oozing from every pore. Then he muttered something under his breath.

"V." I decided to let him off the hook. "We're looking for corroboration here. We already know what Chad said you were doing yesterday."

He lifted his eyes toward mine. I could read the doubt in his eyes as clearly as I could read the headlines in the morning paper.

"Anyway," I said. "Everything you've offered us so far is enough to take you in."

He grimaced.

"I had a few people over. Sort of a party. I was the host. We were watching the football game." His words were tentative. "I had some money on the vi-queens, who lost. The losers."

"Get on with it," Jane said, apparently uninterested in debating the record of the Minnesota Viking's with a fair weathered fan any more than I was.

His eyes sliced toward Jane. All the sexual heat, gone.

"As I said, I was the host. We did a few recreational drugs," He admitted.

"Finally," Jane said. "Let's go."

Louise loosed V's hands. His acne studded face drooped in stunned disbelief. Then the pieces dropped into place and V realized we weren't here to arrest him.

A flood of questions rolled at us, starting with, "You think Chad killed his parents, don't you?"

"We're just covering all the bases," Louise said. "Thank you, for your help."

"Wait!" He touched my upper arm. "What about me?"

I considered him for a moment. "Try to remember to get a name before you buzz someone in the front door. If you don't, you'll never know what you're going to get."

I waited for understanding to show on his face. The only expression was complete confusion.

Chapter Eight

We arrived at the office in time to get a slice of the giant cake the department had purchased for the Chief.

"I'm going to call my boss." Jane stormed away from the streamer festooned break room.

I could almost hear her impassioned plea to her superiors at the paper, the description of the psycho cop who destroyed her recorder and confiscated her cassette tape. My esteemed reputation was growing faster than a kid with new shoes.

After scarffing down a piece of cake and seven or eight cups of punch, I decided to make a pit stop in the ladies room. I entered the stall and locked the latch. The bathroom door opened and someone came in. I waited for shoes to appear under one of the stalls next to me. No shoes appeared. Not so unusual. Maybe she just needed to check her makeup or fix her hair.

I finished my pee break and pulled up my jeans. As I unlatched the lock, the door swung in with the force of a major-leaguer hitting a homerun. The edge of the metal door struck the left side of my face. White-hot pain burst through my sinuses and my eye. Tears streamed down my face. I raised my arms to block another assault and stumbled backward. The back of my calves bumped the toilet halting my retreat.

The door catapulted in again.

I turned but there was nowhere to escape. My shoulder flared with pain. All the air oomphed out of my lungs.

The last thing I remember was falling face first toward the toilet. Then I heard a woman yell, "bitch!" before everything went dark.

Ice-cold hands touched my neck.

"Catherine, can you hear me?"

The voice was muffled and fuzzy.

"Catherine?"

I opened my eyes. Something blocked my left eye and all I could see was white. Then a swell of pain thudded through my head.

"Oh, shit," I moaned. "That fucking hurt."

Louise smiled down at me. "Take it easy, Catherine. We've called an ambulance."

"No." I pushed myself upright. "I don't need an ambulance."

My left hand slipped on the damp toilet seat. That's when I realized the seat wasn't the only thing that was damp. The hair stuck to the sides of my face was soaked.

Louise put her hand up to stop me from lifting myself off the filthy, wet floor. Behind her, a crowd had gathered and heads peaked through the door like a sideways Whac-A-Mole game.

"Wait for the ambulance, Catherine," she said. "You're hurt worse than you think."

"Who hit me, and why am I wet?"

"We don't know, and you fell into the toilet."

Oh God. That was what I was afraid she'd say. The muscles over my shoulder blade cramped and then spasmed. The burning pain sucked the wind from my lungs.

"Crap!"

I hunched forward and panted until the pain receded.

"Help me up. I promise to wait for the ambulance but I don't want to stay on the floor. It's nasty."

I reached my hand out toward her. Louise slipped her shoulder under my right armpit and hauled me to my feet.

"Be careful," she said. "The floor is slippery."

She toddled me out, slow and guarded like a nursing home patient. Pink puddles of toilet water and blood spread into the grout. Three deep impressions creased the outside of the stall door.

Louise led me to the sink. She turned the taps on, hot first and then cold. Investigators crowded the tiny bathroom. The hallway outside roared with the questions of the gathering crowd, wanting to know what happened and if they could help.

Too many cooks in the kitchen.

Louise ran a paper towel under the tap then dabbed at the left side of my face under my eye.

"Can you see out of your left eye?"

"No, only a little blur. My lids are too swollen. Who the fuck did this to me?"

"They're checking the videotape. No one saw anything."

She pulled two clean towels from the dispenser. Again, she ran them under the water, this time she folded them into a square, pressed it over my eye, and held it in place.

"Who found me?"

"Jane."

A hard chill raked through me.

"She didn't see anyone leaving the restroom?"

Louise shook her head. "She said there wasn't anyone in the hallway. Everyone must have been at the party."

The paramedics pushed their way through the hall crowd. My suspicions would have to wait. If Jane Katts had decided to retaliate for me breaking her recorder, the surveillance tape would catch her.

“Well, Detective.” The elder of the two paramedics clicked his ballpoint pen open, and then scribbled some notes on a pad attached to a thick metal clipboard. “You’re going to have one hell of a shiner, but I don’t think you’ll have any permanent damage. You could have a concussion as well, but since you’re refusing to go the hospital, I can’t be certain on either front.”

He clicked the ballpoint closed, and then tucked it into the breast pocket of his white shirt, a half an inch below the nametag that read, Brad.

“You won’t change your mind about going with us to get checked out?”

I pressed the cold compress they’d given me to the side of my face and wagged my head.

“Alright Detective, but do me a favor, if you get any sudden headaches or lethargy, please go see your primary care physician.”

Sudden headaches? My entire head throbbed as an unseen rocker banged out a drum solo on my brains.

“You bet,” I said.

Brad smiled a knowing smile that said, sure you will.

“Ibuprofen and ice for the pain,” Brad said and picked up his kit and left.

Louise scowled at me with her arms crossed over her chest.

“Not now, Louise. My head is killing me.” I covered my left eye with the ice pack. “Literally.”

I slid off the counter top and headed for the door. The hallway had finally cleared of most spectators. My examination had lasted long enough for a shift change and those with families waiting dinner for them had left. A few concerned officers hung around to find out if I was okay, including Shackelford.

“Jesus, O’Brien. Someone messed you up bad.”

“Thanks. Have you found out who yet?”

"The Chief's reviewing the surveillance video now."

Shackelford guided me through the hall by my elbow like a fragile Grandmother. I would have protested my treatment, except with each throb of my pounding head the vision in my good eye swam in blurry tears that obscured my path.

The Chief's voice was clear fifty feet from the doorway of the surveillance room.

"Who the hell was supposed to be on duty?" The Chief bellowed.

His answer came in a hushed voice.

"And where the hell was he when this happened? Where the hell is he now?"

Shackelford helped me navigate between the officers standing in the monitor room receiving the ass chewing from the Chief.

"Whoever he was, was probably at the party with everyone else, Chief," I said.

The tight, anger-wrinkled expression on his face melted like wax to that of anguished concern. For a moment, I wished I had looked at myself in the bathroom mirror before I'd left. I must look pretty bad if my appearance could make the man who had tried to teach me to perfect my emotional detachment crumble like a sandcastle.

"Have you called your husband?" He asked. "You shouldn't be driving."

"I'll take her home, Chief," Louise said from the doorway.

I sent a silent blessing to her. I didn't want to have to upset Gavin before I really had to. He'd drive like a maniac and probably cause an accident trying to get to me.

"Who was on duty here?" I asked.

"Rees," Chief said. "Where the hell is he now?"

"I'm here." Rees lifted his hand from the back of a crowd of officers who looked more like the Vikings defensive line, blocking Rees from the Chief's view. Rees stepped toward me. "Jesus, O'Brien I'm so sorry. I went to get a piece of cake. I couldn't have been gone more than five minutes."

"Long enough for the assailant to obscure the camera in the ladies room hallway," The chief grumbled.

Rees bowed his head like a shamed dog.

I put my hand on Rees's shoulder.

"It was an innocent mistake," I said. "It's not like he took a payoff, chief. Lighten up a bit. It's not your fault Rees."

Rees's lips turned upward, but despite his best effort, he couldn't look at my face.

"How in the world could someone obscure the camera?" I asked. "They're protected by a plastic bubble to prevent tampering."

I moved toward the bank of monitors. Pain pulsed with each step. Rees took my elbow from Shackelford, and helped me into a chair. The videotape machine whirred to a start and the blue screen flashed to life. On the monitor, I saw myself enter the bathroom. Then at the bottom of the picture, in the camera's blind spot, there was the flash of something dark. A spray can nozzle and fingers appeared. Liquid spewed out of the nozzle tip, adhered to the plastic, and obscured the view.

My attacker moved down the hall. There wasn't any way to tell who had kicked in the door. The image on the screen was like trying to see through a veil of Vaseline.

The Chief paused the image. "That's about as good as it gets. I know it's a fuzzy image, but does this person look familiar to you?"

The picture was even more blurry when one of your eyes had swollen to the size of an orange.

"No, I can't make out any of the features."

"Did they say anything when they attacked you?"

"She, not they." I turned to face him. "It was a woman who attacked me. She called me a bitch. That's all, except that she kicks like a mule."

I lightly touched the side of my face. The pain wasn't as intense as it had been a few minutes ago. Adrenaline must have finally kicked in, at least for my face. My shoulder, on the other hand, throbbed with sharp, spiky-needles of pain.

Rees leaned close to my ear. "I'm so sorry, O'Brien. I should have been here to see the cover-up."

The hitch of regret was evident in the strained whisper of his voice.

"You didn't know." I patted the back of Rees's hand. "Anyway it was a party. I'm sorry to have broken it up, Chief."

Chief gave a half grin. "You've made it one memorable anniversary, O'Brien. First the vultures crack and now this."

Realization dawn on me and I swiveled to see the entire room.

"Where is Jane Katts?" I stood and faced Louise. "Where is she?"

"I think she's in the break room."

I shuffled past Louise and out into the hallway.

"Catherine? What's going on?"

I charged down the hall, for the first time not feeling the swoon of pain in my head. The diminished depth perception of my eye caused me to careen right and left down the hallway, like a drunk, first hitting one wall and then the other. Finally, I got smart and ran my hand along the wall to guide me.

I turned the corner into the break room. Jane Katts casually chatted on her cell phone smiling and nodding.

Anger rolled into my chest. For the first time since the stall door had rattled my cage, I was pissed as hell about what had happened.

Before I could think, I reached across the Formica table and batted the cell phone away from her face, like a Catherine pouncing on a mouse. The phone hit the tile floor. The battery skidded one direction and the body of the phone spun away in the other.

Jane's jaw went slack and her eyes wide.

"What the fu—?"

"So you found me?" I said. "How convenient. Then you couldn't wait to get back to your precious little cell phone and report my misfortune to your editor."

"Catherine!" Louise reached for my arm.

Before she could touch me, I jerked my arm away. My shoulder shrieked with pain at the sudden movement. I ignored it.

"Look at me, Jane," I yelled. "Look at what you did to my face. Are you happy? Is this what you wanted?"

Louise stepped between us.

"Catherine, it wasn't Jane who kicked the door. She was in the break room with me right before she found you."

I blinked at her.

Jane stood. "I even had a piece of anniversary cake. I was on the phone with your husband, Gavin, not my editor. I assured him that you're okay and we'd make sure you'd get home safe."

My confidence in all the things I knew, for sure, shook with the force of an earthquake. The room whirled. Then I whirled. The last thing I saw, through my dimming vision, was Louise and Jane rushing forward to catch me before I fell on my ass.

The linoleum tiled floor of the break room felt cold against my back. The chill soothed the pain of the bruises on my battered shoulder.

I took a deep stuttering breath and let it out slow. My left eye had finally swollen completely shut. I opened my right eye.

Louise and Jane hovered over me. Their faces twisted in mangled expressions of worry.

"Well, I'm not dead," I croaked.

The left side of Louise's lips tipped up in a half-grin. "She's fine."

I couldn't see Jane Katts' hand but I felt it on my left shoulder. She pulled me to a sitting position. Then Louise took my right arm. Together they lifted me to my feet, and then bent me into a chair.

I flicked my good eye up to Jane. "I'm sorry, again."

She sat across from me. I was grateful that I didn't have to tilt my head back to look at her any more.

"Don't worry about it." She picked up the two halves of her cell phone. "The only damage was an abrupt hang up that probably freaked your husband out."

Yeah, I would have some explaining to do and I probably shouldn't wait until I got home.

Jane snapped the battery back into place, then flipped open the cover and pressed the power button. The phone chimed.

"See, the phone's fine."

"I'm still sorry." I adjusted in my seat to relieve the pressure of the hard, chair on my shoulder. "Whoever attacked me knew who I was. She targeted me. I jumped to a bad conclusion. You didn't deserve the accusation. You've been playing by our rules through this whole thing."

Jane's eye flicked down to the floor and she nodded.

"I can't imagine who would do this to me."

Louise chuckled. "I could make a multi-page list for you, of just the people I know, who have a grudge against you."

She sat in the chair to my left so I could see her.

"The same list of people who might apply to you?" I asked.

"You got it."

"So who do we know that's pissed about an arrest and has been recently released?"

Louise shrugged. "I don't know. We'll need to check. However, tonight, you need to go home and rest. Gavin is probably freaking out by now."

A lump rose to the soft hollow at the base of my throat when I thought of Gavin's worried face. I wanted to go home, bury my face in his chest, and cry.

Tears burned up to my eyes, and I willed them not to fall.

"I'd better call him." My voice wavered and cracked. "Can I use your phone?"

I held my hand out to Jane.

She gripped the antenna and handed me the cell.

"We'll give you a little privacy," Louise said. "I'll come back in a few minutes to help you to the car. Don't go wandering around by yourself. You're likely to pass out and whack your head again."

From the doorway, Louise called over her shoulder. "See if Gavin can talk some sense into you, and convince you to go see a doctor."

Louise and Jane disappeared around the corner and I was alone. Unease shivered up my spine. Someone wanted to hurt me—had hurt me in the one place I felt the safest, surrounded by fellow officers. Here I was again, alone and vulnerable. I gripped the edge of the table for leverage, got to my feet, then moved so my back was against the wall and I would have a full view of the room.

I flipped open Jane's phone and arrowed down to her call history. Maybe a small part of me was still suspicious of her, but my suspicions disappeared completely when I found my home telephone number in her outgoing calls. I highlighted the number and then pressed send.

The display flashed "calling." I held the phone to my ear. Gavin answered on the first ring.

"Hello?"

"Gavin, it's me."

I steeled myself against the emotional breakdown that threatened to overtake me.

"Jesus, Catherine, are you okay? Some reporter called and said someone attacked you. Then her phone went dead. What the hell is going on?"

His anxiety cracked down the phone line. I swallowed past the stone in my throat.

"I'm fine."

Silence.

"Gavin?"

"You're not fine. I can hear it in your voice. How bad is it, Catherine?"

A hard squeeze compressed my chest. A single tear rolled from my good eye despite my best efforts. I took a deep breath and let it out slow.

"I'm as fine as I'm going to be in the next fifteen minutes. Okay?"

Again, silence.

"Gavin, I'll be home in fifteen minutes. You'll get all the gory details then." I brushed the tear from my cheek. "I just can't do this on the phone."

"I'll see you in fifteen minutes," he said. "I love you, Catherine."

The ache in my chest eclipsed the throbbing pain in my head.

"I know you do," I said. "I love you, too."

I hung up before he could say anything else. If either of us had said another word, I would have bawled like a sleepy child who'd skinned her knee.

Then I was alone. The clock hardwired to the wall above the door makes a strange humming noise that I have never heard before. The break room has never been this quiet before – at least not while I was taking a break.

A rush of panic gripped me. What if the woman who attacked me is still in the building? What if she was watching me and waiting.

A shuffle in the hallway, no more than a mouse scurry, sent adrenaline into every muscle. The effect was something close to rigor-mortis.

Get a grip, Catherine. The voice in my head has always been one no nonsense bitch. *The first shot was a lucky one. A crime of opportunity and you know it. No one is stalking you.*

I flipped open Jane's phone and scrolled through the menu items. A small distraction but enough to keep me from losing my mind until Louise returned.

After a few minutes, footsteps in the hall sent another shot of adrenaline through me. Then I realized the sound wasn't a single set of feet and I relaxed an inch.

"You ready to go?" Louise said as she rounded the corner with Jane and Dave Goldwin.

"Doctor Dave," I said. "What are you doing here?"

"Came to take a look at ya'."

His Minnesota accent seemed thicker than I remembered. Maybe because my appearance had frightened him. From the look on his face, it had.

"I'm not dead yet," I said. "I'm not ready for the autopsy room, Dave."

"I'm still a doctor, smart ass."

He clicked on a penlight and waved it in my face. First my good eye and then my bad.

"I've been checked out already."

He nodded. "By a paramedic who suggested you go to the hospital to be checked out by a doctor, which your stubborn butt refused."

His fingers probed the side of my head. I winced at the sharp, burning pain that made my good eye water.

After a few follow-my-finger exercises, Dave sat back on his haunches.

"Well, she clocked you a good one, but you're pretty hard headed." He reached into his pocket and pulled out a prescription pad and a pen. "I don't think there's any permanent damage. I'll give you a prescription for some Vicodin. Without it, you won't get much sleep."

I doubted I'd get much sleep anyway, but I took the prescription and thanked him.

"Take the day off tomorrow," he said. "Do your body a favor and get some rest."

I stood.

"I don't think so," I said. "I have a feeling my impromptu beauty makeover was connected to this case somehow. Unless I find out how, I won't ever be able to sleep again."

Dave helped me across the room.

"Then at least do me a favor," he said. "Come see me tomorrow morning so I can check you out."

I agreed with the same enthusiasm I have when I tell my gynecologist I'll return in one year for another poke and prod.

After Louise promised to make certain I visited Doctor Dave bright and early, I went home to face Gavin.

Chapter Nine

Gavin waited for me on the front porch, his face twisted in agonized concern. Even KC seemed to be watching me with a look of worry. The light of the front porch only reached across the front steps so far. The dark purple, veil of night still cloaked me from his view. Gavin squinted and strained to see me.

"Catherine." Louise leaned across to the passenger seat. "Don't forget your prescription."

She shook the waxy, white, paper bag toward the window. I leaned in the passenger window and took the prescription.

"Thanks, Louise," I said. "I appreciate you driving me home."

I smiled and rattled the pills. "And the prescription."

In all the confusion, I had forgotten to grab my purse. Louise had anteed up for the Vicodin, which I had been grateful for ten minutes into the drive home.

"Any time," she said. "I'll pick you up at seven tomorrow. Call me if you come to your senses and change your mind."

I nodded my agreement and she drove away.

When I turned back toward the house, Gavin stood directly behind me. I yelped and my heart thudded a fast beat.

"Jesus, Gavin, don't sneak up on me like that."

Dizziness pushed through me and I gripped his forearm to keep from falling on my ass again. He put his hand over mine.

"Who did this to you, Catherine?"

His eyes demanded answers I didn't have. My resolve broke and tears flooded down my cheeks. No sound came from my throat. Instead, I opened my mouth, and a low click, click, click, choked out with each sob.

Gavin's arms, strong and sure, wrapped around my shoulders and I laid the bruised side of my face to his chest. He rocked me from side to side until I regained enough composure to stand upright by myself.

"Let's go inside and get you into bed," he said.

Gavin helped change me into my pajamas and tucked me into bed as gentle as a mother with a newborn. His hand glided over the skin on my left shoulder blade. He let out a heavy breath.

"Catherine. . ."

Without another word, he pulled the pajama top down. I blessed him for his judgment. Now wasn't the time to rekindle the old discussion about me changing careers. Gavin had brought up the subject each of the three times I'd been shot (two of which were only scrapes), but somehow the bruises on my face and body were worse than a bullet wound.

Though I knew the subject would come up later, I blessed him for not making me argue with him while I felt like a warm slab of ground beef.

Gavin slid the prescription bottle from its bag and turned it to read the label.

"You're in luck," he said. "It says take by mouth."

A quick laugh escaped me, which made my head and my ribs ache with effort.

"Quit it." I lay back against the mound of pillows Gavin had arranged behind my head. "Laughing hurts."

"Sorry."

He rolled the pill bottle from side to side again and kept reading.

"And here I thought you'd finally broken down for once and gone to a doctor." He lifted his eyebrow. "What does Doctor Dave know about treating the living? I thought he only cut up the dead."

I shrugged. "Close enough."

Gavin removed the childproof cap, tapped out two pills, and then held them out to me.

I snaked my hand out from under the blanket palm up. He dropped two oblong pills into my hand, and then held up the green glass I keep for water on my night table.

"Do I have to?" I mewled. "I can't swallow pills. I'll gag."

He tapped the back of my hand making the pills dance. "Both of them. Chew them if you have to."

"Eww," I said.

"Then open wide and swallow them."

I chucked the pills as far back in my throat as I could manage without gagging them back out, and then took a swig from the glass. Gavin had given me ginger ale instead of water, and the bubbles went riotous and dissolved the pills before I could swallow.

My cheeks puffed like a chipmunk storing nuts for the winter. The pain on the left side of my face flared from the pressure, and I swallowed the bits of chalky pills as quick as I could.

"Sorry," Gavin said. "I know you like ginger ale when you're not feeling well. I guess I should have warned you."

"I guess." My voice was hoarse from the pressure of soda, which bubbled its way down my esophagus.

KC whined at the side of the bed. Gavin patted the comforter and the dog leapt onto the bed. His expressive little brown eyes glanced from Gavin to me. He ducked his head and whined again.

"He's worried about you," Gavin said.

I had my doubts considering our history but he did look worried. KC ws probably picking up on Gavin's feelings.

He nuzzled my hand. I petted his head. KC laid next to me with his head on my thigh. I kept stroking his fur, which was oddly comforting.

"Looks like you're in good hands," Gavin said.

"Go to sleep." Gavin leaned over and kissed the side of my face. "Hopefully, you'll feel a little better in the morning."

Fifteen minutes later, I was sure that the attack had been my imagination, because all the pain had disappeared. Now I understood how people could get addicted to pain killers. I felt wonderful, bordering on euphoric. Doctor Dave would get a huge thank you for the Vicodin.

My eyelids drooped. My vision doubled. Everything went dark.

At five-thirty in the morning stiff, muscle pain throbbed from the top of my ass to my shoulder.

"Oh, shit!"

I tried to push myself up but the muscles in my back, ground like broken glass under my skin. KC sat up from his place still by my side. He gave a short "woof."

Gavin rolled toward me.

"I'll get your pain killers," he said in a sleepy voice.

"No," I said. "I need to be clear today. Just some ibuprofen."

"Are you sure?"

"Yes. Can you get it though? I need a little something to take the edge off before I can get my feet on the floor."

He clicked on the small lamp on his nightstand and rolled out of bed. His boxer briefs wedged in his butt framed his shape nicely. I found myself wishing I felt better so I could leap across the bed and give each dimpled cheek a squeeze.

Gavin tiptoed across the hardwood floor into the bathroom. KC leapt down to follow him. Bottles clinked against the metal shelves of our old medicine chest embedded into the wall, finally Gavin returned with an industrial sized bottle of ibuprofen.

He handed me three pills. I choked them down with the flat ginger ale.

"Thanks, sweetie."

Gavin yawned and nodded.

"You feel like telling me what happened yesterday?"

He plopped down on the edge of the bed and KC jumped up and laid next to me. The mattress bounced with their weight and I winced.

"Sorry," he said.

"It's okay." I settled back against the pillows. "I was attacked in the bathroom. That's all there was to it."

"By who?"

A shuddering breath escaped me. "I don't know."

Gavin ran his hand along the outside edge of my thigh, a silent encouragement to continue my story.

"Whoever she was, she was smart enough to obscure the camera in the hallway. She knew me. I'm almost positive. Louise and I are going to find out if anyone we arrested has been released in the past few days."

He stared at the wall behind my head for a long moment still stroking my leg. Then his eyes fixed on mine.

"You know I don't want you to go to work today."

I knew. I nodded.

"It doesn't matter though does it?"

I shook my head.

Gavin stood and disappeared back into the bathroom. He returned with a small hand mirror and held it up to my face.

"Look at yourself, Catherine."

The face in the mirror was hardly recognizable as my own. Purple welts had already begun to turn yellowish green in the center. Through the swollen opening of my left eyelids, I could see a brilliant crimson from the broken blood vessels around the colored part of my eye.

"Look what happened to you in the office. Imagine what could happen when you're on the street."

I pushed the mirror away. "I'll feel safer on the street. My attacker trapped me in a toilet stall. Not exactly a high-noon showdown on main street."

The pain in my back ignored, I shifted my legs to the edge of the bed, and lowered my feet to the floor.

"I was more vulnerable in that stall than I will be now that I'm on my guard."

I stood and pain screamed from butt to shoulder. A wave of nausea gripped me. I clenched my fists and took several deep breaths until the feeling passed.

"Catherine, this isn't a joke." He laced his fingers through mine to keep me from walking away. "I'm worried about you."

"I worry about you too, Gavin. That doesn't mean we don't get up, go to work, and live our lives. We can't spend our life running away."

Gavin ran his thumb across the back of my hand, sending a shiver of comfort up my arm. We always came back to this fight but neither of us was willing to budge an inch.

I'd never lied to him. He knew from the moment we met that I was a cop. Somewhere in his mind, to make the idea more palatable, Gavin had created the image of a nineteen-fifties meter maid to help him cope with what I do.

Until the department called with the news of my first shooting. Just a scrape on my arm from a ricochet when we went to arrest a gang banger who killed his girlfriend, but the wound had been enough to bring Gavin face to face with the truth of who he was dating. He ranted and raved that he couldn't be with someone whose job was to get themselves killed. He proposed to me the same week. Gavin said, 'I do' with zero illusions of who I was or what I do for a living.

"Don't give me the fall off a horse, get back on speech." He stood behind me with his hands on my waist. "I'll help you get ready."

Gavin nuzzled my neck. "Just promise me one thing."

"What's that?"

"Promise me you won't take a pee today."

A laugh burbled up, and brought searing pain to my ribs and stomach.

"Oh, don't make me laugh. It hurts way too much."

He kissed my cheek.

"Come on gimpy. You're not fooling me with the brave face. I know you're in an ass load of pain. I can at least help you get dressed."

I relented and put my arm around his shoulder. There were advantages and disadvantages to having someone know everything about you, including when you're lying. If I didn't take advantage of the advantages when they came, I'd be stupid, so I let Gavin help dress me.

We ate breakfast together like two normal people. No talk of killers, attackers, or pain. I talked about plans for this year's Thanksgiving celebration. It was our year to host, so I nagged him about finishing the bathroom in time, while he flicked through the morning paper.

"Oh, shit!" Gavin sat upright and pulled the paper closer to his face.

"What?"

"I think you'd better call your mother, quick."

"Why?" I grabbed the top corner of the paper and gave a light tug. "What happened to my mother?"

"She's going to have a coronary."

He released the paper into my custody and pointed to an article in the center. I read the story.

There was my black and white service photo under the headline, *Veteran Police Officer Attacked in Police Station.*

"Oh, shit!"

Gavin nodded. "I'll get the phone."

Jane Katts had run a story about my attack. At least she'd had the decency to run it on the third page of the metro section instead of page one. It didn't matter; mom had friends that read the paper from cover to cover including the obituaries. Even if she only skipped to the lifestyles section for the *Mr. Fix-It* column and the recipes, her friends would call her and make it sound like there was nothing left of me but a stain on the bathroom floor.

"Hi, Abby," Gavin rolled his eyes at me. "No, we were going to call you . . ."

He nodded and rolled his eyes again.

"It's really not that bad . . ."

He strolled over to my chair.

"Abby— Abby— She's right here Abby." Gavin was now talking like my mother was deaf or stupid. "I'm going to put her on now."

He handed me the phone.

"Good luck," he whispered.

I mouthed, *thank you*, and waved my coffee cup in the air. If I were going to deal with my mother, I would need more fortification. He nodded and left to get the pot of coffee.

"Catherine Margaret, can you hear me?" Tears filled her voice.

"Yes, Mom. I hear you."

Gavin tipped the pot and filled my cup. Fill it to the rim as the old *Brim* commercial used to say. What happened to *Brim*, I wonder?

"You sound terrible," Mom said.

"I sound fine, because I am fine, Mom."

"No you don't. You sound puffy. Are you puffy, Catherine?"

I took a long pull from my coffee.

"Catherine Margaret, are you puffy?"

I sighed. "Yep, I'm puffy, but only a little. I'm not even staying home from work today, that's how non-puffy I am, Mom."

A muffled struggle for the phone came down the line. After a few uttered no's from my mother, I finally heard my Dad say, "Give me the phone, Abigail."

"You okay, kid?"

Tears sprang to my eyes. Something always made me cry when I heard my Dad.

"Yeah, Dad, fiddling fit."

"That's what I told your Mom. I said if it had been serious they would have called."

"I would have called last night, Dad but I was . . ." My voice thinned.

"Never mind," he said, in his no-nonsense fashion. "You needed your rest."

"Yeah."

"See Abby, it's exactly like I said."

Mom told him to give the phone back to her but he didn't.

"You going to work then, kid?"

"Yep." I let out a deep breath. Finally, into a territory I felt comfortable talking about, and away from my health. "I feel pretty good. Anyway, all this is just a bucking horse that I need to get back on."

"That's true," he said. "Do they know who did it?"

"No, but I'm going to find out."

I could almost hear the grin that split Dad's face through the phone line. Whenever I came home bruised from a fight at school and believe me there were many at my Catholic girl's school, he'd have the same grin on his face, and he'd ask, "what does the other guy look like?" Knowing that I didn't stop fighting after taking one hard blow.

"I'm sure you will, Katie."

A shiver raked over my body. Dad was the only person who would ever call me Katie, but if he hadn't it wouldn't have come to me.

Katie.

"I have to go now, Dad." I could feel a culmination of anger and excitement building in my chest. "I love you, Dad. Kiss Mom for me."

The abrupt end to the conversation didn't bother him in the least.

"Will do. Have a good day. Call us later."

"I will, Dad. I love you, and thanks."

He hung up and I pressed the end button on the cordless handset just long enough to reset it and make another call. I punched in Louise's cell phone number. She answered on the second ring.

"Detective Montgomery speaking."

"Where are you, Louise?"

"I'm just down the block. Are you feeling up to today?"

"Oh, yeah!"

"What's going on?" She asked.

"I'll tell you when you get here."

I hung up and then got to my feet. Adrenaline rushed through my veins minimizing the pain in my body, or maybe the ibuprofen had finally kicked in, either way I felt great.

Gavin walked me to the door. He kissed the healthy side of my face and slipped something into the right pocket of my jacket.

"Take the Vicodin, just in case you need it later," he said.

There wouldn't be any point arguing. He had my health and comfort in mind even if it did feel like he was babying me.

Louise pulled up as I stepped onto the front porch.

"It's about time," I said. "What took you so long?"

I eased myself down the steps and practically skipped down the sidewalk.

I slid into the passenger seat and Louise lifted a Venti *Starbucks* cup.

"You're forgiven." I took the cup with the reverence of a priest lifting the sacred chalice.

"Quad shot Venti Caramel Machiato," she said. "I figured you could use a treat today."

With furrowed brows and grimaced mouth, she studied my face.

"Does it hurt?"

The coffee instantly relaxed my body. For years, I have railed against the notion that coffee was a stimulant. For me coffee did a better job than Xanax in taking the edge off any situation. I guess a caffeine addiction was like cigarettes that way.

"I feel great today," I said.

Louise nodded with brows still furrowed. "It's those pills Doctor Dave gave you yesterday."

"I haven't taken any today." She looked doubtful.

"I know who hit me." I blurted the words as if they'd been pressing against the inside of my lips waiting for their escape.

"Who? How?"

"My Dad told me."

She glanced at me from the corner of her eye. "How did your Dad know?"

"He didn't."

"What?"

I took another sip of my mocha.

"Just drive."

"Where to?"

"The office, my dear Watson!" I toasted her with my paper cup. "We have some checking to do."

Louise slid the gearshift to drive.

"I promised Doctor Dave I'd haul your butt in to see him first."

"First the surveillance room," I said.

"First Doctor Dave." She said it like she was addressing a petulant child. "Then we'll find your assailant."

If it was, who I thought it was, we might find more than just my assailant, we might just find our killer.

Within fifteen minutes, I found myself swinging my legs from a metal exam table, next to another table, with a dead body on it, and wondering where my life went all loopy on me. The answer came without hesitation, in a cold unfeeling voice.

The moment you refused to go to the hospital, you chicken. All this, because you're afraid of a little needle.

That statement wasn't exactly true. I also held a deeply ingrained fear of scalpels, antiseptic smells, and doctors in general. Normally, I wasn't the least bit afraid of Doctor Dave, but as he approached me with a thermometer, and I realized where I was, I reconsidered my position.

"No way." I pressed my lips together tight.

"I need to get a temp."

"Then stick that nasty thing in your own mouth. There is no way I'm opening up to say *ah*."

Louise took the thermometer from Doctor Dave.

"Can I keep this?" she asked.

He shrugged. "I guess so, but why?"

"Normally we can't get her to keep her mouth shut. If this little piece of glass does the trick, I want to have it close at hand."

Dave snatched the thermometer away from Louise and shook his head. He scolded her with the thin piece of glass, and then he turned the thermometer to me.

"This is a brand new thermometer," he said. "I just took it out of the box."

He pointed to a torn package on his desk.

I glanced at the body next to me. The thermometer. The body. The thermometer.

"Oh for Christ's sake. This is why I tell my wife I don't work with the living, too many issues."

Dave opened one of the overhead cabinet doors and pulled out a rubber glove. He shoved the thermometer into the index finger of the glove, and then pulled the rubber tight around the outside.

"Happy?" He raised his eyebrows. "Now open up."

"Just let him take your temp," Louise said. "You'll never get to the video tapes if you don't."

I cast one last glance at the body next to me then, reluctantly, I opened my mouth. Doctor Dave moved faster than a shadow against a wall. He shoved the rubber-covered thermometer under my tongue.

"Don't talk." Dave wagged his finger at me.

While I gagged on latex, Doctor Dave waved a pen light in front of my face, and we played follow the light. He pressed his fingers against the skin around the bruises. Then he trailed his fingers along what felt like one giant bruise that ran from the back of my head, down my neck and over my shoulder blade.

"You've got one hell of a muscle cramp here."

He pressed the right side of my shoulder near my spine. Pain shot through me, and an involuntary jump rocked me forward on the table.

"Well," Dave said. "I was going to ask if it hurt, but I guess I don't have to."

He pulled the rubber glove from my mouth, then extracted the thermometer, read the number, and tucked the glass sliver into the pocket of his lab coat.

"Give it to me straight, Dave, I can take it." I hopped off the table. "Will I live?"

Dave set his fists on his hips and widened his stance.

"From what I can tell," he said. "You don't appear to have a detached retina, though those popped blood vessels are nasty. You don't appear to have any broken bones. Did you fill the prescription I gave you yesterday?"

I reached into my right pocket, took out the bottle, and rattled the pills.

"Good, you'll need them," he said. "Don't forget, if you get a headache or any lethargy, go to the hospital. Don't mess around thinking everything will be fine if you ignore it. Have you had a headache?"

I considered a quick lie, but the look on Dave's face said he would know.

"I did yesterday, you can understand why, but today I feel pretty good."

Doctor Dave pressed his lips flat and crossed his arms over his chest.

"I'm serious. The bruises on my skin ache, and when you pressed on them, they throbbed. Other than that, I feel all right. Just a little stiff."

His gaze was steady, and drilled through my eyes as if trying to see the thoughts behind them and determine if I were lying. After a few moments, he nodded.

"Okay, then you're cleared for service. Don't push yourself though."

"She won't," Louise said. "I promise."

From the look she gave me, Louise was determined to keep that promise to Doctor Dave, even if it meant handcuffing me to my chair.

Louise could stand at ease. I had no problem with someone else doing the heavy lifting today. I just wanted to be back in the saddle after my fall.

I slid off the metal table onto the floor, stood in front of Doctor Dave, and raised my right hand.

"I swear, I will take it easy today."

Dave slipped on a new pair of gloves to start work on his next patient, who had been waiting so patiently.

"Just see that you do, O'Brien, and take one of the Vicodin pills now if you're in pain."

I saluted him and we left.

When Louise and I turned the corner into the security-monitoring center, a haggard and drawn Rees hunched toward the main monitoring screen.

"Jesus, Rees, have you been here all night?"

Rees's head came up and he smiled.

"Hey, O'Brien, how are you feeling this morning?"

He came around the console, and then took my arm. His touch as soft as cotton, like he could break me by touching me too hard. From the tired look on Rees's face, guilt over his part in what had happen to me yesterday was what had fueled his all-nighter.

"I'm fine. Thank you, Rees."

I allowed him to direct me to one of the rolling chairs.

"O'Brien, I am so sorry about yesterday. Really, I was just gone for a few minutes."

"It's okay, Rees. I don't blame you for what happened to me. But I'm hoping you've been able to find a suspect on one of the cameras further down the hall."

"I have good news then." His face lit with excitement and his eyes twinkled with life. "I think I found a picture of the woman who hit you."

"It was Katie Dolan," I said.

Louise's tall body went perfectly straight. "How do you know?"

"I told you, my dad told me."

Rees looked confused. After years of working with Louise; we had developed our own form of verbal shorthand, which though efficient, left those around us puzzled.

"You guys want to fill me in on what's going on?" Rees said. "Or do you want to see the image I've found? I'm assuming that's why you're here."

I nodded toward the monitor. "Roll it, Rees. I'm pretty sure I know who my attacker is, but visual confirmation won't hurt when it comes to putting the psycho behind bars."

Louise came around the console and stood behind me.

Rees pushed the power button on one of the side monitors. A still image wavered, on the screen then became clear.

"I paused the image when I found a clear shot, so I could print the face, but I can run the tape back if you want to see it."

Unconsciously, I bobbed my head. Rees rewound the image and then pushed play. The woman ran down the hallway leading to one of the building's exits. When she reached the door she glanced over her shoulder. That's when Rees paused the image again.

"Do you know her?"

I nodded.

"It's Katie Dolan," Louise said. "Catherine, the next time we're stuck on a case, remind me to call your dad and enlist his psychic abilities."

"He's not psychic," I said, still staring at Katie Dolan's face. Her expression was cold and somehow pleased.

I don't know what I'd expected to see, but it sure wasn't pleasure. Katie Dolan was a sick individual.

"Explain to me how your Dad knew Katie attacked you."

"He didn't."

Rees and Louise stared at me with a mutinous look that said, if I didn't pony up with the information, they'd soon make what Katie Dolan did to me seem like a gentle facial.

I let out a deep breath. "It's a stupid story guys."

Louise arched an eyebrow. "Humor us."

"My Dad loves Katherine Hepburn," I said. "So he wanted to name me Katherine. My Mother finally relented but insisted they spell my name with a C instead of a K. I guess it was her little way of giving the great Kate a big 'up yours' for all the times my father dragged her to Hepburn's movies and spent the night breathing heavy over Kate in the back row instead of my Mom."

This revelation elicited a chuckle from Rees.

"Get to the point," Louise said. "How did he know about Katie?"

"I'm getting there. Do you read the last chapters of a book first, too?"

Louise gave me a killer look, then flipped me the bird.

"Anyway, dad always calls me Katie, despite the "C." When I talked to him this morning, hearing him call me Katie made me ill. That's when I realized that I recognized the voice of the woman in the bathroom."

"Katie Dolan," Louise said.

I held my hand out, palm up, and gestured to Louise as if I were serving her with a silver platter.

"And Rees gave us all the confirmation we needed."

Rees reached forward and punched the print button. The laser printer on the other side of the square, cement room gave a high-pitched-squeal followed by a buzzing-whir as it spit out a color photograph.

I pushed myself out of the chair. The short period of sitting had created a stiff pain in my back. The throb of my shoulder made me finger the pill bottle in my pocket. After I had a little food in my stomach, I would have to take at least one to get me through the day.

"Thanks, Rees. I think you should tell the Chief you're not feeling well and take the rest of the day off," I said. "You've earned some sleep."

He gave a weak smile and bobbed his head. "Thanks O'Brien."

Jane Katts was sitting in the same lobby chair she had been perched in yesterday. Again, she had a bag of donuts on her lap. Guilt played across her features when she saw me. Maybe it was the stern look I tried to convey through my mangled features.

Jane stood and held the bag out to me.

Pastries as a peace treaty are almost as insidious as small pox blankets. I wondered how much she's had to spend on donuts in her short career. She should consider buying stock.

"I bought a few extras today," she said and flashed a practiced smile.

The siren song of the donuts pulled at me, and my hand lifted on automatic pilot. I halted the unconscious assent before my fingers closed on the bag. If I took the donuts, I would be a slave to Jane Katts' no good bribery forever. I played off the reach by adjusting my purse strap, and walked past her without comment.

Jane jogged up next to me. "How are you feeling today?"

"Fine."

The metal in my voice was clear to me, if not to Jane.

"You look better," she said.

I stopped walking and stared at her like she was four biscuits short of a picnic. Jane shrugged. Her lips turned up at one side in a pathetic smile.

"Less swollen." She swirled her index finger in the air around her own face, then demured away from my hard stare. "Still a little bruised though."

I proceeded into the bullpen area of our office, and fielded fifty different questions about how I felt. Once I had assured everyone that I wouldn't be dying soon, I had to listen to taunts about sitting on the toilet with the wrong end.

Digs waited for us at the gauntlet finish line, dancing from side to side as if he had to pee. The manila folder he held fanned back and forth with each step. Then he caught sight of Jane and went still.

"Good morning, Digs," Louise said. "What brings you here so early?"

Digs tapped the center of the folder with his index finger.

"I thought you two would want this information right away."

"About the case?" I asked.

His eyes shifted to Jane. "No."

"That means it's off limits to you, Ms. Katts." I made a shooing motion with my hands.

"Where am I supposed to go?"

"Why don't you wait for us on the other side of the room," I said. "We'll call you back when we're done."

Jane leaned forward and deposited the donut bag on my desk, then huffed toward the far side of the room.

"Jane."

She stopped.

"Don't forget your purse."

I picked up her bag, which she had managed to slide onto the desk almost unnoticed, in a slight-of-hand worthy of a master magician. Donuts came in handy as one hell of a diversionary tactic. The strap dangled from my fingertips.

Jane snatched the purse, and whirled away so hard, I thought she might screw herself into the ground.

I called after her. "You didn't bug the donuts too did you?"

The hard clicking of her heels on the floor, as she stalked away, gave me more joy than I'd felt since she forced herself on us two days ago. God, I was one sick puppy.

"What do you have?" Louise asked, once Jane was safely out of earshot.

"I ran some tests to figure out what the substance was that cover the cameras last night." He bounced on the balls of his feet. "It's hair spray. Plus, I was able to pull a shoe print from the stall door."

He handed me the folder.

"Thanks, Digs. That should nail Katie Dolan without a doubt."

I flicked open the file and thumbed through the top few pages. Louise closed the cover, and pinched the folder between her thumb and forefinger. She slid the folder out of my hand.

"Except it's not our case," Louise said.

"What?"

"Come on, Catherine. You're the victim here," she said. "You know you can't investigate your own case."

"Why the hell not?"

She handed the file to Digs.

"You don't see a small conflict of interest in you investigating your own attack?"

Louise cocked an eyebrow at me, and waited for me to see her point of view. Deep inside, I knew what she was saying, though I wasn't prepared to agree with her yet. I wanted to arrest Katie Dolan, and confront her about what she did to me.

I needed to ask her why, even though there would be no good answer. She was completely insane, but I needed to look her in the eyes.

Katie Dolan had made me a victim. This was the side of the fence I don't want to be on. The only way to the other side, where I could be on terra firma again, was to see her face.

"Whose case is it?" I finally asked.

"It's mine." Bob Shackelford had been standing just out of my line of sight. "I promise I'll do a good job, O'Brien."

Louise handed Digs the file. She nodded toward Katie's photo in my hand.

"I know you will, Bob." I held the photo out toward him. "And I appreciate it."

He pressed his lips flat and gave me a smile. Then took the picture and slid it into the file with Digs' reports.

"Her name is Katie Dolan," I said. "We picked her up yesterday in connection with our current investigation. Apparently, she wasn't very happy about it."

I touched the knot on the side of my face and gave a short laugh. Bob laughed too, but his eyes remained focused on the file. He shuffled his feet from side to side.

For several seconds there was an uncomfortable silence while Shackelford tried to find something to say. I couldn't take any more sentiment, especially not from Shackelford. We based our relationship on mutual torment.

"Go get her," I said. "Time's a-wasting. Jesus, who'd you screw to get this job?"

The jab broke the tension. A genuinely relieved smile split Shackelford's face.

"The same person you screwed, O'Brien. You should know that. We all have to screw the pooch for this kind of glory job."

He fanned the file in my face. I winked at him. He winked back and left. I watched him go, or watched the file go, with all the longing of a lover. Letting go of things with grace and magnanimity wasn't my strong suit.

On the edge of my periphery, I could see Jane wave her hand in the air, as if to ask if it were all right to return. I turned my gaze to her and jerked my head to call her over.

"What was that all about?" Jane said with an indignant flap of her hand toward Bob Shackelford's back.

"Another case," I said and turned my back to her. "One that doesn't involve you."

"Are you sure it wasn't about the Luther's case?"

"Positive."

"Okay." Jane jammed her fists into her hips. "What did I do?"

"You broke our deal." I didn't look at her. I couldn't look at her.

Genuine shock crossed her face. "How so?"

"You ran the story about my attack without clearing it with us first," I said. "I knew we couldn't trust you, and now you've proved it."

Jane reeled backward. Her mouth gaped open and her eyes widened. She looked at Louise and Digs for some sort of support but found none. Louise looked through the inbox on the corner of her desk, and Digs glared at her demanding answers.

"You had no right to print that story, without running it by either Louise or me."

Her features smoothed with dawning.

"Ah!"

She made no move to explain herself. Instead, she took a seat, slung her purse up onto her lap, opened the flap, and dug through the contents like a mole burying into the ground. This disregard was more infuriating to me than if she had decided to deny my accusation.

"Well?" I demanded.

She looked up, hands still tucked into her purse. "Well, what?"

"Aren't you going to argue with me?"

She considered the question for a moment, and then shook her head. "No."

"Why not?"

"Because it wouldn't make any difference. I'm sick of fighting with you. I'm going to do my job and your opinion doesn't matter to me anymore."

I grunted and turned to Louise. She shrugged, then held her hands palm out, as if trying to push me away.

I wasn't prepared to give up so easily. "Do you deny that you broke our deal?"

Jane finally located what she was looking for in the bottom of her purse, a tube of *ChapStick.* She pulled off the cap and circled her lips in an exaggerated 'O'. When she had slathered enough wax on them to buff out a Buick, she rubbed her lips together and recapped the tube.

"I do," she said, and dropped the *ChapStick* back into the chasm of her bag. She folded her hands over the zipper of her purse, and then looked at me.

I opened my eyes wider, crossed my arms over my chest, and waited. After a few moments, Jane let out a heavy sigh. She set her purse on the floor at her feet.

"Your attack had nothing to do with the Luther murder investigation. I was not obligated to ask your permission to run the story. Since the department didn't issue a press release, I had an exclusive I couldn't pass up."

"She's correct," Louise said. "It's a separate case. Jane had every right to run the story."

"Did she have the right to invade my privacy? Did she have the right to cause my family undo anxiety? Again."

Louise shrugged. Digs stared at her with the same disbelief I felt, unusual only because Digs would take any opportunity he could to agree with Louise.

"I am sorry," Jane said. "But you two have essentially tied my hands. Journalism is more competitive than you know. You have to keep your name in print or your editor forgets who you are when you pass in the hallway."

She chuckled and shook her head.

"Oh, he remembers your face, but he's pretty sure you're in the obituary department. So, I had two choices."

She held up her index finger.

"I could give up on the Luther case and move on to the next story."

Her middle finger popped up next to her index finger in a peace sign.

"Or I could trust my instincts, stick with the story, and hope for the best. The journalistic equivalent of career suicide."

Jane pinched her second choice between the thumb and forefinger of her other hand.

"That's what I did. What I am doing, trusting my instincts. Each day that passes without some huge revelation to publish, my boss thinks that me being here is a bad idea, and that maybe my time could be better spent elsewhere. So, when a huge story, which could buy me a little more time with my editor, drops into my lap, I won't turn my back and pretend I didn't see. You called the tune, I just joined the dance."

My anger mixed with guilt. Then shame washed over me at my selfishness.

"I am sorry," Jane said again. "If I caused your family anxiety, I *am* sorry."

She meant it.

The sassy voice in my head scolded me with a sharp, *what's your next move slick*?

I considered the question for a moment. The anger I felt in my chest eased, then rippled away.

"Just my mother," I said. "She's in a constant state of anxiety over what I do for a living anyway."

Louise, who had never met my mother, but had the opportunity to speak with her on the telephone on several occasions, laughed and nodded.

"How about we come to an understanding; if I happen to get my ass kicked, again during the time that you're with us –"

A low volley of giggles ran through my audience.

"And you decided to publish a story about said ass-kicking, you will give me a heads up so I can call my mother in advance, and let her know that I'm alright."

Jane stood and stuck out her hand. "Deal."

We shook to seal our pact, which seemed to alleviate the tension all around. Except for Digs who looked at Jane as if she'd been caught kicking his dog.

"Where are we in the Luther investigation?" Jane asked.

I eased into my chair, and pressed my shoulders back. The upper back muscles twitched while I stretched. That was the trouble with adrenaline, it didn't last long enough.

"Personally, I think it's time to sit down and brainstorm. Play a little follow the money, and see where it leads us."

"Good idea," Louise said. "Unless Digs has some new revelation."

"No," he said and shook his head. "I guess I was working on Bob's case."

He sulked out of the bullpen.

"Let's go have coffee." I pushed the donuts away from me. "Fresh pastries with good coffee so we'll have plenty of brain juice working for us."

Louise and Jane agreed. On our way out of the office, Bob Shackelford stopped me.

"Just wanted to let you know a uniform just picked up Katie Dolan. I'll let you know how it goes."

I gave him a quick thumbs-up and left.

Ten minutes later Louise, Jane, and I slid into a booth at the Day By Day Café. The atmosphere of the Day By Day makes me happy. Plastic figures of Scooby-Doo, Smurfs, Batman, and other cartoon characters perch on shelves that run around the entire restaurant. The figures reminded me of when I was a kid, like a *McDonald's* play land for adults.

"It's funny," Jane said. "I've lived in Saint Paul all my life and I've never been in this restaurant before."

"Best breakfast you'll ever have," I said. "Their toast is made with homemade bread. It reminds me of my Grandma's house."

That and you could actually get a fried egg and hash browns, instead of egg substitute and tofu browns. Lately many of my favorite haunts in the downtown area had gone health-food-chic. As Hank, the three hundred fifty pound operator of my former, favorite, breakfast hang out so aptly put it, "I gotta keep up with the time no matter how repulsive I find what I'm feeding the mindless masses." He finally confessed after I grilled him further that he eats at home these days.

The Day By Day was also one of the only places you could get a decent cup of coffee, without paying primo prices. Just a plain cup of java but the staff of the Day By Day knew how to make plain Joe sing.

A pretty, young woman who wore black rimmed glasses (which looked like they belonged on the miniature face of a three year old), and multi-colored, dread locks, approached our table with an order pad. She'd piled the dreads into elastic at the back of her head so the colorful ropes of hair fanned out in a corona around her head.

A flicker of surprise ran through me when I noticed that the rest of her outfit didn't match her face and hair. She wore khakis and a non-descript, black T-shirt. It looked like some creative child had removed modern art Barbie's head, and stuck it on Yuppie Barbie's body.

The girl took our order and then left to retrieve our coffee.

"Alright, who do we think did it," I said.

Louise unrolled her silverware from the paper napkin and laid them out on the table.

"We have to put Katie Dolan at the top of the list considering what she did to you yesterday."

I grimaced.

Jane caught Louise's meaning immediately.

"You know for sure that Katie Dolan attacked you?"

I gave Louise a sharp, hard, look.

"Oh, what," Louise said. "I didn't give anything away. Thanks to Jane's story yesterday the department is probably already overrun with other reporters asking questions. The Chief will have to issue a statement identifying your attacker and stating that she's in custody."

Jane's excitement dissipated at the realization that she no longer had the exclusive. Too bad the local papers didn't run multiple issues per day anymore. She might have been able to scoop everyone before Chief issued a report this afternoon.

"Okay, so we have Katie Dolan," I said and riffled through my purse. "Does anyone have paper?"

Jane laid the notebook she'd been using throughout the investigation on the table, and then slid it toward me.

"Thanks," I said. "Who else do we have?"

"Put that V guy on the list." Jane shivered and stuck out her tongue. "He really creeped me out."

I motioned for Jane's pen. If we had to wait for me to find something to write with in the bottom of my diaper bag of a purse, we'd be here until long after breakfast.

"We can't just put Vincent on the list because you don't like him."

"Sure you can," she said. "It's my notebook. I want him on the list."

I found a clean page, scratched Katie Dolan's name on the top line, then reluctantly a V on the second line. Jane nodded her approval.

"Linda and Jack Meyers are players in this somehow." Louise's face was contemplative. Despite our juvenile behavior, she was undistracted, as serious, and professional, as she had ever been. "And as much as I hate to say it, Chad is still a suspect."

"Really?" I wrote the names on the page. "I'm not so sure about Chad."

Our waitress returned balancing a circular, brown tray with coffee cups, and a gold thermal pot. She set a cup at each place, filled them, set the pot between the three of us, and then left to flirt with a table of young men dressed in paint stained overalls.

"Chad was the first person to find his parents," Louise's tone was no bullshit. "There's no evidence to rule him out yet."

"He has an alibi," Jane said.

"From a drug dealing, burn out." I drew in a deep whiff of my coffee. "Not exactly a model citizen. A good attorney could tear that alibi apart in ten seconds of fast talking. Anyway, if Chad has an alibi, then so does V and we'd have to remove him from our list."

Jane shrugged and took a pull from her coffee, grimaced, then reached across Louise for the small dish of cream near the wall.

The cell phone clipped in a sling to the outside of Louise's purse began to chime. She flipped it open and looked at the caller ID.

"It's the office," she said. "Detective Montgomery."

She listened for a few seconds then said, "We're on our way."

Louise tucked the phone back into its case.

"Looks like breakfast will have to wait."

"Why?" I asked and gazed longingly at my coffee. "What's happened?"

"Chad Luther has been attacked."

She pulled two twenties and a ten from her purse and tossed them on the table. More than enough to pay for the breakfast we wouldn't eat and a generous tip.

I drank my coffee in one long swallow and felt the burn all the way down to my stomach.

The three of us piled out of the booth like the building was on fire, and headed for the door. Our waitress looked distressed.

"Sorry," I said and showed her my badge. "We have to go. There's money on the table."

She gave a hesitant half smile and then nodded. "Have a great day."

Squad cars blocked the parking lot of Chad Luther's dorm. A red and blue glow from the squad's lights, strobed off the windows of the brick buildings, and lit up the common with a dance floor glimmer. The uniformed officers had blocked the entire common, so we parked on the street.

"Big time overkill for an assault," I said.

"I guess they're not taking any chances after what happened to his parents." Louise showed her badge to the officers at the steps and signed us in.

She was probably right, but it still seemed like more firepower than needed to protect one kid *after* the fact. One or two squads parked out front would have been sufficient.

A buzz of activity greeted us when we reached Chad's ground floor dorm room.

"What happened?" I badged the officer keeping gawkers at bay.

He winced when he focused on my face. "Someone busted out the kid's window and jumped him when he entered the room."

I glanced down at my watch. "This morning?"

He nodded.

"Is he hurt?" Louise asked.

"Rabbit scared, but he doesn't look too damaged."

We nodded our appreciation and stepped into the crowded dorm room.

"Well it's about time you arrived." Linda Meyers stood near the window at the far end of the room with her hands on her hips. "Are you satisfied? I tried to warn you she'd do something like this."

Chad sat on the lower bunk bed with his head down. He held a blue icepack to the back of his neck. His eyes flicked up briefly, and then returned to the space between his feet.

I knelt next to the bunk bed. "Chad, do you know who attacked you?"

"Yeah," he said. "It was my Mom's cousin Katie."

I looked up at Louise. Jane Katts took a deep breath and said, "B –"

I snapped my fingers and shook my head.

"I told you." Linda pushed her way past two officers toward us. "You didn't listen to me and now she's trying to hurt Chad."

"Is that true, Chad?" I said.

"Yes!" Linda shot back.

"Mrs. Meyers, please wait in the hallway until we're finished here," I said.

"I'm not going anywhere. Someone needs to protect Chad and it sure as hell hasn't been you."

She stabbed an accusing finger in my direction. I motioned to the officer closest to her.

"Take Mrs. Meyers into the hallway please, Officer," I said. "We'll be finished here in a minute."

He took Linda Meyers by the arm. Part of me felt a twinge of guilt. She bitched her way out of the room and thrashed out of his grasp. Linda Meyers was going to make him work for his money today.

"Chad," I said. "Can you please tell me what happened?"

He sat up and leaned against the support post of the bunk headboard. His eyes focused on me for the first time.

"Jesus, what happened to you?"

"Car accident."

"That sucks." His brows knitted together. "I bet it hurts."

"Yeah, it does. How are you?"

Confusion flickered across Chad's features. His eye alighted on the ice pack in his hand, and the confusion on his face cleared. He put the pack back on his neck.

"I'm fine." He shrugged. "Or I will be."

I moved closer to Chad in an effort to block the rest of the room. I wanted him to forget there were others watching and listening, to forget that his Aunt was ranting in the hallway. Forget everything except what I wanted him to focus on.

"Tell me exactly what happened."

"Katie was waiting for me in my room. She hit me on the back of the head and I ran for the hallway." His eyes shifted to over my right shoulder. "That's it."

"What did she hit you with?"

"Ah, I don't know."

"When was this?"

Chad gave a one-shoulder shrug. "Maybe a half an hour ago."

That explained the parade of police cruisers outside. The officer who arrived on scene first, believed Chad's attacker was still somewhere on campus.

"We're going to take you to our office. You'll be safe there."

For a moment, I smiled at the thought that I no longer believed my office was the safest place to be. Not for Chad and not for me. How ironic, that the person Chad thought he needed protection from, was the person who had changed my idea of security forever.

Chad nodded his agreement and got to his feet.

"I'll take him to the car with me," I said to Louise. "You wrap things up here."

I winked at her and Louise's head tilted forward in acknowledgment.

Once in the hall, Linda Meyers pounced on us.

"Where are you taking him? What's going on?"

"Mrs. Meyers." I tried to use the same tone that Louise did when she was dealing with hysterical people. "We're taking Chad to our office. He'll be safe there."

"I'm going too." She crossed her arms over her chest daring me to say otherwise.

"Of course." I inclined my head to the uniformed officer behind her. "Would you please escort Mrs. Meyers? Our car will be full."

The officer rolled his eyes skyward then nodded. I was going to owe him a lunch for sticking him with Linda for that long.

By the time we reached the parking lot, word must have come down that the suspect in the attack was no longer in the area. Only two squads remained with their lights flashing, the rest had returned to their regular patrols.

I squeezed into the back of Louise's Toyota with Chad.

"Where were you this morning?" I asked.

Chad looked startled as if he didn't realize I was next to him, or I had just pulled him back from a very deep thought.

"What?"

"This morning when Katie broke into your room, where were you?"

His gaze was stony. "Why?"

"No reason. I was just wondering if the University has early classes or something?"

"No." He turned toward his breath-fogged window. "I went to the Union for breakfast."

I looked out over the common.

"I missed breakfast this morning. Do they have daily specials?"

"Why?" He turned toward me. "Do you want to know what I ate? Just say so. I had two eggs, soft boiled, sausage – patties not links – wheat toast with strawberry jam and orange juice. It's what I have every morning."

Chad's breaths came out in short, angry, puffs.

I held my hands up at my shoulders, palms out. "Sorry, Chad. I'm just not really good at uncomfortable silences. I tend to want to fill the emptiness. It's not personal."

He relaxed against the seat, satisfied with my explanation. His features hung on his face like an old man who'd been down many bad stretches of road in his life.

"Louise, my partner –" I jerked my thumb toward the dorm, "is better with people than I am. When she's not around I'm sort of . . ."

I wiggled the fingers of my right hand as if I'd be able to grasp the word from the air.

"Awkward." Chad provided.

"Yes." I nodded. "Awkward. Thanks."

Chad's lips melted into a flat smile.

"Did you call your Aunt before you called the police?"

"No." Chad looked as if a cattle prod had been rammed into his back. "I called the police first."

"Then you called your aunt?"

"Yes."

"It's nice to have someone who cares so much," I said.

"Yeah, it is."

Louise and Jane emerged from the arched, stone, dorm doorway. Louise opened the driver's door letting in a cold rush of wind before she got in and closed the door. She glanced at Chad in the rearview mirror.

"How are you doing?"

His response was automatic. "Fine, thank you."

The ride back to the office passed in silence, except for the occasional uncomfortable outburst from Jane Katts. The officer transporting Linda Meyers arrived before we did, which didn't surprise me. He had probably used his lights and sirens all the way to the office, then up the stairs to the right floor.

Linda paced furiously in the lobby. From the red that tinted our receptionist's face, Linda had been ranting since she arrived.

I pushed through the glass door followed by Chad, then Jane, and finally Louise.

"Chad." Linda Meyers rushed toward him, but Chad turned away before she could embrace him. She settled for rubbing her hand across his shoulders, as if she were soothing a crying baby.

"Are you alright, Chad?"

He crossed his arms over his chest, head down. "Fine."

"I demand that you arrest my cousin." Linda ranted into Louise's face. "How many members of my family does she have to kill before you believe me?"

The placid, unreadable, but friendly expression that Louise used like a mask, when confronted with an irate member of the public appeared and seemed to do its job. Linda eased back, maybe only an inch or two, but enough.

"Mrs. Meyers." Louise's voice was calm and even. I envied her ability to switch off any personal feelings. My natural instinct when under attack was to attack back, defend myself.

"We need to get an official statement from Chad and he has to press charges. If we do everything by the book, when we bring her in, we may be able to find evidence, which helps us with your sister's murder. If we rush in, a good defense attorney, which with her money wouldn't be hard to find, would have any evidence we found regarding the murder thrown out of court."

All that was left of Linda Meyers's anger dissipated. She considered Louise as if trying to decide if she could be trusted or not.

"I apologize," she said. "I'm just a little upset about everything that's been happening."

"We understand, Mrs. Meyers," Louise said. "We need to speak to Chad alone."

Louise swept her hand toward the front desk.

"Rebecca can get you something to drink. She'll show you to the lounge where you'll be more comfortable."

Rebecca gave Linda a hesitant smile.

Louise placed her hand on Linda's shoulder.

"We'll only be a few minutes," she said. "We'll come get you in the lounge."

I held my breath until Linda Meyers was out of sight, afraid she would realize she was being led away, and change her mind. She didn't. Instead she followed Rebecca and gave Chad only one backward glance.

We escorted Chad to a hallway that leads to the interrogation rooms.

"Chad," I said. "Are you sure Katie attacked you?"

Part of me wanted him to say, no. Here was his chance, and I wanted him to take it.

Chad didn't hear opportunity knocking. He only heard a simple question. He turned hard eyes toward me.

"I saw her. She hit me. What part of that is hard for you to grasp?"

I took Chad's elbow with more force than I probably needed to, jerked open the door to my right, and pushed Chad through the opening. Louise and Jane followed me inside and I closed the door.

Chad faced the glass. I stood beside him and crossed my arms over my chest. On the other side of the one-way mirror, Katie Dolan gestured wildly at Bob Shackelford.

"You caught her?"

"Yes," I said. "About forty-five minutes *before* you claim she attacked you. Can you grasp that, Chad?"

His eyes narrowed at me. "Why did you arrest her?"

"For attacking me." I pointed to my face. "You see, she really did attack me."

Chad turned toward Louise looking for confirmation. She nodded. He let out a deep breath and moved to one of the viewing seats. He dropped into the chair, propped his elbows on his knees, and held his head in his hands.

"Shit."

Louise sat in the chair next to him and I moved to the mirror and blocked the view of Katie Dolan. We'd give him a few more minutes to decide if he would try to concoct another lie, or tell the truth. I was routing for the truth.

To my surprise, Jane Katts settled against the back wall and held her tongue. In the last few days, Jane hadn't proven herself tactful in these situations.

Chad lifted his head and fixed his eyes on mine.

"She did that to your face?" he asked.

"Yes, she did," I said. "Are you sure you want to stick with your story? Do you know the penalty for filing a false police report?"

"Why, Chad?" Louise asked.

He sagged against the back of the chair and scratched at his left eyebrow.

"Is there really a good reason?" He said. "I can't think of one. Can you?"

"Then tell us the truth bad or bad," I said. "I've gotta tell you Chad, the suspense is killing me."

"Oh, then maybe I should hold out a little bit longer." Cold cruelty fixed in the expression on his face. He reminded me of a kid caught kicking a dog that shows no remorse.

"Funny," I said and jerked my thumb over my shoulder. "Maybe I should go in there and tell your cousin that you're trying to frame her. My guess is you, and your Aunt Linda, have decided to not only frame her for your attack, but also the murder of your parents."

A cocky swagger washed over him. In my mind, I had given Chad the status of frat-boy-wannabe-punk but as we pealed back the layers, Chad was slowly changing from wannabe, to professional punk.

"Chad if you don't tell us what's going on we're going to have to arrest you," Louise said. "Do you know something about Katie's involvement with your parents? Is that what this is about?"

Chad scratched at his eyebrow again. "Linda said Katie was involved with my parents somehow. The attack was her idea. She said it was my word against Katie's and with her record, no one would believe her."

Linda Meyers had probably been right. Had she executed her plan, before we picked up Katie for questioning, I would have been willing to believe Katie capable.

"What's the big deal? It's not like she was going to face the death penalty or anything." His gaze returned to the floor. "They'll just send her back to the looney bin, which is where she belongs anyway."

"From what I can tell, you and your aunt, belong in cross-your-heart, white jackets next to her."

Chad gave a low chuckle.

"Yeah, maybe mental illness runs way down deep in the roots of our family tree."

Louise stood and moved to my side.

"There's more to this ruse than framing Katie," Louise whispered in my ear.

I nodded in agreement.

"Please don't egg him on anymore." She bit each word off under her breath. "I think I can get it out of him."

I rolled my eyes up to the acoustic ceiling tiles, then looked at her, and nodded again. Louise circled on Chad, cocked one foot out, leaned back on the other and crossed her arms over her waist.

Too bad my mouth worked quicker than my brain in certain situations. If I could keep those two in harmony more often, I'd be a better detective. I guess that's why the chief had partnered me with Louise. Louise could get top-secret information from a dead spy.

"Does your Aunt have any proof that Katie was involved with your parent's deaths?" Louise asked.

"No."

"Then why is she so het up to have your cousin locked away?"

"God, you guys are dense." He let out a laugh and shook his head. "If Katie is put away who do you think gets the money? Let's think for a second." He put his index finger to his temple. "If Katie is free."

He jumped up, eyes wide, as if he'd just come up with an important revelation.

"Oh yeah, and Katie's guardian, is dead. Then a judge is appointed guardian."

He tapped his temple again.

"But if Katie is arrested for murder, and put away for life, then she won't need that money any more. So who gets it?"

Chad looked from Louise to me and then back to Louise.

"Any guesses, *DETECTIVES*?"

"Alright," I said. "We get it."

"Oh, good. I'm so glad I didn't have to s-p-e-l-l it out for you."

Katie Dolan was the fatted calf that Linda Meyers was prepared to sacrifice. In the twisted aftermath of the last two days, Chad Luther had become just a plastic pawn in the game of who gets the family inheritance.

"It's not insanity that runs through the roots my family tree," he said. "It's greed. One of the seven deadly sins."

His eyes narrowed and he gave a cynical laugh.

"My family has always been full of over achievers."

The soft rustle of paper drew my attention to the back of the room. Jane flipped the page of her miniature steno book over and continued to scribble notes without looking up. I had forgotten she was with us.

"Chad, we're going to leave you here," Louise said. "There will be an officer outside the door if you need anything."

Louise didn't wait for him to respond. She closed the shade in front of the mirror and then headed for the door. I motioned for Jane to follow.

Linda Meyers sat at the table closest to the door of the lounge where she wouldn't miss us when we entered. Not that the room was huge, but during shift changes, the small area became quite crowded, like now. Linda spun the paper coffee cup like a top on the table in front of her, waiting for it to rattle to a stop before spinning it again.

When she finally saw us, she got to her feet.

"Where's Chad?" she said, without preamble.

"Mrs. Meyers," Louise said. "We need to speak to you."

We led her into interview room four, but she refused to sit until we told her what had happened to Chad. So, we sat and waited for her to come to the conclusion that we'd go no further until she calmed herself.

She paced for a few moments and then finally took a seat. Linda twisted her hands on the table in front of her.

"What's happened?" She turned pleading eyes from Louise to me. "What did Chad say?"

"Well, he didn't say much." I leaned back and stretched my arms out in front of me. "After we told him that

Katie Dolan was in our custody at the time he claimed she had attacked him."

Linda's eye narrowed in suspicion. She looked between the three of us, finally fixing on Jane. Jane looked surprised by the sudden scrutiny.

"You're lying." Linda directed her statement at Jane. "You don't have Katie in custody."

Jane straightened uncomfortably and cleared her throat. Louise took a deep breath, readying herself to jump in and rescue Jane, but I tapped her elbow. Louise looked at me and I shook my head.

If Jane Katts wanted the inside track on this investigation, she might as well jump in and help.

"We do actually." Jane's voice was tentative.

She laid her pen and paper on the table and laced her fingers over the top of them.

"Katie Dolan was arrested early this morning."

"That's a lie," Linda said. Her words came out like a gunshot of an accusation. "I don't know why you're playing games with me. Chad told you it was Katie."

"Because that's what you wanted him to tell us," Jane said.

I sucked in a deep breath. Jane had just made the worst of rookie mistakes. You never lay all your cards on the table at once.

"I'm calling my lawyer," Linda Meyers said. "I am going to sue you and this police department. You're harassing me, and my family, during a very difficult time. I need a phone so I can call my lawyer."

Louise and I stood and headed for the door with Jane in tow.

Once in the hallway and out of hearing distance of Linda Meyers, Jane turned to us and asked, "Why did we leave? She would have slipped up if you'd kept asking her questions."

"Maybe she would have," I agreed.

"Then why didn't we keep talking?"

"Because she asked for a lawyer," Louise said. "Anything we found out after that request would have been thrown out of court. Especially if we'd kept asking questions before giving her access to a phone."

"Now her lawyer is going to tell her not to talk to us at all," I said.

"We know she's lying. We know she put Chad up to this scam, and we can't do anything about it?" Jane stomped her foot like a spoiled brat. "That really fucking sucks."

I nodded my agreement. "That's the law."

Jane stared as if there would be some loophole in our logic. There wasn't.

"So what do we do now?"

Amusement rolled through me at Jane's personalization of what was happening. Finally, she was beginning to understand what we did every day. She would never be an impartial bystander again, not after coming this far with us.

The cell phone in my purse chirped to let me know I'd received a text message. I slid the phone from its pocket.

"Now we visit Digs," I said and wiggled my phone in the air. "Digs just sent me a message that says he needs to see us 9-1-1."

"Very punny," Louise said and shook her head. "Does he say why?"

I scrolled through the entire text.

"No. He does like his dramatic reveals. I guess this is one of them."

Chapter Ten

"We have a ballistics match."

Digs didn't even wait for the door to close before making his announcement. Anti-climactic for Digs who liked to play Monty Hall, what's behind curtain number two, every chance he got.

"I knew you'd want to know about it right away." He was panting with excitement.

Jane, caught in Digs' enthusiasm, gave a quick round of applause. Louise and I just waited. There had to be more. A ballistics match meant nothing. He could have matched the bullet to another unsolved murder, and our lives would have just become more complicated. Not much to get excited about.

Digs held up a report. I took it from him, and skimmed down to the facts I wanted.

I blinked at the information written at the bottom of the page and then looked up at Digs. He nodded at my unasked question.

Louise took the paper from my hand. Her eyes ran down the report just as mine had. Neither of us cared for the appetizers, we always went right for the chocolate dessert.

"What?" Jane asked. "What does it say?"

Digs rushed to tell her. "The gun is registered to Jack Meyers."

"Holy Shit!" Jane hopped up and down with Digs in a modified Snoopy-dance of joy.

Louise handed the report back to Digs. "Who would murder a family member with a registered gun and then not run? Or at least try to hide? It's just stupid."

Digs and Jane stopped their Snoopy-dance and turned gimlet eyes toward Louise.

"Come on guys." She shook the paper for effect. "This report is nonsense. Someone stole Jack Meyers' gun to frame him."

"Which proves it had to be a family member," I said, adding my nod of agreement. "That narrows our focus."

"To the exact same suspects?" Jane said. "You haven't focused on anyone except the family."

"Not true," I said. "We've eliminated your favorite suspect, V. Plus, part of me still considered Walter Wren a suspect."

The three of them gave me the your-last-cookie-has-crumbled look.

"The old man?" Louise asked.

"Yep."

"Why?"

"The ring, Digs found in Susan Luther's throat."

Digs gave a hesitant glance at Jane.

"Don't worry," I said. "She knows all about the ring."

Jane arched her eyebrows at me and crossed her arms over her chest. It was a look I had seen many times before but usually from Louise.

"Well maybe not everything about the ring." I had confiscated her tape before Jane could listen to all but an excerpt of our meeting with Digs. "But she knows about the ring."

I waved my hands in the air as if trying to erase my words and felt a sharp pain in my left shoulder. I would eventually have to break down and take one of the pain killers Doctor Dave had prescribed

"Never mind. It's not important. Anyway, I focused on more than the family."

They didn't look completely satisfied, but they let it go. Chalk it up to another Catherine moment of addled confusion.

Louise drummed her perfectly manicured nails on the file cabinet she was leaning against, and stared out into space. Finally, her brows drew together and she focused on Digs.

"What about the ring?" she asked.

Jane edged forward as if straining to hear. This was the meat of the story and she had waited for it for two days.

"What have we found out about the diamond?" Louise asked. "You said the stone was local."

"It is, but I've run up against the retailer's wall of silence."

I rolled my eyes and let out a frustrated grunt. We lost too much time to retailers, who hid behind privacy laws, so afraid of lawsuits, if they gave any information to the police. The real world certainly wasn't like the cop shows on television.

"I got as far as narrowing it down to the right shop, but now I need a warrant."

"Who's issuing?" I asked.

"Judge Todd."

Finally, we'd received a break. Judge Todd signed off on warrants like a celebrity on the red carpet signing autographs for fans. I had personally seen him approve four search warrants without more than a cursory glance over the pages.

I tapped the plastic case of my cell phone and then pointed at Digs.

"You call us the instant Judge Todd signs off on the warrant."

"Where will you guys be?" Digs asked.

"Trying to find out if Jack Meyers really is as stupid as your ballistics report says he is."

Chapter Eleven

If Jack Meyers were guilty of the murders of Susan and Jonathan Luther, he sure wasn't making any effort to hide from the police. We found him lounging in the reception area reading a copy of *National Geographic.*

"He must be trying to throw us off his trail," I whispered to Louise. "We could be dealing with a criminal Einstein."

Louise smiled, but the gesture was for Jack Meyers benefit not mine. Jack spotted her and stood.

"Are you through with my wife?" His wary dog look had returned. "Can I take her home now?"

"Not yet, Mr. Meyers," Louise said and extended her hand.

Jack gave her hand a perfunctory shake, but didn't make eye contact.

"Would you like a cup of coffee or a soda?" I asked. "She could be awhile."

Jack nodded.

"Come with us," Louise said. "We'll find you a more comfortable seat, and some current magazines to read."

We brought Jack into the lounge. I bought him a *Coca-Cola*, and a crackers and cheese from the vending machines, then located a more current *National Geographic*. If he had felt the slightest bit of hesitation about talking to us, when we found him in the lobby, I was certain we had managed to pull his defenses down.

He took a sip of his soda, then set it down on the coffee table in front of him. "What happened to you?"

I touched the side of my face. "Accident in the bathroom."

"You need to buy a bathmat. Most home accidents happen in the bath."

"I know."

We shared a laugh.

"When can I take my wife home?" He asked. "Your coroner left a message saying Jon and Susan's body will be released tomorrow."

He clasped his hands together and leaned forward on his knees. Then he dropped his voice to above a whisper. "We have to make arrangements. I'm really not good at those things. That's always been Linda's department."

I took a seat on the shabby sofa next to him.

"She might be delayed," I said.

Jack's head snapped toward me.

"Why?"

There was a brief pause while I tried to decide how I was going to handle him. From sharp look in Jack's eyes, I decided that I should treat this as a delicate situation.

"Mr. Meyers, your wife has called for her attorney," I said.

Jack Meyers sat up straight and turned his knees toward me.

"Why does she need an attorney? For Chad?"

His tone was almost hopeful, as if he'd been waiting for us to arrest his nephew. I took a deep breath and shifted in my seat.

"No."

"Then what?" Jack's spine stiffened and his eyes widened. "You've arrested, Linda?"

"No," I said, without hesitation. "We wanted to ask your wife some questions, and she decided she needed a lawyer."

"Questions about what?" Anger bit in every word.

Louise shifted his Coke from its place on the coffee table and sat on the edge.

"Mister Meyers, Chad claims your wife told him to accuse Katie Dolan of attacking him this morning."

Jack considered Louise's statement, like a man weighing a major life decision. Do I take the job or not? Can I beat the train? Should I switch fabric softeners or not? One of those really tough decisions.

"That's a lie." The vein at his temple throbbed with the driving beat of a man that was about to have an aneurysm. "You can't believe anything Chad has to say. He's lying to save himself."

"I believe him," I said.

"Of course you do." Jack laughed like I couldn't be more of an idiot. "He's a good liar. He's had a lot of practice."

"What time did your wife receive the call that Chad had been attacked this morning?" I asked.

Jack sat back, disarmed by the question. "I don't remember."

"You don't remember?" I was on the scent now. "The call had to come in fairly early this morning, and you don't remember the phone ringing?"

"No." He scratched at his head. "No actually, I don't remember the phone ringing at all."

"Linda arrived before the first Officer. How do you explain that?"

The creases in Jacks forehead smoothed. "I can't."

"Then maybe you can help us with another nagging question." I edged closer, pinning him with my eyes. "Can you explain how the bullet we pulled out of Jonathan Luther came from a gun registered to you?"

Jack's wide eyes glossed with tears. He swallowed hard, and then blinked away the tears before they could fall.

"Please tell me that is not true." He turned to Louise. "Please tell me."

Louise shook her head. "I can't. Do you want to wait for your lawyer to arrive before we continue?"

He lowered his chin to his chest and stared at the floor. Deep heaving breaths ratcheted from his lips.

"No." He shook his head. "I think I want to talk. This family has kept secrets for far too long."

Jane's face took on the kid in the candy store look. She was on ground zero for the full airing of the Luther family's laundry. Scooping the competition didn't quite cover this, decimating would be a better term.

"Linda became irrational after Susan was killed. I thought she was just in shock."

Jack rubbed at his temples.

"The other morning, when you came for a visit, I had just realized my gun was missing. I wanted to have it for protection."

That explained his nervous behavior when we arrived that day.

"Protection from who?" Louise asked.

"I said from Chad, but my Wife insisted we were in jeopardy from Katie."

He reached for his can of soda and drank a long draft.

"Jesus Christ. Katie is unstable but I never felt threatened by her." Sad eyes turned up to meet mine. "My wife is a little unstable at times too. The whole family is. There's a history of mental illness."

The police reports we'd read about Susan and Jonathan Luther's background showed their families as more than unstable. I shifted uncomfortably away from him.

"I guess you already know," he said. "How much of it do you know?"

"All of it, I think."

Pity throbbed in my heart at the crumpled look on his face.

"I love Linda. More than I even knew until just this moment. She's a good person, but she gets a little mixed-up from time-to-time. The truth is the phone never rang this morning. I know because I was in my home office at about six this morning. I was waiting for a call, so I would have known."

"Mister Meyers," Louise interrupted. "Maybe you should wait to speak with your lawyer before saying anymore."

"Why? So he can put a glossy finish on what I'm saying?" Jack pushed at his temples again. "No, I don't need anyone to spin what I'm saying. What I've said is the truth as cold and ugly as it is."

Jane perched on the edge of her seat and wrote so fast, she'd never be able to read the hash marks and swirls that ejaculated from the tip of her pen. The thought that she'd just fill in what she couldn't read, with her memories of this conversation worried me. Should make for interesting reading, since she was writing too fast to hear what was being said.

Two of the administrative assistants I'd passed in the hallway, but never gotten their names, came into the lounge. They waved a quick hello, and then turned their attention to the vending machines and their coffee breaks.

Louise suggested we move to somewhere more private to continue our conversation. Jack agreed and we moved to an interview room, where we had a tape recorder and a video camera, to document Jack's bleaching of his family's laundry.

"Mister Meyers," Louise said and took a seat across from him. "What you're telling us is that your wife called Chad this morning."

He nodded. “She had to have called him. There’s no way Chad called her.

Since the murder, Linda’s insisted that we arrest Katie. She insisted it was the only way. When I asked, ‘arrested for what’, she just smiled and told me everything would be fine.”

Jack fumbled with a button on the right collar of his pale blue, button-up shirt. The fingernails on his right hand were neatly manicured, except for the thumbnail, which had either been gnawed on or run through a grater.

“What would be fine?” Louise’s voice was so gentle she could have been humming a lullaby.

“My wife has a problem.” He held his hand in the air between us, and then rubbed his thumb and index finger together. “With money. She gambles. She spends. I don’t even know how or where, but the money disappears. A few weeks ago, I found bills for credit cards she’d taken out in my name, stuffed in one of her winter boots.”

“How much?” I asked.

He lifted his left shoulder in a defeated shrug. “I have no idea. Hundreds. Thousands. Tens of thousands.”

His fingers set to the task of attacking his button again.

“That’s why I was up this morning.”

Jack let out a resigned breath and pressed his palms flat on the table in front of him.

“I hired an investigator to find out exactly how much Linda had spent. How far in debt we are. He was supposed to call this morning, but Linda must have been on the phone with Chad.”

A question that should have been asked days ago finally occurred to me.

“What kind of car does your wife drive?”

Jack Meyers blinked at me. The question had put him off the rails of his story, and his mind was searching for the direction of my little red wagon.

“Her car is an old Buick Regal.”

"What color?"

"Dark blue."

It fit. Bernice Leigh, the Luther's neighbor across the street, had said she'd seen a dark car, one she thought was dirty green. She could have been mistaken. Even with her binoculars, a trick of fall light and the veil of dirt could have fooled Bernice's vision.

He rolled his hands around each other. "We've been saving for a new car for her, but now . . ."

His voice trailed off then he pressed his hands flat on the table again, almost as if doing so steeled him against reality.

"Depending on how much Linda owes, it might be a long time before she gets a new car. Mine's paid for by my company so we'll at least have one decent vehicle."

While Jack was distracted with his transportation concerns, Louise's telepathy had kicked in.

"Do you know where Linda was the day of the murders?"

Jack went ramrod straight. He edged to his feet, sliding the chair backward, with a slow grind of the metal tipped chair legs on the Linoleum.

"No, I don't."

His answer was deliberate and his voice had taken on a menacing edge.

"I know what you're implying Detective, but you are on the wrong track. My wife and her sister were close. When we first got married, I would have said too close, but they went through a lot of shit together as kids. All they had was each other."

"Please, Mister Meyers, sit." Louise fanned her hand in the air, as if he were being silly. "No one said she killed anyone. We need to cover all the bases or some slick defense attorney will. He'll uncover your wife's money problem, and out her in court if we don't prove beyond any question that your wife wasn't involved."

He considered her for a moment, and then dropped into his chair. He lifted his hands to his head, and rubbed his temples.

"This whole situation is a fucking nightmare."

Jane Katts flipped her notebook page and continued to scratch like mad. Jack turned his eyes toward her.

"What are you writing? Isn't the tape recorder and the video camera enough? What the hell could you possibly be writing."

Trapped in the intense scrutiny of Jack Meyers' gaze, Jane tightened her grip on the notebook, as if he had lunged for the tight spiral of the header. She averted her eyes from his.

"I'm here to observe. I'm just noting my observations." She lifted her eyes. "I tend to overthink things if I watch a video or listen to the tape. I like to capture my insights as things are happening."

The anger on Jack's face fizzled. What an adept liar she'd become in the last twenty minutes.

"I can stop if you'd like," she said.

"No. Sorry. I'm just having a bad day."

Jane smiled. "I understand."

"I can find out where Linda was the day of the murders," he said. "I know her and she won't tell you. Hell, our lawyer is going to tell her, not to tell you anything."

An offer we couldn't pass up. Louise took Jack to the room where we had plunked Linda. I went to still the throbbing in the side of my face by taking two of Doctor Dave's magic pills.

I swallowed the pills, with a mouthful of day-old coffee, and then rested the undamaged side of my face on my desktop. Dave had prescribed rest, so I felt no guilt in taking a breather while Louise and Jane did the legwork.

There was however, the slightest twinge of guilt at the sight of all the filing stacked on the edge of the desk. The files on top were recent cases, but the ones further down were a bit fuzzy.

With the backlog in the courts, they'd be in the file drawers before anyone needed them.

The Luther case would never make it to the stack, too high profile. This case would hit trial quickly. Thanks to my big mouth, the case was more sensational than it warranted.

My cell phone blipped to life in my pocket. I pulled it out, flipped open the case, and pressed the phone to my ear without lifting my head.

"O'Brien here."

"Here too."

Just the sound of Gavin's voice made me smile.

"Hi, honey," I said. "You must have known I needed to hear your sexy voice."

"Yep, my wife-dar went off right before I dialed your number."

"Ha-ha. Whoever told you, you were funny lied. I keep trying to tell you."

"What do you mean?" he said. "This stuff is pure tarnished tin."

I gave him a complimentary laugh.

"How are you feeling?" he asked. "Any better?"

"Like someone drilled through my face."

The piercing whine of a table saw chewed through the phone lines.

"Where are you working today?"

"Same place," he said.

I hesitated. "That's good."

Gavin gave a low chuckle. "You never hear me when I talk about work, do you?"

I squeezed my eyes shut. Gavin always listened to me talk about my day. He gave support when I needed and even helped work through difficult cases, not to mention the best foot-rubs on earth. For some reason every time he talked about his construction jobs, I tuned out.

"Of course I listen."

"Liar."

I groaned and sat up. "I'm sorry, honey. I really am. I'm listening now."

The Luther's file lay on the paper mound to my right. I pulled it from the stack and flipped it open.

"I'm working on the mall project," he said.

"Oh, right. The school to strip mall conversion." I flipped to the forensic reports and scanned the page. "Seems like that's taking forever."

"Good work takes time."

"And you are the best."

I scanned Digs' notes, as surprised as ever at his thoroughness, he'd even analyzed Chad Luther's vomit.

"That and my client keeps changing her mind. She's had two retailers drop out of the project, so we've had to reconfigure the space for a different retailers needs."

"Um, hmm."

"Catherine? What are you doing right now?"

"Nothing. I'm listening to you."

"No, you're not."

I was going to owe him big time. Only thirty-seconds before I'd sworn I was listening and my mind had wandered back to the case.

"Sorry, the drugs Doctor Dave gave me are kicking in and I'm really tired."

Hell holds a special place for people who manipulate other's sympathies to cover their own asses. The flames licked at my high heel boots from time to time, just to remind me of my place.

"Maybe you should knock off early and go home to rest." His voice was full of concern.

"I'm kinda resting at my desk," I said. "The Chief's letting me take it easy today."

No amount of Hail Mary's or Our Fathers would get me out of this one.

"I'll let you go," Gavin said. "You'll be home for dinner then?"

"I should be."

I lied. I had no idea where the rest of the day would take me. From the look of Chad Luther's toxicology report, the day might be far from over.

"I'll make a light supper then. Chicken salad sound good?"

"Sounds wonderful."

The call waiting beeped.

"I have another call, Gavin. I have to let you go."

"Okay. I love you."

"You do, don't you?"

"Very much."

"I love you, too."

Gavin hung up and I clicked over to the in coming call.

"O'Brien here."

"I got the search warrant from Judge Todd." Digs panted into the phone as if he were running a marathon. "I'm on my way to see you now."

He hung up without saying another word.

Chapter Twelve

Louise and Jane arrived at my desk about three-tenths of a second before Digs burst through the double doors of the bullpen area, waving a sheet of paper.

"I got it!"

"What does he have?" Louise asked.

"The golden ticket. He finally gets to visit the chocolate factory like he's always dreamed," I said and grinned at my own humor.

"Oh, God." Louise shook her head. "Don't tell me you didn't get enough sleep last night."

My sense of humor kicked into overdrive on sleep deprived days. I fanned the air.

"I'm fine. It's the drugs."

Digs dashed between the desks like a pro receiver dodging tackles with the goal line in sight. He slid to a stop within inches of slamming his thigh into the edge of my desk.

"Judge Todd issued the warrant for the jeweler."

He bent at the waist and took two wheezing breaths. It reminded me of the asthma kid in high school after track and field days.

"Jesus Digs, did you run up three floors?" I patted him on the back.

"Yep." He nodded. "Judge Todd authorized the search warrant, and just the threat of cops showing up during business hours made the jeweler fax the information we needed."

Digs passed the crumpled fax to Louise. After a few seconds of scanning the page, Louise's eyes opened wide.

"What?" My heart skipped a beat in anticipation. "It was Susan Luther's ring, wasn't it?"

"No." Louise shoved the paper toward me. "It was *Marion* Luther's."

On the top of the page was the logo for Panaterros Jewelers, one of the largest, and most respected, Jewelers in Saint Paul. You had to go through armed security just to enter their showroom. No wonder they hadn't wanted police to visit. A raid by police was enough to frighten away their skittish high rollers.

Below their elegant, swirly logo was an official statement from the Panaterros' corporate lawyer, stating their compliance with warrant number, blah, blah, blah. I flicked my eyes to the confirmation of purchase. Marion Luther's name and address in McCann County were printed in bold italics.

"So what does this mean?" Jane asked.

"In and of itself, nothing," I said. "But put it together with some other information Digs, our eager beaver, brought to light, and it means a whole hell of a lot."

Digs grinned then frowned. "What information."

I took a seat at my desk, and shoved the stack of filing to the side. Filing would wait another day. I logged onto my computer.

"There's one more item I need to check first."

I pulled up the Driver Vehicle Services record check window.

"If the answer is what I think it is, we're all going home early tonight." I looked across the desk toward Jane. "And you will have the scoop to beat them all."

"Can I help?" Jane smiled.

"Yeah, call the funeral home in McCann County and find out if Marion was buried with her ring."

"How am I supposed to get them to tell me that?"

"I don't know," I said. "Use your press clout. Tell them you're planning to expose a theft ring at their funeral home."

Jane nodded and took out her cell phone. I tossed Marion Luther's file across the desk to her.

Louise slid into her chair. "What are you onto, Catherine?"

"I don't know yet, but I need you to do a bank records search." I jotted a note and handed it across to her.

She reviewed the note then turned to her computer. "Sounds like this is getting good."

Chapter Thirteen

When all of the calls had been made, and Louise, Jane, and I had a chance to conference about what we'd learned, we were ready. It looked like I would make it home for dinner after all.

For the first time in my career, all the players were assembled in one place like an Agatha Christie novel.

Chad sat at the table in the interview room with his hands wrapped around a coffee mug. He looked up when we entered and gave us a halfhearted smile.

"Am I being sprung or what?"

"Not yet Chad," Louise said. She held the door open behind her.

An officer ushered in Linda Meyers. Chad's brows drew into deep furrows.

"What the hell is he doing here?" Jack Meyers said as he followed his wife through the door.

Chad cocked one arm over the back of his chair. The swagger, and bravado, Jack had described to us when we first met was in full force.

"Good to see you again too, *Uncle Jack*."

A lanky man in a gray three-piece suit stepped through the door carrying a briefcase. There were so many wrinkles on his face that he bore a striking resemblance to a Shar Pei puppy. Where his eyes should have been were two furry caterpillars, and a thick roll of skin. To my amazement, the caterpillars drew up and expose two gray eyes.

"I'm Mr. and Mrs. Meyers's attorney, Patrick Bennett."

There was a phlegmy quality to his voice that made me clear my throat.

"If there are any questions for these two, they should go through me."

He pressed his lips together and the creases at the sides of his mouth drooped into swagging jowls.

"Please have a seat, Mr. Bennett," Louise said. "We're not quite ready for questioning."

Linda, Jack, and Chad exchanged pointed, hate-filled glances for several tense moments. At last, the door opened again and revealed the remaining branch of this twisted family tree.

Jack Meyers gave a cynical laugh and folded his arms over his chest. "Perfect."

"What the fuck!" Katie's eyes darted around the room. "I'd think this was an intervention, but none of these people care that much about me."

She finally turned her narrow eyes toward me and leaned in to give the bruises a good examination. She laughed.

"Pretty," she said. "You've really gone down the toilet since I saw you last."

Bob Shackelford, who had escorted Katie in, shoved her into one of the straight-backed chairs.

A giggle escaped me then turned into a full-fledge laugh. Stunned silence muted the room.

Louise leaned toward me. "Is it the drugs?"

"No." I wiped a tear away. "That was funny. Then I thought what's even funnier, is the next time Katie has a chance to use a toilet with a door, will be in about twenty to life."

"For felony assault?" All humor had left Katie for the moment. "I don't think so."

"She's right," the Meyer's Shar Pei-lawyer said looking up from his yellow legal pad. "Three years with a six-thousand-dollar fine max."

"Interesting." My voice dripped sarcasm. "Except she's not going away for assault. She's up for murder."

"Oh," Mr. Bennett said. "Then you're correct."

He returned to scratching notes on his legal pad. I briefly wondered from which phone directory they'd selected his name.

Katie Dolan went calm. Too calm.

"I didn't kill anyone."

"Maybe not directly," I said. "But you helped."

I pulled out the plastic chair in front of me, took a seat, and then folded my hands together on the table.

"This entire investigation was like a puzzle, with no picture to guide you, and too many corner pieces."

I glanced back over my shoulder toward Louise. "I'm not stealing your thunder am I?"

"No." She leaned her back against the cinderblock wall. "Frankly, I'm curious to see where the heck you're going with this analogy."

For once, she was letting me drive. Normally, my theories were so convoluted that Louise questioned my law enforcement background. Part of me knew that if we hadn't had our pow-wow earlier she would be doing the pee-pee dance of nerves behind me. I gave Louise the Groucho Marx eyebrow waggle, and winked, before returning to my assembled suspects.

"You see, I started this puzzle expecting a square but all the extra corners seemed to fit. It wasn't until the center of the puzzle was finished, that I realized what we were dealing with was an octagon and not a square."

I glanced up to make sure the red light on the video camera was running. A speech this poetic was going to make the training rounds.

"First there was, Katie." I swiveled in my seat to face her.

"I didn't fucking kill anyone."

"Your motive was strong enough for murder, and you had threatened to kill the victim in the weeks prior to her death."

My hand drifted up and touched the side of my face.

"Then you attacked me, and I was sure you were violent enough for murder. The only problem is you don't have a car. So unless you took a cab to the murder, how would you have gotten there?"

The Shar Pei-lawyer grunted and nodded his approval, then scribbled more notes on his legal pad.

Jane, who had taken up residence in the corner behind Chad, rolled her eyes toward the ceiling and shook her head.

"You have a car though." I faced Linda across the table. "A dark blue car, which would fit the description of the car spotted outside your sister's home when she was killed. Plus, the victims were killed with a gun owned by your husband."

The caterpillars on the Shar Pei-lawyer's face arched up and he cleared his throat. "My client has an easily corroborated alibi."

I held up my hand to stop his lawyerly ramble.

"I'm sure she does, Mr. Bennett. We'll get to that later."

Linda let out a caveman like grunt. "I didn't kill my sister."

"Shut up, Linda," Katie said. "The sooner she's finished, the sooner we can go."

Linda lunged forward. Her grab, halted by the width of the table, fell short of reaching her cousin.

"I'm as innocent as you are."

"Whatever," Katie said.

Jack Meyers eased his wife back into her seat. He put his arm around her shoulder to comfort her.

"You ready to jump in yet?" I asked Louise.

"Nope, you're doing a bang up job so far."

"Well, just tell me if you feel like you want to add anything."

"I'll be sure to let you know." She nodded.

I continued.

"Then there's Chad, who seemed too broken up to be involved in his parents death."

"I have an alibi too," Chad said.

"That's right." I drummed my fingers on the tabletop. "You were getting high, and drinking with some of your friends."

Jack Meyers clicked his tongue against his teeth. "It figures."

"Fuck off, *Uncle Jack.* I know you do blow."

Jack's eyes darted around the room as if he were looking for an escape.

"You're a liar, Chad."

"Oh, right." Chad nodded and gave a feral grin. "I guess you've got white powdered snot then."

Chad tweaked the end of his nose and sniffed for effect.

"You little bastard!"

I slapped my palms flat on the table. The loud crack made Linda jump, and stick her fingers in her ears. The rest of the room stopped their bickering and turned their attention to me. All except Bennett, who's scratching pen, was the only sound in the room.

"I'm not finished talking yet!" I raised half out of my seat and looked around, daring any of them to make a sound. "When I'm done, I'll lock you all in a room, and you can beat the crap out of each other. Until then, I have the floor."

Jack returned his comforting arm to his wife's shoulder. Linda pulled her fingers from her ears and curled in close to him.

"Okay, since you're all getting a little antsy, I'll get to the point."

I put my butt back down onto the chair.

"I think you all see my dilemma," I said. "Whenever I tried to pin the murders on any of you, the pieces didn't fit."

The Shar Pei-lawyer raised his hand like a grade-schooler.

"Yes?"

He tapped his pen on his legal pad. "So, if I'm following you correctly, no one in this room murdered the Luther's?"

"That's what it looked like," I said.

Shar Pei smiled. He'd just won the gold star from the teacher.

"Until I found the final puzzle piece. The one that made all the others come together into that beautiful octagon shape."

I spread my fingers in the air as if describing the sunrise.

Bennett frowned down at his notes, and then shook his head. "What piece was that?"

"The toxicology report on Chad Luther's vomit."

Linda Meyers blanched. "The what?"

"Chad stuck his finger down his throat, to give his discovery that added bit of authenticity," I said.

"What the fuck are you talking about?" Chad said. "You're crazy."

"No, I'm not. You had a fleck of vomit on your nail polish when we saw you at the neighbor's house that day. At first, I thought the polish had chipped, but it was puke. If you hadn't been wearing black nail polish, it probably wouldn't have been so noticeable.

Of course, if you hadn't vomited in the first place, you wouldn't be facing a murder charge right now. Along with your Aunt Linda and your Cousin Katie."

Bennett drew two business cards from his gray flannel pocket. He slid one toward Katie, and the other down the table toward Chad. He went back to writing notes without noticing the shocked expressions on the faces of everyone around him.

"Okay," Jack said and made the timeout symbol with his hands. "Just bullet-point this whole thing."

"Chad's tests came back negative for drugs and alcohol, which erases his alibi. Except we spoke with Markus Vincent, and he says you were with him that day. Aside from being a drug peddling ass, why would he lie?" I shrugged. "That led me to check his bank records."

"I checked them, actually," Louise said.

I pointed over my shoulder. "That's right. Detective Montgomery checked the bank records. Markus Vincent had a one hundred thousand dollar wire transfer from Katie Dolan the day before the murder."

Bennett tisked and shook his head. "That doesn't look good."

"Shut the fuck up, you old fool," Katie snarled at him.

Bennett's brows snapped up, and his jowls drooped. He reached across the table and took his business card back. I guess no amount of money was worth taking abuse from a psychopath.

"Then I did a little more checking." I held my hands in the air. "No actually, in the interest of accuracy, my friend Jane in the corner did the checking for me."

Jane tipped her pen in a wave. Bennett gave a cheesy smile, wiggled his fingers at her, then went right back to making notes. Louise, Jane and I exchanged amused glances.

"Jane contacted the funeral home in McCann County to find out if Marion Luther was buried with her wedding ring."

"Why?"

I expected the question, and as I expected, the question hadn't come from Chad. Instead, it had come from Linda Meyers.

"What does that have to do with anything?"

"Whoever killed the Luther's had something to prove. Right, Chad? You loaded the diamond, from your Grandmother's ring, into the shotgun shell before you killed your Father. Apparently, you didn't realize how thorough an autopsy is, because we found the ring's setting in your Mother's throat."

Linda took a deep shuddering breath and choked out a, "no."

"How do you know the ring was Marion's?" Jack patted Linda on the shoulder.

"The stone was laser engraved and registered," Louise said and I sent up a silent thank you. I still didn't understand the whole diamond registry bit, and I really didn't care, as long as it pointed me to a suspect.

"The only problem is," Jane took the floor with more confidence than she'd had earlier in the day. "Marion Luther was buried with her wedding ring. At least she was according to the funeral records."

"Whoever took the ring attended Marion's funeral. This left Linda and Chad, since Katie was barely on speaking terms with Susan at the time."

The Shar Pei-lawyer scrubbed at his forehead. "This is very confusing."

"I know," I agreed. "But I'm almost at the end, so stay with me."

He nodded.

"My theory is Chad took the ring. You saw who murdered your Grandmother, didn't you Chad? The Sheriff in McCann felt that a family member committed the murder, and he was right. Your father killed his mother, didn't he?"

Large soupy tears rolled down Chad Luther's face in twin streams of grief. He'd been holding the truth in for a long time.

"I saw him."

"Jesus," Jack Meyers whispered. "You can't be serious, Jon killed his Mother?"

"From the hospital and court records, Marion Luther, and her husband were *spare the rod and spoil the child* parents," Louise said. "There's evidence that Marion abused her son."

"That's a fucking lie!" Chad dragged the back of his hand across his face and wiped the tears from his cheek. "She was a good person. She loved me. Grandma was the only person who did, and my dad took her away from me. He deserved to die, and my mom did too. She fucking knew dad killed grandma. Mom just spent the money like she wasn't sleeping with a murderer."

"Chad, I can't believe you did this." Linda cradled her head in her hands.

"Then how do you explain your car at the scene of the murder, Linda?" I asked. "The neighbor across the street remembered seeing a dark, late-model vehicle. After Chad's alibi fell apart, I still couldn't make the car fit. His car is a red Spyder, so I did a DVS search on you Linda. You have a dark-blue late model vehicle, don't you?"

Jack Meyers pushed away from his wife. He covered his mouth with his hand and his eyes went wide with horror.

"Then there's the matter of your husband's shotgun."

I edged forward in my seat, clasped my hands together, and leaned on my elbows.

"You gave Chad the gun and your car."

"Linda, my God." Jack slid his chair away from her.

"That's why you kept telling Jack everything would be fine. Katie would pay you for your help with the murder, which would have solved all your money problems. Except she forgot about the provision in her Father's will, which appoints a guardian for Katie, should anything happen to Susan."

Jane gave me a thumbs-up from behind her folded arms to let me know I was on track.

"A small detail, easily over looked. That's why you tried to frame Katie for both murders, by concocting the early morning attack on Chad."

Katie sat bolt upright. "You what?"

"Oh, that's right. You don't know about that little bit yet."

"You fucking cunt!"

Katie tried to stand. Bob Shackelford's beefy hand on her shoulder drove her back into her seat with the force of a sledge.

"Revenge and greed," Louise said. "The oldest reasons in the world to commit murder."

I stood and nodded toward the one-way mirror on the far wall. The door to the interrogation room opened, and two more uniformed officers came in.

"Katie Dolan, Linda Meyers, and Chad Luther," I said. "The three of you are under arrest for the murders of Susan and Jonathan Luther."

Chapter Fourteen

"That was brilliant!" Jane skipped down the hall beside me. "I can't believe you nailed them. Do you think you can make it stick?"

Louise pushed open the double doors of the bullpen and stood aside. "I don't think prosecution will be that hard. On his way out, Chad was trying to make a deal to testify."

"That's great." Jane shook her body. "Do you get this kind of high every time you arrest someone? I'm vibrating all over."

Louise and I shared a smile.

"No, never," I said. "I think your anticipating your big story."

Jane clapped her hands together. "That too."

In deference to the pain that made itself known, I gently swung my coat over my shoulders. Then I picked up my purse.

"Where are you going," Jane said. "We have to write the story. You can't leave."

I touched my left shoulder. "I'm feeling a bit stiff and I'm really tired."

Louise flicked on her computer. "I guess that leaves me to write the report."

"Thanks."

She smiled.

"But you can't leave," Jane said. "I have to go to press with this, *tonight*. By tomorrow, every news outlet in the Twin Cities will have the story."

I fished my keys out of my purse, then flicked through the pile of metal, until I found the one for my car door. My car should still be in its space where I left it yesterday.

"Well, Louise is too busy to help you, and I'm going home to rest, per Doctor's orders."

"This is just fucking great." Jane's day-one pout returned.

"I guess that means you have to write the story by yourself," I said.

"I guess." She stared at the floor for a few seconds until she realized what I'd said. Her head snapped up. "Are you serious?"

"What do you think, Louise? Can we trust her?"

Louise pursed her lips and scrutinized Jane. "I think we can. If not, we can always shoot her."

"Agreed," I said. "You be nice or we'll shoot you."

Jane leaped forward, and before I could protest, gripped me in a bear hug. Pain rocketed through my entire body and seemed to discharge through the bottom of my feet.

"Ouch!"

Jane let go. "I'm so sorry. I just got excited. I'm so, so sorry."

"It's okay," I said. "Go hug Louise, or anything else, if that will move you out of my way."

She laughed and stepped aside.

There could never be anywhere more inviting than your own front door. The troubles of the world dissipated like magic, each time my feet landed on our welcome mat. I stood for a moment and breathed in the clean, fall, air. The tension of the past few days ebbed.

Before I'd made an effort to find the key, Gavin swung open the door. KC stood next to him wagging his tail. The little mutt actually seemed happy to see me. Gavin helped me inside like a little old woman. I forgave him for making me feel old, the instant my nose registered the delectable smell of Gavin's world-famous, grilled, lemon chicken salad.

He took the purse from my shoulder, and tossed it under the table in the entryway.

He laid a gentle kiss on my cheek. "Are you hungry?"

"I wasn't, but I am now."

"Excellent." He rubbed his hands together in his best Mr. Burns impersonation. "Did you have a good day?"

"I did. After I got off the phone with you, we wrapped the Luther case."

Gavin pulled out one of the heavy oak dining room chairs and helped ease me in. KC curled up on the floor next to me. On the table in front of me were a Diet Coke, and a bottle of Western dressing.

He knows me so well.

"That's wonderful news," he said. "Your mother's been calling all afternoon. She's a little miffed that you cut her off this morning."

"Poor, Dad." I took a sip of Coke. "Sometimes I wonder why he married her."

"I'm glad he did." Gavin set a big bowl of lettuce in front of me. I helped myself to a large serving and smothered the plate with dressing. "If he didn't marry your mother, I wouldn't have you."

"Even if I don't hear you when you talk about work?" I tilted my chin down, and gave him my best puppy-dog eyes.

He tweaked the end of my nose. "Even in spite of that fact."

Dressing dripped down the front of my shirt with the first fork-full of food.

"And in spite of your table manners."

I flicked a gob of salad dressing at him. The orange goo landed just under his left eye.

He wiped the dressing away. “I see we’re feeling better this afternoon.”

I giggled. Then a large piece of lettuce hit the side of my face with a wet smack.

The ensuing food fight led to a joint shower. And because of my injuries, Gavin was particularly cautious during the best sex we’d had in a long time.

Acknowledgements

Time to thank everyone on Team Stacy! Go Team Stacy! Go Team Stacy!

First, a special thank you to my team leaders; my daughter and my husband who both love me unconditionally and accept the time I spend locked in my office pounding away at a keyboard as mommy's "work time." Thank you for allowing my creative impulses to come forward and indulging every crazy notion I have. Thank you for not running for the hills when I say, "I have an idea. . ."

This book is dedicated to my parents. There aren't enough thank you cards or gifts on this earth to show my appreciation for the years of guidance, support, love and for just letting me be the wacky me that I am. You are counted in my greatest blessings.

Thank you to Elizabeth Goldstein for all the editorial work. I'm so grateful for your expertise, your honesty and your talent. Welcome aboard the crazy train that is Team Stacy!

Thank you to Grandma Gimse whose strength is an inspiration to me and always has been. Thanks for being on my team before there was a team. I love you.

For my Team Stacy flag wavers: My sister Jennifer, Jim, Tony S., Nancy, Brian, Tony J., Joanna, and Christine. What could I have accomplished without all of you cheering me on? Um, pretty much nothing because I would be a hopeless shut-in. Thanks for helping step out into the light.

I have to thank all the book bloggers who have supported the Catherine O'Brien series and me. I am grateful to include you as part of Team Stacy. The work that you do for the love of a good read is awesome. I have been so impressed with the professionalism with which you all handle your blogs. I have met some of the most intelligent, well-read, articulate people during my blog tours. I appreciate your grace, your kindness, and the love you've shown me and my characters. Yes, I know you love Digs and Louise more than you love me but I still love you!

Thank you to all the readers who have stuck with Team Catherine and Team Stacy. I love your comments and criticism. Yes, I listen but I don't always hear. It doesn't mean I don't care though. Sometimes I have to go my own path.

Last is most. Thank you to God for all the opportunities He's given me. Though I may not have made the most of the gifts I've been given and opportunities He's put in my path (what with free will and all) I am still grateful. I am blessed.

To anyone I forgot, it wasn't intentional. No, I am not mad at you. You know I love you, but I'm getting old. I don't know when it happened. It just snuck up on me when I wasn't looking. We'll go out for drinks to make up for my oversight. Just give me a call, because I won't see your post on Facebook. You know I won't so why do you bother?

Many Blessings To You All!

~S~

About the Author

Stacy Verdick Case lives in Minnesota with her husband and her daughter. Stacy is currently hard at work on her fourth Catherine O'Brien mystery.

Visit Stacy on the web at: http://www.StacyVerdickCase.com

Join the Willing Accomplice mailing list and receive exclusive subscriber only content, advance notice of contests, new releases, murder, mayhem, and more!

Sign up today at ww.StacyVerdickCase.com or scan the code below:

Praise for the Catherine O'Brien Series

A Grand Murder

ISBN: 978-0-9837137-0-8

A Luring Murder

ISBN: 978-0-9837137-4-6

Available in Paperback, eBook, and MP3 Audiobook Download

Kirkus Reviews:

Spending time in Catherine's world is plenty of fun, and hopefully Case has more novels in store. An entertaining addition to an enjoyable series.

Midwest Book Review:

. . .a spicy, fast-paced, first-person detective saga that produces winning characters and a satisfyingly-compelling mystery that will keep readers guessing to the end. ~ D. Donovan, eBook Reviewer

BellaOnline:

"This clever new series is only going to get better!" - Edie Dykeman reviewer

TracyRiva.com:

"She made me laugh, cringe, get heart-ache, and want to shake someone – in all the right ways. ... I look forward to reading more Catherine O'Brien mysteries; I feel the characters and the author both have a bright future ahead." ~ Kathy LaMee Reviewer

Pearls Cast Before A McPig (mcpigpearls.blogspot.com)

"All in all I really enjoyed this book and I'll certainly read more books in this series once released and if I can get my trotters on them.". ~ Sullivan McPig

PracticalFrugality.com

"I really enjoyed how Catherine and Louise are able to play their personalities off of one another as they conduct interviews. You can really detect the bond that has developed between these two partners." ~ Karen Puleski

Also From Before the Fall Books

Bookended By Beauty Queens

★★★★★
"Eye & Mind Opening Read." ~ Barbara Hightower *Babs Book Bistro* & *Amazon Vine Voice* reviewer

★★★★★
"A riveting read." ~ K. Duncan *Write About* blog reviewer

★★★★★
"Hilarious and touching." ~ Lisa M. Amazon Reviewer

★★★★
"A Journey Rich in Character and Emotion" ~ Tia Bach *Mom in Love with Fiction* blog reviewer

Buy *Bookended by Beauty Queens* Today!

Available in Paperback, eBook, and MP3 Audiobook Download
ISBN: 978-0-9837137-2-2

Visit us at www.BeforetheFallBooks.com

CPSIA information can be obtained at www.ICGtesting.com
Printed in the USA
LVOW11s1105291014

411054LV00002B/52/P

9 780983 713760